T0265844

A LONESOME
PLACE FOR DYING

A LONESOME PLACE FOR DYING

A NOVEL

Nolan Chase

CROOKED
LANE

NEW YORK

Published in the United States by Crooked Lane Books, an imprint of The Quick Brown Fox & Company LLC.

Crooked Lane Books and its logo are trademarks of The Quick Brown Fox & Company LLC.

Library of Congress Catalog-in-Publication data available upon request.

ISBN (hardcover): 978-1-63910-777-3
ISBN (ebook): 978-1-63910-778-0

Cover design by Jerry Todd

Printed in the United States.

www.crookedlanebooks.com

Crooked Lane Books
34 West 27th St., 10th Floor
New York, NY 10001

First Edition: May 2024

10 9 8 7 6 5 4 3 2 1

For C.R.

For J. L.

1

Ethan Brand stood on his front porch, watching the coyote over the horizon of his coffee cup. The animal had run a few yards into the grass the instant he stepped outside, but now she was regaining her courage. Something hung from her mouth, large and an earthy red.

If the kids had been staying with him, Ethan would have chased her off. But he was alone now, had been for several months. The animal's movements were tentative, a cautious intelligence behind every footfall. Her coat a beautiful ghostly yellow, reminding him of desert sand. The red something fell from her jaws to the front step, almost as if she were offering it back to him.

"Get going," he told her.

The coyote didn't move.

"Don't you have someplace better to be?" He took two steps, eyes not leaving the coyote, and bent for the object. "Me neither."

His free hand grasped something wet and rubbery, heavier than it looked. Sized between a baseball and softball, and mostly intact. A heart, he realized.

Examining it, he saw that the main blood vessels had been severed cleanly. By its heft, too large to be human. How did an animal heart get to the front porch of his house? The one-floor structure was on a half acre, the front yard overgrown since Jazz and the kids had left. No carcass on the lawn, nothing to clue him to where the organ had come from. Too heavy for the coyote to have carried any great distance. The animal licked its jaws and paced.

"What you might call an auspicious start to the day," Ethan said.

He wasn't superstitious, didn't believe in signs. The world could turn violent or sweet, but it rarely told you which ahead of time. But of all the days to find something like this. A person more open to messages from the heavens might call it a bad omen.

Turning back to the house, Ethan saw the note stuck to the door, chest height, hanging from a piece of gaffer's tape. Computer printed in block letters, in one of the common fonts.

QUIT NOW.
LEAVE.
THIS IS YOUR LAST WARNING.

Ethan Brand took a sip of coffee and read the note again. No signature. The paper was letter size and white, as common as what they used in the department's copy machine.

The coyote had loped around to the side of the porch, its pale blue eyes tracking him. He'd never seen one with blue eyes before.

"You didn't happen to get a look at who did this?" he asked the animal.

No answer. Whoever had taped up the note had likely also placed the heart on his porch. An anonymous warning. His first day as chief hadn't even started, and already he was getting death threats.

* * *

Ethan Brand was forty-two, and had never envisioned a career on this side of the law. As a kid he'd loved westerns, but rarely rooted for the town marshal. The saddle tramp, the cowpuncher, the brave—that life of adventure and movement had appealed to him. He'd spent a good portion of his teens raising hell, his early twenties at loose ends, roaming, working odd jobs, avoiding college.

At twenty-three he'd joined the Marines, 2nd Light Armored. Spent two tours in the Helmand Valley, barreling down roads in the belly of a LAV, hiking across broken terrain, attempting to sort friend from hostile while men and women younger than him died at his side. His time in Afghanistan had wiped away any romance of violence. A roadside IED had wiped away everything else.

Medevacked to base camp, to a hospital in Frankfurt, and finally on to Bethesda, Maryland. He woke up in Walter Reed with what remained of his left foot in bandages. In the months after, he'd cling to two things: the memory of a week spent in bed with a civilian translator, and a growing desire for the nullifying effect of OxyContin.

His mother had died while he was overseas. For a year he haunted the empty rooms of her home, doing nothing, feeling as little as possible. He'd done his damnedest to block out the world. Blaine, Washington, in the upper northwest corner of the country, was as good a place as any to lie low.

And then one day he'd had a visit from Chief Frank Keogh. The heavyset Black lawman had come up the drive and sat down on his porch. Saying nothing for a long while. Letting Ethan Brand wallow in his shame.

Eventually Frank said, "I heard a rumor Agnes Brand's son was asking around town where he could score some hillbilly heroin. That really what you want, Ethan?"

He'd been too ashamed to respond.

"You really want to pursue that life, it's not too hard," Frank said. "I won't say I know what you been through because I don't, and I really don't care. Got my own sack of woes to tote around."

"So then why are you here?" Ethan asked.

"Call it a recruitment drive," Frank said. "Blaine is growing, more folks crossing the border every day. The department needs another body. I got good kids working for me, college kids, but I figured it wouldn't hurt, having someone knows their way around a gun."

Frank Keogh had taken a pack of Wrigley's Spearmint from his front pocket, offered it to him, then unwrapped two sticks for himself.

"Understand me, son. The *last* thing I need is some cowboy who draws first and asks questions never. But a fellow who knows what it means to take a life, who can walk a situation back from violence—a fellow who's clean, and not prone to moping around his house—a fellow who's got his shit so together he can wipe his ass clean with one square—that's a fellow maybe I can use."

The moment was as close to an epiphany as Ethan had ever had. Fifteen years later he still remembered the feeling. One moment life had felt gray and static, the next a horizon of challenge and possibility. As if he'd just been handed a viable future. In a way, that was exactly what Frank had done for him.

The chief told him to apply a month from now, giving him time to cleanse the toxins out of his system, put his house in order, and find out if he could still hit the broad side of a mountain. Frank Keogh left him with words he'd remember the rest of his life.

"You want to find anything worth looking for, son, you need to look beyond yourself."

So he had.

* * *

Ethan drove to the station with the heart on the seat next to him, wrapped in newspaper, and the note on his dashboard. The truck had been his mother's, a beige and white Dodge with more scrapes, scuffs, and miles on it than the department's entire motor pool. Randy Travis played from the tape deck. "Forever and Ever, Amen."

Blaine had a population just above six thousand. To the north, the town limit was the Canadian border, on the territory of the Semiahmoo Nation. To the south along I-5 was the city of Bellingham, Seattle ninety miles beyond that. Blaine saw higher than normal criminal activity for its size, most of it born from economic desperation. In the summer months, fishing and tour boats crowded Drayton Harbor, and businesses swelled with travelers en route to California or Mexico. It was April now, the morning pleasant but on the chill side.

The town looked different to him this morning. Part of that was the weight of responsibility. *His* town now. Last night had been Frank Keogh's retirement party, and Ethan had the mild headache of a hangover to show for it. His swearing-in ceremony was this afternoon.

The other reason for the difference was the death threat. More likely than not, it had come from someone he knew in Blaine. Someone who right now was waking up inside one of the small clapboard houses, drinking coffee at the Ocean Beach Hotel or Lucky Luk's Café, or getting ready to open one of the shops along Peace Portal Drive. Someone who wanted him scared, or someone who wanted him dead.

He still loved westerns, and deep down a part of him would always root for the outlaws. But a threatening note, paired with a heart—where did you even start looking for the kind of person who'd do something like that?

There were the people he'd put away, and the ones he was still trying to. Maybe the heart was a way to intimidate the new

5

chief, or to protect a criminal operation. The McCandless family weren't above trying something like that.

Or the motive could be political. Wynn Sinclair had put his considerable wealth and status behind Brenda Lee Page's campaign for the position of chief. Brenda Lee was a good officer, and he couldn't say why Frank Keogh had put Ethan's name forward instead of hers. This morning he hoped to take Brenda Lee aside and smooth out their working relationship going forward. But there might be more animosity there than he suspected.

Were there others who felt the job should be theirs? Or who worried about what Ethan would do with the office? As if he knew that entirely himself. The political nature of the job was new to him.

What if the note was from someone close? He hadn't lived a life of pure virtue. There were friends he'd lost, both in the corps and in the days after. People he'd failed to protect, still others he'd harmed unintentionally, doing what seemed right when there were no perfect choices. Doubtless some of those people might hold him responsible, or their loved ones would. In one or two cases he'd agree with them.

There'd been a married woman he'd been seeing since his separation, though Steph had called that off. Still.

He pulled the Dodge into his usual spot in the station's parking lot, next to Brenda Lee's Subaru and the empty space reserved for the chief of police. *His* spot, he remembered. Ethan reversed, three-pointed, touched bumpers with a prowler, cursed, and backed into the chief's space.

Nothing could ever be simple.

2

The Blaine police station was one story, brick on three sides, white clapboard along the front. Built in the 1980s, its clean and quaint exterior contained catastrophe and disarray. In the summer the building was sweltering, in the winter the pipes froze. The basement flooded every other spring. Between renovations, exterminations, the updating of computer and electrical systems, and the use and abuse heaped on it by officers and citizens alike, every day Ethan marveled that the building still hadn't crumbled to a fine powder.

The department comprised fourteen officers, plus civilian staff, auxiliary officers, and volunteers. Jon Gutierrez, the senior civilian administrator, nodded from behind the front desk and handed him a sheaf of message slips.

"Morning, Chief. Still feels a little weird calling you that. No offense." Jon noticed the newspaper bundle under his arm. "Fish or a fragile antique?"

"A heart," Ethan said, garnering a quizzical look from the office manager. "Long story. Any hassles?"

"Quiet morning. Officer Ruiz is responding to a 10-23 at the scrapyard, which seems to be the work of our favorite rock chucking high school brigade. And Officer Page is—"

"Present and accounted for," Brenda Lee Page said, emerging from the booking station with her hand extended. "Good morning, Chief. Sincere congratulations. I wish you all the best."

Brenda Lee's manner of speech was always a tad formal, a match with her posture and fastidious workspace. More mannered than usual this morning, though. This was her concession speech to her former rival.

"I appreciate it," Ethan said, stepping behind the desk into the shared office space. "What do you have going right now?"

Brenda Lee Page had joined the department a few months after he had, graduating from U of W with a degree in criminology. They weren't exactly friends, but they'd worked reasonably well together for more than a decade. Brenda Lee clearly felt as awkward about the change in their professional relationship as he did.

"We're still considering our options," Brenda Lee said. "Terry has his real estate license, and we have a good amount saved in our joint checking. There's a possible opening for an assistant chief in Kelso next year. Wynn—Mr. Sinclair—also mentioned that if I was no longer required in Blaine as an officer, but wanted to stay in town, Black Rock has need of security personnel—"

"I meant what do you have going this morning," Ethan said.

"Oh."

The thought that Brenda Lee worried he might fire her, or that she might quit, hadn't occurred to him. Would she have fired him under the same circumstances?

Her posture shifted closer to at ease, or as close as she got to ease. "I was just typing up notes from a car theft. Seeing if it matched any others. Nothing pressing. Why?"

He set the newspaper on his desk—his former desk—and unwrapped the heart.

"Most people bring in doughnuts," Brenda Lee said.

"Someone left this on my porch, along with a note. You know anything about that?"

"Absolutely not, Chief."

"Ethan."

"I don't know anything about this."

He believed her. Brenda Lee Page took a more hard-line approach to the job than he did, and in her personal life leaned toward the conservative side. She'd never been untruthful to Ethan's recollection, certainly not when it came to the job. If anything, Brenda Lee could be a little too truthful at times.

"Don't tell anyone else about this," he said, placing the heart in an evidence bag.

"Understood."

Ethan shoved the bag onto a shelf in the small evidence refrigerator. It was eight fifteen by the wall clock. He hadn't finished his coffee this morning, and the emptiness of his stomach was getting harder to ignore.

"You have time to grab breakfast at Lucky's?" he asked Brenda Lee.

"I already had yogurt, but I wouldn't turn down a cup of tea. Let me just finish my report."

He left her to type, crossing H Street, passing the war memorial cannon on the corner. Blaine was waking up. He nodded at Sally Bishop, smoking an electronic cigarette while sitting on an overturned milk crate out front of the Super Value Food and Drugs. His destination was Lucky Luk's Café. The old-fashioned neon sign, which announced the restaurant name and cuisine in three languages, wasn't lit, but the blinds were raised, and Mei Sum could be seen inside, filling the cups of the morning customers.

Mei was the seventeen-year-old niece of the restaurant's owner, Walter "Lucky" Luk. She was also what the school called an "accelerated learner," what Ethan would call a genius. Of all the people he saw in the course of a normal day, Mei was the one Ethan found it easiest to talk with. He wasn't sure why. Maybe because Mei's intellect seemed as much a gift as a curse for her. He sympathized.

"Heya, New Chief," Mei called, snapping off a salute with the cleaning rag still in hand.

"At ease."

He took a seat at the counter. Mei kept a magnetic chessboard behind the fortune cat. He'd been trying to beat her for a year now. So far he was zero for twenty-six, with two stalemates and a draw.

"How does it feel being top cop?" Mei asked. "Must feel great to know you could arrest anyone you want."

"Touch and go," he said. "Any chance of coffee?"

"Pot's on. The usual?"

His usual was an over easy egg, rice, and red eye gravy, which Lucky's made with hoisin sauce. Mei moved the chessboard in front of him. They'd started a match days ago, and while he studied the positions, Mei cracked an egg on the grill and poured coffee.

Ethan slid his bishop over to G8, capturing a rook. "Wouldn't do that." Mei put his coffee down and hopped her knight over to the empty square, which he realized far too late gave her an attack on both the king and queen.

"Gotta watch for the fork," Mei said.

The game was over by the time Brenda Lee Page joined him at the counter. The officer accepted a mug of chamomile tea, one sugar, and adjusted the volume on her radio.

"Seems to be a normal animal heart," Brenda Lee said. "Beef would be my first guess. On my way over, I asked at the butcher counter if the Super Value was missing one, but they couldn't say.

There's little demand for organs, though certain cuisines do consume the heart, for both dietary and spiritual reasons."

Ethan nodded. "And the note?"

"Seems to be from someone who doesn't like you."

"Would you add your name on that list?" When she hesitated to answer, Ethan said, "This is you and me talking. I can't replace you, even if I wanted to, which I don't. But I'd like your read on our relationship, where you and I stand, and where we go from here."

"All right."

Brenda Lee turned her stool a quarter toward him, propping her elbow on the counter. Her take on a relaxed and informal pose, he guessed.

"Respectfully, Chief, I mean Ethan, I believe I would have been a much more suitable candidate for the job. I think Frank Keogh made a mistake. I think he let his personal favoritism for you outweigh my experience, education, and temperament. Yes, temperament. I think you can be a little, well, lackadaisical."

"Good word," Mei called from behind the counter.

Ethan took a drink of coffee and looked at his hopeless position on the chessboard. "I didn't campaign for the job," he said.

"That's my point. It was handed to you."

"Frank Keogh made a recommendation, which City Council took. Not like I came in off the street."

"No," Brenda Lee said. "You're a very good officer."

"Thank you."

"I just happen to be better."

A matter of opinion. He let it go.

"Why did you want the job?" he asked. "I mean, what would you do differently from Frank?"

"I won't say the salary wasn't a factor, because it was. I'm long overdue for a raise." Brenda Lee placed the tea bag on the corner of the saucer. "Were I chief, for certain I would be tougher about parking violations. The beachfront lots should get ticketed twice as often. That's a source of extra revenue right there. Operationally, I would target the McCandless family, chiefly their cross-border operations. And as far as personnel goes"—here Brenda Lee hesitated—"I would terminate Cliff Mooney."

Ethan was somewhat surprised. Mooney had been suspended with pay for over two months, having been caught tampering with evidence in the case of a suicide. He'd claimed it was accidental, that the diary from the dead woman's apartment had been lost somewhere between his prowler and the station. Ethan himself had investigated Cliff Mooney's ties to the deceased, finding that Mooney had not only been in a relationship with her, but had arrested her previously for solicitation and petty theft. Whether their arrangement was business or romance, the officer had bent the rules to keep the woman out of trouble. Ethan had found video footage from the courtyard of a motel that showed Mooney accepting money from her. Whether the diary contained evidence or not, it would likely have showed their relationship was improper.

The decision to fire Clifford Mooney should have been an easy one. But Mooney denied he'd done anything intentionally wrong. He'd lost the diary, and anything beyond his mishandling of evidence was part of his personal life. That was headache one. Headache two was Mooney's family connection. Cliff was the nephew of Eldon Mooney, mayor of Blaine, and a longtime supporter of Frank Keogh.

Frank was too moral to let Cliff rejoin the force. He also knew that an outright firing would alienate the department from City Hall, probably wrecking the career of anyone Frank endorsed. So Cliff Mooney had sat at home playing video games since Valentine's Day, drawing his salary, in law enforcement limbo.

Ethan wanted to fire him more than anything. What shocked him was finding out that Brenda Lee Page felt the same.

"You'd take the political hit?" he asked her.

"I would, yes. Cliff is a disgrace to the uniform and what we represent."

He wondered exactly what that was. "Firing relatives of the mayor could make someone a short-term chief."

"True, but the increase in revenue from parking would help offset any—"

The radio erupted, Heck Ruiz's voice calling a 10-38, request for backup. His voice rising in pitch, breaking code and saying, "Ethan, Brenda Lee—anybody—I'm at the train tracks, a mile and change south of the scrapyard on Portal Way. We've got a, well, I forget the designation, but it's important you come here quick. Follow the tracks."

Heck was a new hire, and the rookie's excited tone almost certainly meant a body. From the sound of it, not an accident. Ethan threw back his coffee, left money next to the abandoned chessboard.

"After you," he said to Brenda Lee, and to Mei, "Game to be continued."

He followed his senior officer out to the motor pool, thinking the day was getting stranger by the minute. Considering how it had started, that was no mean feat.

3

Mo's Scrapyard had been in the Singh family for three generations. The property was southeast of the town center, past the point where Peace Portal Drive turned into Portal Way. An industrial area, the road was abutted by train tracks and a thicket of blackberry.

They drove in the Dodge, Ethan realizing that Frank Keogh hadn't turned over his keys to the chief's SUV. He'd get them from Frank at the swearing-in ceremony this afternoon. Assuming their current business didn't interfere.

"About that heart," Brenda Lee Page said. "I noticed impressions in the tissue. Possibly stab marks."

"Bite marks, actually. There's a coyote that's been skulking around my property. She got to the heart before I did."

"A coyote."

"With blue eyes. Ever seen one like that?"

"You should call Animal Control," Brenda Lee said.

"There are bigger problems at the moment."

She nodded. "Like who might want to kill you."

He'd actually meant the business they were driving toward. Portal Way hewed close to the train tracks, the coastal spur of the Great Northern Railway that connected the Pacific Northwest to

14

the rest of the continent. Blaine hadn't had a train station of its own since the early 1980s, when the salmon canneries and lumber mills were still operating, and the Empire Builder ran passengers between Seattle and Vancouver. The closest station now was in Bellingham.

Brenda Lee Page had lived here all her life, aside from college. She'd seen the town pivot from salmon and lumber to warehouses, freight, and beachfront condominiums. The two largest employers were Black Rock Logistics and Sinclair Developments. Both companies were controlled by Wynn Sinclair. Maybe that was why Brenda Lee had so eagerly sought Wynn's endorsement.

"My opinion, Ethan, for what it's worth, I'd take this threat seriously. The person who wrote the note was smart enough to use common paper stock and a generic typeface."

"Could've been what they had on hand."

Brenda Lee nodded. "But they probably didn't have a heart on hand, did they? Ergo, it's safe to assume some planning went into this."

"Ergo," Ethan said. "Good word."

"Don't underestimate this person. They feel wronged by you, you personally, and they very much want you dead."

Ethan turned down the gravel road leading to the scrapyard. Tendrils of blackberry thumped the windshield and the side of the truck. The road was pitted, slow going. A mile ahead of them, he could see the silently alternating lights from Hector Ruiz's patrol car.

"Suppose you and I were to make a list of suspects," he said to Brenda Lee. "That's first supposing I could convince you to stay on, perhaps with an increase in salary."

Brenda Lee smiled. "Suppose I'm with you so far."

"Whose names should go on that list?"

"Anyone you've angered recently," she said. "Anyone motivated by professional jealousy, or a feeling of persecution, or romantic betrayal. Let's take them in turn."

"Who do you think wants my job?"

"I haven't spoken with Heck or Mal, but they might have designs on being chief. Of course, I'd add my own name, if I wasn't known for my rigorous ethics." Adding, after a pained silence, "That was a joke."

"Thanks for clarifying," Ethan said. "Who else?"

"Jody McCandless may feel you're likely to persecute him, given the history between you and his brother."

"We all worked to put Seth away."

"But your testimony clinched it," Brenda Lee said. "Didn't he threaten you in court?"

"Seth McCandless makes a habit of saying stupid things," Ethan said.

"He could have asked his brother to deliver the threat. Or his sister, come to think of it."

Sissy McCandless owned a travel agency in town, and didn't seem to want anything to do with her family business. Ethan had barely spoken to Sissy, beyond exchanging hellos during her brother's sentencing hearing. Jody McCandless, the younger brother, was running things now. Jody was dangerous, hard to predict.

"What about Cliff Mooney?" Ethan asked.

"So obvious I shouldn't have to mention it. Both the first two categories apply—he could feel he deserves to be chief *and* that you'll take his job away."

"He's only wrong about the first part," Ethan said. "What was the third category? Romantic betrayal?"

"If you'd rather not say, Chief."

"Not much *to* say."

He and Jazz had separated almost a year ago, as amicable as a separation with two children could be. In the summer she'd taken a job in Boston, where her parents lived, where the boys were now going to school. Not a divorce, not yet anyway.

Though not generally prone to grand gestures, Ethan had woken up one morning last November, packed an overnight bag, and taken a week's leave, vowing to return with his family. He'd driven cross-country, through blizzards and downpours, stopping twice to sleep and once to have the Dodge's transmission replaced. He arrived in the suburb outside of Boston in time to walk his sons to school and have coffee with Jazz before she started work. Then he'd driven home to Blaine.

There wasn't a place for him there, in the East. The knowledge had broken his heart. It had also woken him up, like an open window on the highway during a nighttime drive. He was where he was, *who* he was, someone who hurt deeply but fell in love easily, and that wasn't likely to change. It was time to move on, he'd decided.

Easier to say than to accomplish. Since the separation, he'd dated some, and there was a married woman he'd loved, perhaps still did. Steph had ultimately decided to stay with her husband. If that counted as romantic betrayal—but there wasn't time to discuss it.

Ethan parked the truck behind the prowler and they clambered up the gravel embankment to where the tracks began their curve away from town. A long gray slash through dogwood and Douglas fir, green leading into more green. Hector Ruiz waved from a patch of trampled undergrowth, on which rested the unmistakable form of a body. Hector, known as Heck for an aversion to profanity that led to sayings like "when the shoot hits the fan," and "spit out of luck," wore the drawn expression of someone slowly coming back from shock. The compact, handsome officer avoiding looking directly at the corpse. Next to him stood Gurvinder Singh, the current operator of Mo's Scrapyard and the grandson of its founder, a slender, bearded man in overalls and heavy boots.

Before clearing his mind of everything except the scene, Ethan asked himself if Heck had designs on his job. He doubted it. Heck Ruiz was twenty-four and green, and on occasion his inexperience would plunge him into situations the young officer wasn't prepared for. But Heck was smart enough to realize this tendency, and had matured a great deal in the few months he'd been on the job. If Heck had ambitions at present, they were to keep his breakfast down and not step in anything vital.

"Nothing got touched by us," Heck said. "Gurv called in a broken window, and we found part of his fence bent up. Kids, we figured, full of pee and vinegar. Seemed like they were following the tracks, so we followed them back, and . . ." He inclined his head toward the body.

"What time was this?" Brenda Lee asked.

"Took the call about eight oh five. We started walking, found the body around eight thirty."

Ethan glanced back down the tracks. "We're about a mile and a quarter from the scrapyard. Quite a distance to walk just to follow up on a broken window."

"You know how it is, Ethan." Heck's body language stiffened. "*Chief.* I almost forgot. You know how it is, Chief. You start walking along a train track, tell yourself you'll head back at the next turn. First morning it hasn't rained in a week or so."

Without discussing the division of labor, Brenda Lee drew Gurv Singh to the side to begin taking his statement, while Ethan adjusted the gun on his belt so he could haunch comfortably and examine the scene. The dead body appeared to be female, white. She was lying with her face turned away from the tracks, one arm beneath her, legs bent. Brown hair matted to her cheek. She wore slip-on shoes, black with beige soles, black jeans with designer rips in the knees. A gray pullover hoodie with the word HOLLISTER in white along the left sleeve. The sweatshirt was pasted to her left side around the ribs, the fabric dark with blood.

The woman had landed on buttercup and fireweed as well as the all-pervading blackberries. Sprays of yellow and purple surrounded her. The eyes were open, the features not yet set in rigor mortis. Her expression registered shock and something else Ethan couldn't put a name to. *Wisdom* might be the closest, and that was far from the mark. A dying person knew things the living didn't—maybe that there was nothing left to know.

"Late twenties, maybe," he said to himself. Not a kid, but older than the clothing suggested. Her fingernails had been painted but not recently, half moons of bare cuticle below a flat chipped red. Nothing in her pockets, no wedding band, no jewelry around her wrists or neck. No visible tattoos.

Ethan pried up the hem of the sweatshirt, sticky and wet, exposing what had been a white cotton tee. Two horizontal rents in the fabric. Stab wounds, he guessed. The clothing had absorbed much of the blood, though the woman's right hand and sleeve were caked with it.

The shirt and jeans looked new, clean, the shoes more appropriate for pavement than the brush. Was she out jogging, maybe? Walking a dog? You didn't wear your best runners for a turn through the woods.

"When did it stop raining yesterday?" he asked Heck Ruiz.

"It was still spitting when I went on shift," the officer said. "Maybe midnight, one AM?"

"Her hoodie isn't wet." Ethan stood, aware of an ache in his left ankle. "Not with water, anyway. No mud on her shoes. See?"

Heck made himself look at the woman. "Yeah. Weird to be doing this without the chief, isn't it? Sorry, I mean—well, you know what I mean."

Ethan nodded. Frank Keogh had a way of assuming authority over a scene, everyone so used to it that both officers and citizens naturally set to work. He wondered if he'd earn that same deference one day. Maybe it was something you had to claim.

"Take photos," he told Heck. "Mal is on call, so let's get him out here to help with the canvass. The broken window at the scrapyard might be connected to this. She might even have been the one to break it."

He didn't think that was likely. The body was slightly turned toward the yard, northerly. The way the limbs were bent, the choice of footwear—it didn't fit with someone running from an act of vandalism.

More than that. There were no footprints around the body, no trampled brush aside from the patch where the woman lay. A person wouldn't leave traces if they were walking along the tracks themselves. But there would be signs of a struggle, of attempted escape, of a killer fleeing from the act. A blood spatter. *Something.*

"You call the ME?" he asked.

Heck shook his head. Behind him, Gurv Singh was pointing out to Brenda Lee the spot along the tracks where they'd noticed the body.

The distance from the tracks to the body was less than six feet, though on a steep gradient. Had she fallen from a passing train? Jumped? Or been pushed? Ethan climbed up, resting his foot on a rail tie, and surveyed the scene. He imagined himself falling that distance, a wound in his side, life pouring out of him.

However the woman had ended up here, it was a long way from anything, and a lonesome place to die.

4

The morning wore on. By the time it had worn out, leaving a listless gray afternoon, Ethan Brand had advanced his understanding of the unknown woman's death only a little.

Gurvinder Singh had woken at seven, as he normally did on a weekday. Feed the cat, fill the percolator, check the news feeds and the price of his mutual fund, then bring a cup of coffee with sugar to his wife in bed. The three-story Singh household sat diagonal from the scrapyard, separated by a raspberry field his grandfather Mo still tended. Only this morning, as Gurv waited for the machine to burble, he chanced to look across the field, at the corrugated metal hangar that housed the scrapyard office and work space. One of the square windows had been punched out.

It wasn't the first time it had happened. Vandalism and trespass were almost rites of passage for students at Blaine High. The kids either climbed over the barbed wire at the top of the fence, or peeled up the chain link at the bottom, or simply cut their way through. The office held no money, nothing that was both valuable and portable. While Gurv was upset at the break-ins, it was mostly irritation at having to order a new pane of glass and clean up whatever mess the kids left.

As a rule, minor vandalism wasn't the sort of thing the Singh family would report to the authorities. If the trespassers had stolen a hubcap or a section of copper pipe, well, those weren't objects likely to be recovered. The kind of hard-luck person driven to steal such things wasn't usually in a position to make restitution. The call was for insurance purposes. Gurv Singh had accompanied Officer Ruiz along the tracks mostly for the exercise.

The witness had never seen the dead woman before. Could think of nothing else important to the case. Gurv had gone to bed early the night before, around ten. His wife would swear to this.

"Did the train come through at the usual time this morning?" he asked.

"I don't even notice the sound anymore." Gurv scratched his bearded cheek. "This is not an accident, is it?"

"Doesn't look that way."

"I never got my wife her coffee," Gurv muttered. "She's gonna be pissed."

Ethan was certain the scrapyard owner had nothing to do with the crime. But he sent Heck Ruiz home with Gurv to verify the alibi and talk to the rest of the Singh family. Who knows, one of them might have seen or heard something.

Brenda Lee Page was phoning the various railroad authorities. The Amtrak Cascades passenger train left Vancouver every morning at six, passing Blaine around six fifteen on its way to Oregon. The return trip left in the late afternoon, usually passing by around nine at night. Freight lines ran between these times, most of them in the morning hours. The trains could reach 150 miles per hour, but delays, sidings, and unexpected stops could all affect the timetables.

If the woman had been a passenger on the train, maybe a conductor in one of the stations was puzzling over an unclaimed suitcase or a jacket left on an empty seat. There might even be footage of the incident. The *murder*, he corrected. A crime aboard the train wouldn't necessarily be in his jurisdiction. It could be federal, even international.

There had been two homicides in Blaine in the decade and a half Ethan had worked there. Though not well-practiced, his people knew the importance of crime scene preservation, evidence collection, chain of custody. Whoever ended up with the case, they'd be dependent on the work his people did now.

His people. Still odd to think that. With Brenda Lee on the phone and Heck disappearing up the train tracks with their witness, Ethan was alone with the body. He took photos, sketched the scene in his notebook. He was measuring the distances when the prowler cut across the divider from the road, bumping down the incline and parking behind his truck. Malcolm Keogh got out, carrying an evidence collection kit.

"An honest to God murder, huh?" Mal's enthusiasm dropped as he saw Ethan's expression. The young officer slipped into professional mode. "What would you like me to start with, Ethan?"

Ethan, not Chief. "The hands, if you please."

Careful not to move her fingers lest anything preserved under the nails be lost, Mal began bagging the dead woman's hands. Mal, the former chief's son, was bespectacled and stocky, and the most well-schooled of the officers in forensic preservation. The opposite of his father in a lot of ways, Mal was more comfortable with data, at home in the digital realm. "Raised by his mother and the damn internet," Frank would say. For his part, Mal seemed to view his father as a throwback. Ethan wondered if Mal viewed him the same way.

"You weren't at your dad's retirement party last night," Ethan said.

"The family had dinner before. And parties aren't really my thing."

"You're okay with it, though? His retirement?"

"Why wouldn't I be?" The hands done, Mal shifted to collecting samples of the bloody branches. There weren't many. "You know what my dad's got planned?"

"No, what?"

But Mal smiled, shook his head, and didn't say.

The medical examiner's van parked on the shoulder of the road, and Dr. Sandra Jacinto crossed the grassy divide to the tracks. The Whatcom County medical examiner was a former professor of biology, a Filipina in her late fifties who dressed as fashionably as her morbid career allowed, and who usually had at least one assistant in tow. Today she was alone.

"How are you settling in, Chief?" the doctor asked, swapping her dress shoes for rubber boots. "It's about time they gave the job to someone cute."

"Nothing like jumping in with both feet," Ethan said.

"Let's see what we've got."

He left her to examine the body. Brenda Lee was on hold with Amtrak. Pressing the phone into her shoulder, she told Ethan that the morning train was between Centralia and Kelso at the moment, but would be stopped and checked thoroughly when it pulled into Portland.

"Are they missing a passenger?"

"Too early to tell."

Feeling helpless, the odd person out of his own investigation, he called the Bellingham PD and Whatcom County sheriff. Better to loop them in ahead of time. Blaine shared forensic resources with the larger departments, and the sheriff's office operated the county jail. Neither had information on a missing person matching the dead woman's description.

When he was done on the phone, Ethan wandered back to where the medical examiner was making notations. "Can you tell me anything about time of death?"

"Some time before now," Sandra Jacinto said without looking up from her clipboard. "Hollister and TOMS footwear. Oh, to be young again."

"Any chance you could ballpark the time?" Ethan asked.

"Less than four hours, going from rigor and temp, but don't expect me to write that down."

Ethan nodded. "A passenger train went by here two hours ago."

"Consistent." With the end of her pen, Dr. Jacinto pointed at the bloody patch in the dead woman's side. "It was probably quick. The puncture under the arm probably cut the axillary artery, and the other got close to the heart. An upward thrusting motion. Not much blood considering they struck two vital spots."

"Someone who knew what they were doing?" Ethan asked.

"Or got very lucky." The medical examiner put her clipboard back in her case, and removed a blue body bag. "I'm minus a student this morning. Strep throat. Be a doll and help me lift her."

Maneuvering the body into the bag was cumbersome, but they managed to accomplish it without disturbing the hands. The van's gurney couldn't make it over the divide, so he asked Mal Keogh to help the medical examiner carry the body.

Mal was standing above them on the tracks, training his cell phone at one of the ties. "Busy here," he said. "Can someone else do it?"

Authority issues already, Ethan thought, as he and Sandra lugged the corpse to the van. One more headache. Mal had gone from college directly to the department. As far as Ethan knew, he'd never worked a job where the boss wasn't also his father. A blessing and a curse to that, he reasoned.

The medical examiner was surprisingly strong. She held her end one-handed as she unlocked and opened the back doors of the van. They slid the body onto the trolley. Sandra Jacinto retied her ponytail, a gleaming pale silver.

"The sooner you can autopsy her, the better," Ethan said.

"I'm short-staffed, but since it's your special day, I'll do what I can."

"It's appreciated."

She smiled. "Exactly how much?"

The flirtation was a part of their working relationship, one-sided, but he didn't object. Dr. Sandra Jacinto was attractive, and he was single now. More or less.

With the body removed, he could view the impression left. The ground had sopped up some of the blood. In places the foliage was already regaining its former shape. A fact about death: it stopped nothing.

A piece of paper was tangled in the crushed flowers, folded in half and smudged with blood. Mal slid it into an evidence bag. A receipt for $69.62, paid for in cash. Two pale ales, two rum and Cokes, a cheeseburger supreme, and a bag of Tim's Salt and Vinegar potato chips. Steep for four drinks, a sandwich, and a side.

"Seems pricey," Mal said. "Maybe we should be looking for a robbery suspect as well."

There'd been no wallet or change purse around the body, nothing in the woman's pockets. So how had she paid? Why hold onto the receipt? And was the food and drink all hers, or had someone shared it with her?

Ethan called in two auxiliary officers to guard the scene, then told Mal he'd need to help with the canvass. The forensic expert seemed disappointed at the task.

"There's clay on the rails here," Mal said, showing Ethan the photo he'd taken. A few gray scuffs on the weathered steel. "As if someone paused there to scrape their shoes."

"Lot of people walk these tracks."

"Not since the last time it rained."

"It's good work," Ethan said. "But right now I need you to walk south a pace and see if there's more to our crime scene."

After an awkward pause, Mal nodded, hiding his reluctance as best he could. "A piece of advice, Ethan?"

"I'll take all I can get."

"Don't try to be my dad. His ways don't work anymore. I don't know if they ever did."

He watched the young officer start down the side of the train tracks, wondering exactly what was meant by that.

5

By noon Ethan Brand was at his desk, shaping his notes into a preliminary report on the Jane Doe homicide. His first time occupying the chief's small private office, looking out through the glass walls, through venetian blinds a dirty cream color. A bank box of Frank Keogh's personal items sat on the filing cabinet. Lena, Frank's wife, and a teenaged Mal grinned at him from a framed photo.

He had nothing to replace the photo with, no decorations to make the space his own. That would have to wait.

The canvass along the tracks had yielded nothing so far. Ethan busied himself checking reports of missing persons throughout Washington State. None matched Jane Doe's description.

His ankle was sore.

At one o'clock, with every other hand busy with the homicide, he took a wildlife call from the Orca Fin Motel. One of the guests had left their door propped open to fetch ice, and come back to find "a giant wolf or mountain lion" munching their continental breakfast.

The motel owner handed him a key card without looking up from the television behind the check-in desk. Ethan crossed the courtyard, thinking this was where he'd caught Cliff Mooney accepting money from a woman who'd later killed herself. The motel staff asked no questions. He'd spent a few afternoons in these rooms himself, after the split with Jazz. He and Steph had been serious about each other—serious enough she had considered leaving her husband. But guilt and responsibility had beat out romance, and they'd broken it off.

A fact of living in small towns, Ethan thought. Whether on the Washington coast or in the mountains of the Hindu Kush, your life happened within sight of everyone else. A true unknown, like his Jane Doe, was rare.

A shirtless man stood outside room 14, smoking a cigar. The hair on his chest formed a white diamond.

"Finally," the man said. "You gonna shoot it?"

"Let's see what we've got first. Step back, sir."

Ethan opened the door and shook his head.

"You again," he said to the coyote.

The blue-eyed animal looked up from the empty plate, saw the open door, and trotted out. Almost sauntering, Ethan thought. The man beside him winced and froze. The coyote licked her lips as she passed them, darting through the hedge along the border of the parking lot. As soon as she was gone, the man turned bellicose again.

"You should put those things down," the man said. "Attacking innocent people."

"Seems like all she attacked was some powdered eggs and bacon. But if you want to write a formal report, sir."

The man shook his head, muttering. "Knew I shouldn't a stopped here."

"The Chamber of Commerce thanks you," Ethan said, heading back to his truck.

*   *   *

At two thirty he was finished the report. Brenda Lee Page entered the office to tell him the morning train would be stopped in Seattle, tickets checked, and a cursory search conducted. She was heading south now to assist. The rail company would send a list, including crew members, before the end of the day.

"Best they can do," Brenda Lee said. "Trains normally don't count heads when passengers leave."

She lingered in the office chair, wanting to say more.

"I'd like to lead the investigation. With your supervision, of course."

"You haven't led a homicide investigation before," he said.

"You haven't supervised one."

Ethan nodded, a fair point. "This means you're staying on?"

"I make no excuses for wanting your job," Brenda Lee said. "But I do like mine. And, frankly, you need the help."

"I appreciate it."

"And you did mention something pertaining to a salary bump."

* * *

By three, his foot was bothering him. Something about the incline leading from the train tracks to the body had jolted his ankle the wrong way. He drew the blinds and unlaced the boot.

The injury itself didn't pain him any longer. A partial foot amputation, the outermost metatarsals removed. The tissue had healed smoothly, and the hinged foot plate which compensated for the two missing toes did its job reasonably well. He could walk just fine, even run when he needed to. But on steep inclines or uneven terrain, if the plate got jostled, it would send a throb up the ankle.

When the injury was new and he felt that pain, he'd take pills, usually several at a time. No more of that. These days, Advil was as far down the road of pain medication as he was comfortable traveling.

No sooner had he adjusted the plate than he heard "shave and a haircut" knocked on the glass. Ethan briskly replaced the boot as Frank Keogh poked his head through the door.

"Good afternoon, Chief," Frank said. "I heard you caught a body your first day. If it weren't for bad luck, what would we have, huh?"

Ethan put on his most professional administrative smile. "Hello, Frank. I'm going to need you to go back to reception, please. We don't allow civilians back here."

"You're kidding, right?"

"I'm afraid it's policy."

Ethan held the tight smile as long as he could, and when Frank shrugged and began to withdraw from the office, he grinned and stood to hug his former boss.

"Almost had me," Frank said. "I thought I'd grab you before the ceremony for a quick drink."

Ethan hadn't put anything in his stomach since breakfast. "How about a spring roll instead?"

Together they walked across First Street in the direction of Lucky Luk's. Frank wore a brown poplin jacket and tan Dockers. The former chief was only sixty-two. Until a few months ago, he'd never so much as hinted about retirement.

"You're limping," Frank said. "Everything all right?"

"Took a wrong step at the crime scene, that's all." Ethan didn't know if Frank was aware of his injury and prosthetic. He suspected so. Frank didn't miss much. But they'd never spoken of it.

He'd decided to hide it, or at least hide the extent of the damage. A decision he'd made out of pride and stubbornness, one he sometimes regretted. The doctor who handled the department physicals had lost a brother in Iraq, and hadn't noted the injury in Ethan's file. Workwise, the injury had never proved an issue.

An electric blue Mazda pickup was idling in front of the war memorial. As they crossed H Street and entered Lucky's, Ethan watched a rangy man peer at them from the driver's seat of the truck. Nobody he recognized.

"Twice in one day, Chief," Mei said. "And the old chief, too. This is gonna be the safest café in town."

They took a table in the corner where Ethan could keep watch on the truck. Frank noticed this, shaking his head with amusement as he ordered a plate of spring rolls and a beer.

"Old habits die hard, they say. Me, I'm happy to kill as many old habits as I can. Let younger shoulders carry 'em."

Ethan ordered his usual with a side of broccoli. He drank some coffee. The blue pickup was still there, the man inside still watching them.

"You ever receive a death threat, Frank?" he asked.

"I'm a Black man who spent thirty years writing tickets on white folks in pickups. What do you think?"

Ethan showed him the note. "Found this taped to my door this morning."

Frank broke out a pair of reading glasses, examined both sides of the note. "Rare anyone takes the time to print something out these days. Got an idea who left it?"

"Brenda Lee says someone who either wants my job, is afraid of what I'll do, or who I wronged romantically."

"Smart lady," Frank said. "You make things right with her?"

"I think so." Ethan had a few bites before asking, "Why didn't you consider her for the job?"

"Who says I didn't?"

Frank poured soy sauce on his plate and wiped a spring roll across it.

"It was a tough decision. Brenda Lee is smarter than you. More ambitious. Her personal life is a damn sight more stable. On the other hand, you're better with folks. Less apt to throw the book at them. You got to police everyone fairly in this job. And fair doesn't always mean equal."

"So what clinched it?" Ethan asked.

"I had to put it to one thing, that day at Black Rock."

He remembered. Two months ago a fire had started in a warehouse owned by Black Rock Logistics. A pair of forklift operators had been working the night shift. Both were hospitalized for smoke inhalation.

The fire was started with a Molotov cocktail, in protest over a new pipeline project that Black Rock was involved with. Most of the protests had been peaceful, and the project was under reconsideration when the bomb had gone off. The site staff caught two suspects sneaking back onto the shipping yard. The two barricaded themselves in the break trailer, an angry mob of workers soon surrounding it.

Brenda Lee Page and Ethan Brand had taken the call. By the time they arrived, bottles were being smashed against the trailer, the windows already broken. Weapons were moving through the crowd—bricks, box cutters. There was talk of building a fire and smoking the dirty rats out.

They pushed their way through the mob, talking the protestors into letting them inside the trailer. The perpetrators were nineteen and seventeen years old. Both were scared, the younger one bleeding from the broken glass.

The trailer began to rock. Backup was called. Brenda Lee drew her service weapon. Threats flew back and forth through the broken windows.

In the end, Ethan had opened the door and stepped out to face the crew. He spotted rifles and jerry cans of gasoline. Someone told him to get out of the way.

33

He stood his ground. Couldn't remember what he said in the moment, but it amounted to a warning. If he drew his gun, someone was going to die. The mob could no doubt get him, but he'd take a few down with him. Down all the way.

In the end he didn't have to draw.

"Partly it's a matter of temperament," Frank Keogh said, pointing at him with the chopsticks. "Part of it's the look, that tall drink of water Eastwood thing you got going on. But mostly, son, it's the fact you don't default to violence. Force as a last resort. Can't teach that."

"What about Brenda Lee?" he asked.

"You'll never find a better officer, but I'm not comfortable how quickly she sidled up to Wynn Sinclair. The wealthy tend to get their way, law and order-wise. But you can't make it too easy on them."

They finished their meal. He asked what Frank had planned for his retirement.

"Weed," the former chief said, surprising him. "I'm officially in the marijuana cultivation business. Lena's brother offered me a quarter share of his farm. Don't think the irony escapes me."

Only a few years ago they'd been stopping people for smoking pot—or more often than not, looking the other way. Legalizing marijuana had pushed the grow-op crews into other avenues of commerce. Cocaine, methamphetamines, prescription pills, and weapons.

And now the former chief was a pot grower. Ethan remembered what Frank's son had said about the old ways not working anymore. Maybe Mal was right. And maybe Frank Keogh had realized that sooner than anyone else.

Outside, he asked Frank for the keys to the chief's vehicle, and any last words of advice.

"Remember what I told you, that time I came to see you? About looking beyond yourself?"

Ethan nodded.

"As chief, now, people are looking to you. How to act, what to do. They'll test you. You're gonna have some ugly decisions to make, son. Try and make the ones that keep your people safe, and let you put head to pillow with a clean conscience. Reasonably clean, anyway."

As he listened, Ethan noticed the door of the blue pickup open. The driver made his move, darting across the street, causing a station wagon to stomp on the brake. Ethan walked toward the driver, holding up a hand to stop. The driver was carrying something wrapped in a black plastic bag.

"This is for you," the driver said.

"Put it down." Ethan's voice was sharp to his own ears.

The driver complied. "There's a note that goes with it."

He looked at the blue envelope with his name on it. "Who's this from?"

"They don't tell me that, sir."

Ethan toed the edge of the black bundle. "What's in there?"

"*Opuntia albispina*," the driver said.

Behind him, Frank Keogh began to laugh.

Inside the bag was a potted cactus shaped like a series of waffle griddles. "She's called an angel wing," the driver said. "Put her near a south-facing window and just watch her flower beautifully."

Ethan teased out the note. It was signed by Jazz and both of his sons. *Happy first day, Dad*, it said.

6

Considering how his first day as chief had started, it didn't seem possible for it to get stranger. But it was, and it did.

The rail company sent over the passenger manifest, along with a list of crew members working the morning line. Brenda Lee had begun combing through the names. The problem was, there was no way of verifying that a passenger who bought a ticket, say, for Tacoma, actually got off at that stop. Tickets weren't checked at every station. The train ended the trip in Oregon with all crew accounted for. But if they were short a passenger, no one had noticed.

Worse, the train itself was cleaned at the end of the line, before Brenda Lee's request not to disturb it had been relayed. Then it had been sent on its return trip north. When Brenda Lee asked the company to hold it in Seattle for an hour, they'd agreed. But traffic on I-5 was so congested, she was late reaching King Street Station. Brenda Lee arrived in time to watch the last car snake out of the depot, while she simultaneously called the next station and maneuvered her car back onto the interstate. If there had been proof the body came from the train . . . but proof was what she was looking for.

At Edmonds, Brenda Lee and a representative from the rail company combed each car again, to the irritation of the passengers and crew. They found nothing. No blood, no signs of a struggle, no luggage unaccounted for. No connection between the dead woman and the crew.

Dr. Jacinto would perform the autopsy tomorrow morning in Bellingham. Ethan wanted to be present. The postmortem was a chance to ask questions, to get a palpable sense of the death, what caused it and how. He also felt attending was the proper thing to do, a way to pay the dead woman respect.

At a quarter to four he walked to City Hall. A spitting rain had started, and by the time he arrived, the epaulets of his dress uniform were beaded with water. He'd forgotten his cap.

"City Hall" was a bit of a stretch. Blaine's civic government occupied several floors of the Banner Bank Building, a modern steel and glass structure with a barrel-vaulted roof. The council chamber was a medium-sized conference room with a curved dais for the council members, a few rows of seats for the public. The town seal and a brocaded flag were the only trappings that hinted at the official business conducted within the room.

Ceremonies weren't Ethan Brand's thing to begin with. But he took his spot in the front row while the council filed in. After ten minutes of officiating, he was called to stand before the dais. The city manager, Arlene Six Crows, asked if he'd faithfully and honorably discharge the duties of chief of police.

"I will," he said, glad it was over.

"Would you like to say a few words to the council?"

"Nope, I'm good."

Arlene gave him a quizzical look. *Of course* he was supposed to make a speech. It had been on his list to do this morning, before the heart, before Jane Doe, and before the chaos both brought with them.

"Are you sure, Chief Brand?" Arlene was the closest thing to a friend he had on the council. Full-figured and fierce, her hair in a long plait, Arlene had been born on the territory of the Nooksack, and she'd earned her law degree from Tulane. Her firm would defend any Indigenous person free of charge, though it specialized in corporate and treaty law. Arlene had butted heads with Wynn Sinclair when his proposal for a seaside resort had encroached on a parcel of land governed by the Lummi Nation. Sinclair hadn't been happy about that.

Speaking of whom. Blaine's wealthiest private citizen sat on the far right of the dais, a square-shouldered and handsome man a few years older than Ethan, with bottle black hair. In addition to his development company and a controlling share in Black Rock, Sinclair owned the Ocean Beach Hotel and Supper Club, along with swaths of real estate around town. His father had served on City Council, and his mother had been the first female mayor. Whatever else could be said about him, Wynn Sinclair had inherited a sense of civic duty. If he wasn't enthused by the council's choice for head of law enforcement, he wasn't broadcasting that fact. But Ethan thought he detected a glint of malicious joy as Sinclair watched him squirm.

"A few words, Chief?" Arlene repeated.

"Just, ah, that this is sure an honor, I mean for me, and I want to do a job that's good."

He could see Jay Swan, the one-person newsroom of the *Blaine Skyline*, copying down his words as fast as he could stammer them. Ethan faltered, took a breath, and started again.

"I'm not big on speechifying, and truth be told, it's been a hell of a day. So I'll do us all a favor and cut this to the quick. I take pride in this job. The man who vouched for me is about the best person I know. I won't let Frank Keogh down, or you, and I'll do my level best. Thanks kindly."

The smattering of applause told him it had been enough. A photo was taken. Soon the ceremony was over and he was surrounded by outstretched hands. Arlene was first, insisting on a hug.

"Congrats," she said so only he could hear. "I'm looking forward to whupping your butt in court and making you look silly."

"It's a date," he said.

The mayor was next. He knew this would be the most dicey conversation of the evening, and wanted to avoid bringing up Cliff Mooney's suspension. But the mayor had other ideas.

"Kudos to you, Ethan. I know you'll be fair. Speaking of fair, I'd like to bend your ear a bit about my nephew. Two months of Frank's hand-wringing is punishment enough, don't you think? The kid deserves a square deal, and another kick at the can."

Eldon Mooney's folksy manner didn't disguise his intent. The mayor's definition of a square deal meant full reinstatement. Cliff hadn't been kicking cans, though, he'd been abusing his authority as an officer. It wasn't a simple call.

"Cliff deserves a fair hearing," Ethan said, as diplomatically as he could.

Mooney clapped his shoulder. "Glad to hear it. My office at ten. See you tomorrow."

Before he could get his bearings, Jay Swan had cornered him, asking for a brief interview. Jay, a slim nonbinary person wearing a short-sleeve dress shirt and tie, said the paper was starting a new podcast, and "your story would be a high-octane way to kick it off." Ethan found himself agreeing to a sit-down interview at lunch tomorrow. An autopsy, an interview, and a talk with the mayor. Tomorrow was filling up quick.

Frank Keogh had entered the chamber during the ceremony. Frank shook his head in mockery. "What a speech, Ethan. Really dazzled the hell out of them."

"That bad?" Ethan said.

"I'll put it like this. If you spoke like that trying to get out of a ticket, you'd end up serving twenty to life in Clallam Bay."

Outside, the rain had paused. They saw Sissy McCandless, a gawky woman in granny glasses and the red vest of her travel agency uniform, heading up Martin Street. Sissy nodded at them.

"There goes the white sheep of the McCandless family," Frank muttered.

Ethan looked around, thinking it would make sense to shake hands with Wynn Sinclair. Show there were no hard feelings, and despite any personal animosity, Wynn could expect fairness from the department. But Wynn had retreated during the congratulations, and his Porsche was nowhere in sight.

His wife was, though. Ethan spotted her approaching from the direction of the waterfront. A tall woman with red-black hair, freckles around dark eyes, wearing a black cotton dress patterned with violets. His heart lurched and Brenda Lee's phrase ran through his head. *Romantic betrayal.*

"Congratulations, Chief," Steph Sinclair said formally. "My husband would like you to join us for dinner tomorrow. Could we expect you for seven at the club?"

* * *

He'd gone back to the office and paperworked himself into the evening. Trying his best to avoid thinking of her. Stephanie Ann Sinclair. The name provoked something wild in him, something uncivilized. The more he tried not to think of Steph, the more undeniable his thoughts became.

The first time they'd met, he'd pulled her over for speeding. The radar gun had clocked her Lexus going ninety in a residential zone. Steph glared at him, almost daring him to write a city councillor's wife a ticket. So he had.

Later on they'd been able to laugh about it, lying in a motel bed together. "You acted like it was the first time you hadn't been able to talk your way out of being written up," he said.

"It was. Men are damn fools." Steph spoke plainly about her own sexuality, as a fact about herself, but not the dominant one. Her candor was one of the things he'd loved about her.

Loved. That had surprised both of them. Those first months after his separation, he'd avoided going home as long as he could, spending hours walking the streets, sitting in Lucky's or the Blue Duck Saloon, taking overtime whenever he could. Anything to escape that house with no lights on inside, no toys on the front lawn.

On one of his midnight rambles, he passed the Ocean Beach Supper Club. The restaurant closed at ten, yet the light in the front dining room was still burning. Steph Sinclair was at a table alone. Reading glasses on, the day's receipts in front of her. Her eyes were closed.

He'd rapped on the glass. Asked if she was all right. When she said she was, he observed that the night was warm for October, and did she feel like walking with him?

"My face is probably a mess," Steph said. Up close he could see the marks of tears.

"Who's around to notice a little smudged eyeliner?"

"You noticed," she said.

They'd walked, mostly in silence. The next night, when he returned, Steph told him about the problems at home. Wynn had become frustrated when his resort project fell through. He was drinking a little more. They'd been arguing more, too. Then one evening Wynn had thrown a potted plant at the wall, in front of their daughter Jess, showering the teenage girl with dirt and broken roots.

Steph grew melancholy talking about it. "Something between Wynn and me broke that night. Brushing Jess's hair, I kept overhearing myself tell my daughter that her father loves her, that he's not a violent man, he's just exhausted these days from work. Making excuses for him. All of which are true, but I found I didn't care anymore. I *couldn't* care. Does that make sense?"

"It does to me," Ethan said. "So what'll you do?"

"I don't know. But I dread going home and facing him."

Their nightly walks became routine. Ethan found himself telling Steph Sinclair about Jazz. His wife had thrown a few things in their decade of marriage, though never in front of the kids. "Cooking brings out the devil in her," he told Steph. "She's not good at it, and she's used to being good at everything. Jazz once pitched a brick of butter at my head, on account of I asked if her cottage pie was supposed to smell like that. And not underhanded, either. She Nolan Ryan'd that damned thing."

Steph's tired laughter was soft music. "Did she apologize?" she asked.

"Not with words, but later that night, yeah." Normally bashful about matters of sex, and not understanding why he didn't feel that way talking to her, he added, "We'd be arguing one minute, the next we're naked, fooling around. No apology or explanation. Passions run close for us. *Ran*, guess I should say."

"You don't seem easily riled," Steph said.

"Jazz taking a job across the country, moving the kids to Boston, that did the job."

Steph had asked him a question that cut through the storm of everything he felt. "Do you accept your wife's reason for leaving?"

Maybe she thought it was innocuous, or she might have been looking for answers to her own domestic problem. Either way, asking the question changed his answer, and changed his life. What he loved about Jasmine Soltani, how cultured she was, how enthusiastic about experiencing the world, were qualities that were stifled by their life together in Blaine. Jazz wanted more for herself, more for the boys. Access to the best the East Coast had to offer. She wanted to give her sons part of the life she'd had. Ethan understood that reason. But he hadn't accepted it till then.

"I suppose I have to," Ethan said. "Her mother's a history professor, dad's a retired diplomat. They're good folks, and it's nice the boys get to spend time with them. But it's time they're not spending with me, and that hurts."

"You still love her?" Steph asked.

"Always, from the moment I saw her without a helmet on," he said. "I was escorting a group of civilians from the DoD, heading to Camp Dwyer, this outpost in Garmsir. There was some trouble on the road, but there was *always* trouble on the road. They hunkered down in the Humvee, wrapped up like goalies—pads, helmets, the whole works. We took some live rounds but get through okay. Inside the base, I see this gear come off, and the most stunning lady I'd ever seen asks me where the hell in Afghanistan she can get a drink."

Steph smiled. "Love at first sight?"

"And then some. We became pretty friendly, then I didn't see her for a few years. When we met again stateside, it was like time started up again."

He touched his chest above his heart.

"That woman's name is burned here forever. I had to become a better person to be worthy of her. And I have no idea what changed to make me lose her."

"You're a true romantic," Steph Sinclair told him.

"Try not to be, but here we are."

"And that rules out anyone else?"

"It has till now."

They'd found themselves walking in the direction of the Orca Fin Motel.

* * *

43

Ethan had installed a motion sensor on his porch light, so he never had to come home in the dark. First thing, he checked around the house, the shed, to see if there were any more notes or vital organs. Nothing. He was alone, on the night of his biggest career celebration. That was acceptable. He didn't feel much like celebrating.

The word *lonesome* kept coming to mind. The spot on the train tracks, the town itself in some ways. Something deeper than loneliness, an ache, a sense of life being unsettled, of playing out in a way it shouldn't have. There was no other word that seemed to fit.

After months when his feelings for Steph only seemed to grow more intense, she'd been gone as well. Right when it seemed she'd made up her mind to leave Wynn. He'd been looking forward to having Steph and her kids at his place. Today's brief word was the first time they'd spoken in almost a month.

A quick call to Jazz to thank her for the cactus, then a shower, then bed. Turning on the faucet, Ethan stripped down, taking care with the left sock and footplate. If you didn't scrutinize too hard, the prosthetic looked pretty natural.

He couldn't look at the injury without feeling a profound mix of loss and gratitude and guilt. Brad Dobbs and Ben Henriquez hadn't been so lucky. Maybe this, too, was another way of feeling lonesome.

Now that Frank was gone, no one in the department suspected his injury. The physical demands of the job often caused him considerable pain, as it had this afternoon when he'd stood on the train tracks. He wasn't the fastest sprinter, but he wasn't the slowest, either, and made up for it with an endurance born of orneriness. The only people in town who knew were his physician, Dr. Lau, and the women who'd shared his bed. Including Steph Sinclair.

Did Steph tell her husband? he wondered, drying off and readying for bed. She had stayed married in the end, remaining Mrs. Wynn Sinclair. Maybe for the sake of Jess and Wynn Junior. Or maybe because Ethan had cautioned her about her use of prescription pills, something he'd found all too seductive at one point in his own life. Everyone had their secrets.

Next to his bed sat a copy of *Middlemarch*. Jazz had never canceled her membership in the Blaine Women's Book Club. Every month a new tome arrived. He loved getting mail, enjoyed most of the books. They connected him to his ex-wife, and they nurtured a faraway hope that one day his family would come back.

He read a chapter before giving in to fatigue. His mind ran to other thoughts. Somewhere in the basement of Bellingham General Hospital, a young woman with no name was also lying alone. Only instead of an empty bed, Jane Doe occupied a stainless steel drawer in the medical examiner's refrigerated storage. Her killer, name also unknown, was still at large.

Tomorrow Ethan would do his damnedest to change that.

7

At seven the next morning, Ethan Brand stood in the chilly autopsy room in the hospital basement, gripping a take-out cup of coffee he'd lost interest in. He watched as Dr. Sandra Jacinto removed Jane Doe's brain from the cranial vault. Placing the brain in a pan, and the pan on a digital scale, she weighed it, dictating something into her headset too soft and too technical for Ethan to catch.

You could learn something about a person watching how they reacted to an autopsy. Frank Keogh had made sure every one of his officers had observed Sandra at work. Brenda Lee Page made no attempt to hide her fascination with the process, the mechanics of the body. Heck Ruiz found it gruesome and unpleasant, crossed himself, but didn't look away. Mal Keogh had seemed bored. Cliff Mooney made a show of not being fazed, cracking jokes and checking his phone.

Ethan himself was known for having an ironclad stomach. In fact, autopsies affected him greatly, the vulnerability of a person, the pity and terror of seeing the body's secrets on display. Like they were trusting you with that knowledge. During his first deployment, he'd cultivated a stony expression, businesslike in matters of death. It calmed those around him and helped him focus, acting as if it were true, until it *became* true. But that wasn't at all how he felt.

Washed and drained, the stab wounds in Jane Doe's side were narrow and ragged. The doctor made note of how deep they went and what anatomy they damaged. As the doctor had suspected, the wound closer to the armpit had cut the axillary artery. The other had nicked a lung on its way to pierce the heart.

The murder weapon would be a long, thin blade, dull judging by the bruised edges of the wounds. Applied with force. The wounds were on the left side.

"Left handed killer?" Ethan asked.

"Right-handed, I'd say, or ambidextrous. Average height. Look."

On the right hip was a collection of oval bruises. Finger and thumb impressions. The killer had gripped the side of their victim using their free hand, holding the torso in place for the stabbing. A jailhouse move, Ethan thought. Sneak up behind, grab and stab.

Jane Doe was in her late twenties to early thirties, had fractured her tibia sometime in the last decade, and her appendix and tonsils had been removed decades ago. She was healthy, had pale skin and smooth hands, which might point to an office job. Her teeth were intact and in good care. Dental records and fingerprints would be checked.

The medical examiner replaced the organs and sewed up the chest. Ethan waited in Sandra's small, neatly appointed office, as she finished her dictations and washed up. On the floor next to him was the plastic cooler he'd brought along.

There was something indistinct about Jane Doe. The word that kept coming to his mind was *generic*. Pretty, but lacking the imperfections which made a face memorable. Picking her out of a crowd would have been difficult.

Generic. Behind that word was an idea that seemed important, a clue. He couldn't access it. Why would a nondescript face be significant? Had he seen her somewhere before and not realized it?

After a few minutes, Dr. Jacinto came in carrying a tray of samples. Vials containing blood and body liquids, tissues, scrapings from the nails.

"I'll tell the lab to put a rush on these," she said. "No great mysteries, from what I've seen. Exsanguination leading to hemorrhagic shock. No blood means no oxygen to the brain, equals death."

"The weapon?" he asked.

"A dull stabbing implement, tapered, approximately seven inches long, one point two inches wide, and point zero one seven inches thick. Rounding up, of course."

"If I happen to find the knife, could you match it?"

"I could tell you if it was consistent with the wounds," the doctor said. "Peppermint tea?"

He accepted a cup, which smelled better than the morgue, but didn't take the place of a second coffee. Sandra pursed her lips and blew steam from hers. She looked down at the cooler.

"Early for beer and sandwiches, isn't it? Or am I finally getting a picnic with Blaine's most eligible bachelor?"

"I'm still married," Ethan said.

"Technically."

Sandra Jacinto was an attractive woman, maybe a decade older than he was. There was some sort of chemistry between them, but nowhere to go with it, especially at a quarter past eight in the morning. But the attention was flattering.

Lifting the cooler, Ethan said, "It's actually a heart. I was hoping you might take a gander."

The doctor opened the lid and held up the baggie. She prodded the indentations the coyote had made.

"Get hungry on your way over?" she asked.

"Coyote. Found this on my porch yesterday morning."

"Another adoring fan," the doctor said.

She moved back to the autopsy room and put the baggie on the scale.

"Two point two pounds," she said. "Too heavy to be human."

"I figured it was beef," Ethan said. "Also figured some high school kid might have stolen it from his biology lab."

"Wrong on both counts." Sandra opened the baggie and held it for Ethan to sniff. "What do you smell?"

"Heart, I guess."

She nodded. "And what you *don't* smell is formaldehyde. Dissection hearts usually contain preservatives."

"Maybe Blaine High is going farm-to-table this year."

The doctor smiled. "Say I tell you what this is," she said. "Would that buy me dinner and dancing at the Blue Duck this weekend?"

He was too tired to blush, and made the deal.

"A two-pound heart is twice as big as human but small for a cow. However, it's the ideal size for certain varieties of game. My guess, this is an elk heart, Ethan."

"So I'm looking for a hunter or a butcher," he said.

"Or someone who knows a hunter or butcher." Sandra closed the lid and slid the cooler back to him. "This has been fun, but unless you need to know what subspecies of elk, I have an afternoon class to prepare for. See you Saturday night at seven."

* * *

"Elk?" Brenda Lee Page asked.

"That's what the doc said. Supposing you wanted to get your hands on an elk heart, where would you go?"

"I would go hunting."

"If you were in a hurry," Ethan said.

They were on opposite sides of his desk, going over the strategy for the day. Brenda Lee would tackle the passenger list from the train, contacting each person to make sure they were alive, and ask if they'd seen anything suspicious. Mal Keogh would assist her. Heck Ruiz would talk to someone at the school, find out who might have broken the window at the scrapyard. The vandals could have stumbled across the body, might have seen something. The bushes around Portal Way would be searched concentrically, moving out from where the body had been found. The fingerprints had been run through AFIS, but returned no matches, meaning Jane Doe had no criminal record in the US. Until she revealed her name to them, these were the best leads they had.

With another coffee in his stomach, Ethan felt halfway human. In an hour he'd sit down with the mayor and Cliff Mooney. The first major political meeting of his career. He wasn't looking forward to it.

This morning's *Skyline* carried only the most basic details of the body found near the train tracks, along with an appeal to anyone who might have information. Today the department would have to issue a formal statement. Another task he wasn't looking forward to.

"There's a new butcher shop that opened near the harbor," Brenda Lee said. "La Petite Boucherie. They specialize in wild game. Terry got some lovely bison sausage from there."

"Worth checking. Anyone else you can think of who deals with elk?"

Brenda Lee hesitated, stirring an extra sugar cube into her cup.

"The McCandless family used to," she said. "For a flat fee Seth McCandless would break down a carcass, grind sausage, even make jerky. My brother took a mule deer to Seth once. He said the conditions weren't very sanitary."

"Seth is in prison," Ethan said.

"Just thought I'd mention it."

Ethan hadn't gone hunting since his teens. He and his father had done the butchering themselves, dressing the kill, an old-fashioned process, hanging strips of meat, tanning the hide. His father had been something of a hermit, something of a survivalist, and something Ethan still didn't understand. Jack Brand's belief in meeting nature on its terms had cut his life short.

"Could be from a restaurant," Brenda Lee offered.

"Organs are a poor person's meal, aren't they?" He'd eaten his share as a kid. "Who's serving Heart Surprise on their menu?"

"You laugh, but chefs treat that sort of thing as a challenge. Liver, tripe, even kidney and brains—disguising cheap cuts or making them taste good takes a lot more skill than flipping filet mignon."

He tried not to think of the autopsy, Sandra's matter-of-fact weighing of organs. "Point taken. I'll talk to someone at the Supper Club."

"You're having dinner there with the Sinclairs, aren't you?" Brenda Lee asked.

He wasn't sure how she knew that, or what business of hers that was. Despite the awkwardness the meal would bring, being close to Steph again was an appealing thought.

But right now it was time to see the mayor. On his way out, Ethan looked at the shift schedule behind the front desk. Malcolm Keogh had clocked in on time, but wasn't to be found in the station.

"Seen Mal?" he asked Jon Gutierrez. "Brenda Lee needs help running down the passenger list."

"Mal said he had someplace to go," the office manager said. "He told me he'd be back before noon."

"Didn't say why?"

Jon shook his head. "Nobody tells me nothing, Chief."

"I'm starting to feel the same way," Ethan said.

8

Eldon Mooney's passion was sailing. When he wasn't busy at City Hall, he could usually be found on his yacht, the *Sassy Bess*, or in the private room at the Marina Club. Mooney's office reflected that passion—model schooners, a lacquered ship's wheel mounted to the wall. The lapel pin of his navy blue suit was a diamond-studded anchor.

The mayor shook Ethan's hand, pointed his new chief of police toward a guest chair, and perched himself on the edge of his desk. A short man with curly hair dyed chestnut brown, lighter than his eyebrows, Eldon Mooney's ruddy face displayed an easy smile, even when the topics turned difficult.

His nephew hadn't stood when Ethan entered. Cliff Mooney wore a tight red and white striped T-shirt which displayed impressively muscled shoulders and arms. His legs were short and contained in beige slacks. His fair hair was thinning. Cliff had a weak chin usually covered with a goatee, though today he was clean-shaven. He'd missed a spot below his left sideburn.

Ethan elected to stand.

The mayor coughed, staring at his nephew. Cliff stood up with palpable reluctance, a thirty-year-old man sulking like a teen, and stuck out his hand. When they shook, Cliff applied more pressure than necessary, as if crushing fingers would show he was strong enough to deserve his old job. Ethan was glad to have his hand back.

"All right, gents," the mayor said. "We have ourselves a little quagmire to steer through. Cliff, you have something you want to say to our chief?"

Cliff Mooney had sunk back into his chair. "I know what I did wasn't right. I still don't think you shoulda followed me around and ratted me out to Frank."

"*Cliff.*" The mayor's voice was chiding.

"I'm sorry. Sir. I'd like another chance to come back to work. Sir."

As a performance, Ethan had seen better at his sons' school pageants. If Cliff felt any remorse, it was for being caught—"ratted out," as he put it. Frank had told Ethan to tail Cliff Mooney and report on what he saw. Ethan had done that and nothing more.

"Very big of you, Cliff." The mayor turned to Ethan. "All three of us recognize what the kid did was wrong. It can't happen again, no ifs, ands, or buts. The question is, is two months on the sidelines a reasonable enough punishment?"

"I'm not sure that *is* the question," Ethan said.

"Well then, what is?"

Why hadn't Frank Keogh fired Cliff? True, what the officer had done was mostly off the clock. That didn't change the fact that Cliff used his authority to start a relationship with a troubled woman, take money from her in exchange for providing protection and looking the other way. When the woman had killed herself with pills, Cliff had done his best to hide their relationship, removing her diary from evidence and breaking the chain of custody. By even the most generous standard, he wasn't fit to wear a badge.

Could he be *made* to fit, though? That was the question that troubled Ethan. Dominica Smith had been troubled long before she met Cliff Mooney. Smith had arrests for solicitation and drug possession going back years. The mayor's nephew hadn't created her troubles, merely added to them and, if Ethan was correct, profited from them. If Cliff showed genuine remorse, truly understood what he'd done, and was willing to take counseling and training to improve . . .

The answer was still no. Certain things were simply unforgivable, spoke to a fundamental lack of fitness to hold a position of authority. And anyway, Cliff Mooney wasn't interested in forgiveness. From the half-assed apology, it was obvious Cliff felt he'd done nothing wrong.

Open and shut, an easy decision, except for the very powerful man related to Cliff, the man whose office they were standing in. Maybe Frank hadn't fired Cliff because he didn't want Eldon Mooney for an enemy. Someone entering the marijuana business, dealing with permits and red tape, probably wouldn't want to damage his relationship with the mayor.

Which left the decision on Ethan's shoulders.

"The question for me, before anything else, is whether your nephew is willing to be honest about his relationship with Ms. Smith. Full, frank, and candid. Exactly what his role was in her life, what he knows about her death, and exactly what he did afterwards and why."

"That's my damn private life," Cliff said, appealing to his uncle. "He's so interested in sharing secrets, why doesn't he tell us all why his wife left?"

Ridiculous, Ethan thought, two grown men talking to each other through a third. He looked at Cliff, waited for the suspended officer to meet his eyes.

"I don't know if I can trust you," he said. "Or if you're contrite."

"The hell's contrite?" Cliff's eyes flitted between Ethan and his uncle, still looking to the mayor for help.

"Contrite means acknowledging what you did was wrong and feeling bad about it," Ethan said.

"He just wants to trap me so I spill my guts, Uncle El."

The mayor had crossed his arms while listening, as if to signal neutrality. Now he held up his hands.

"Ethan, my wife and I have spoken to young Cliff many times since he was sent home. We're both satisfied that he's contrite, and remorseful, and ready to move on. I believe the issue isn't his relationship with the girl, whatever that may have been. The issue is the removal of a diary from her apartment."

"Of evidence," Ethan said. "Tampering with a crime scene is a criminal offense."

"The kid was embarrassed," Eldon Mooney said. "He's young and full of beans. Who among us hasn't—"

The phone on his desk clanged, a sound that reminded Ethan of a ship's bell. Maybe it was all the nautical memorabilia in the room. He looked at a crocheted sailboat on the wall, the words *Clear Skies and Calm Seas* above it.

Mooney spoke into the phone, then handed it to Ethan. "For you, Chief."

He'd left his radio at the office, along with the cell phone Frank Keogh had dropped off. Jon Gutierrez came on the line briefly, connecting him to Mal Keogh in the field.

"I found something, Ethan," Mal said, excitement and triumph in his tone.

"You're supposed to be assisting Officer Page."

"I know, but this is major. Meet me at the old church on the turnoff."

So Mal had gone to the ruined church after clocking in, taking off without telling anyone. It sounded like the officer's hunch had paid off. Unless Mal had another motive to get him out to an abandoned building.

"On my way," Ethan said.

Both uncle and nephew looked to him for a decision.

"You'll have my answer, end of the day," he told them.

*   *   *

In 1914 Icelandic Lutherans had built one of the earliest churches in Blaine. Over the next century and beyond, the congregation had grown, split, reunified, and built and rebuilt three churches. Grace Church, with its steepled bell tower, was the most prominent in town. The Second Lutheran had been abandoned in the eighties. The concrete slab and a swaybacked skeleton of ruined lumber now stood alone in a field of overgrown grass.

How firm a foundation, Ethan thought. The church always brought to mind his wife. His second year on the job, Ethan had decided to contact Jazz. They hadn't seen each other since that week in Afghanistan. She'd left the Department of Defense and was working at a college in Seattle. He drove down. They spoke long into the night, and from then on whenever they had spare time, they were together. The first time he'd taken Jazz home to Blaine, they'd driven past the ruins of the Second Lutheran. Jazz remarked that it was the loneliest building she'd ever seen.

"It reminds me of that poem by Philip Larkin," she said. "'Churchgoing.'"

Ethan had never given the building much attention before. He'd been impressed, both by the lines and by her ability to recite them from memory.

"Poems and grievances," Jazz told him, smiling. "I never forget either one."

Ethan stopped the truck on the grassy shoulder behind Mal Keogh's prowler. The former chief's son swallowed some water and tossed his empty bottle on the passenger seat. He led Ethan through the grass toward the side of the foundation.

The ground they crossed became boggy. Ethan wondered if that was one of the reasons why the church had been moved. Hard to ask people to put on their Sunday-go-to-meeting duds and wade through a swamp to attend service.

His left boot stuck, sucked into the mud. He lifted the leg carefully, twisting it free. The ankle began to throb.

"If I'm making this trek just to see dirt," he said.

"Not dirt, clay." Mal had on gum boots and was moving fast. "I knew I'd seen it before somewhere."

They walked over fallen boards from the church's side. Mal pointed at a depression where the earth had been turned. "There used to be a well there, but it was filled in. See the clay? Same rusty color as what I found on the tracks near the body."

Narrow tire treads crisscrossed the depression. Dirt bikes, maybe, from the width of the tracks.

"Good find," Ethan said.

"It gets better."

Mal trudged to the back of the ruined building, reached behind an ancient potbellied stove. His gloved hand emerged with a mustard-colored canvas backpack. Herschel brand, no name written on the cloth. The bag looked empty inside.

"Wanna bet this is Jane Doe's?" Mal shook the bag. From one of the pockets came the jingle of coins. "She paid in cash for those drinks on the train, right? So this could be change from—damn, look at that."

Turning the bag slightly, he held it up for Ethan to see. Along the side of the pocket was a swipe of dark red.

9

Hours were chewed up searching the rest of the churchyard, walking stooped across the grass, wading through muddy patches. They found no more tire tracks or items belonging to Jane Doe. Each time his foot caught, pain shot up the ankle. Ethan was almost hobbling by the time they concluded the search.

Back at the station, Brenda Lee Page made a point of meeting them at the door. She and Mal Keogh began speaking over each other, Brenda Lee asking why he thought he could disobey orders, Mal explaining that he was the only one who could have followed up that lead.

"No one else here knows jack about soil composition or forensic geology," Mal said.

"But we do know something about chain of command."

"I found the dead woman's backpack," Mal said, as if that meant the end of the discussion. "There's blood on it, which means we have evidence, and we're one step closer to finding out her name."

"Laura Dill," Brenda Lee said. "What do you think I was doing all morning? Sweeping?"

The former chief's son didn't answer that.

Laura Rae Dill had booked a round-trip ticket, Bellingham to Vancouver and back. She'd gone over the border two days before her murder. Laura was thirty-one years old, born in Whatcom County. Brenda Lee hadn't found a current address for her, but Laura's father Robert Dill lived at the Royal Coachman trailer park in Lynden, half an hour southeast of Blaine.

Brenda Lee had even found a photo of Laura, taken from an abandoned social media account. The woman resembled Jane Doe, though maybe ten years younger, hair longer and eyes hidden behind shades. Laura Dill flashed a peace sign at the camera.

"I'd have more if you'd actually done the job you were assigned," Brenda Lee said.

"So sorry that I played a hunch," Mal said. "Which totally paid off, in case you didn't hear."

"If you can't do your job—"

"Thought the job was to solve this—"

"Good work, the both of you," Ethan said, louder than normal to quell the dispute. "Finish up talking to the passengers and crew. I'll pay a visit to the father."

In his private office he unlaced the boot, chased an aspirin with cold coffee, and massaged his ankle. Not so bad. He'd tracked mud through the station, though. Clay, he corrected himself.

Brenda Lee Page and Mal Keogh had never been chummy, but they'd also never squabbled like that before. Maybe that was his doing in some way. A new boss and the first murder investigation in years: that was a lot of change for a small department to absorb. Each officer wanted to know where they stood.

He left the office to break the news to Robert Dill. An unpleasant task, but if there was a relative to notify, he'd spare them hearing the news from Brenda Lee Page. His senior officer was naturally blunt. Knowing this, she tended to lean to the other extreme. He'd once seen her sit with a woman for nearly an hour, after which the woman thought her missing cat had been located. "Actually it's your father we found," Brenda Lee had told the woman. "He's in Lincoln Park. And he's dead." Better to do this himself.

Jay Swan was waiting for him outside the station. The *Sky-line*'s lead reporter had a satchel of recording equipment slung across their chest.

"Lunch, remember, Chief?" Jay said. "We were going to record that podcast."

It was the last thing on his mind. He liked Jay, and had watched them grow up, hiring them as a babysitter when he and Jazz needed a night out. Being a nonbinary person in a small town couldn't be easy. Neither could being a journalist with an entire town to cover.

"Can we push it an hour?" he asked, heading to the truck. "I have an errand to run that takes priority."

"I could ride with you, kill two birds?"

He was too hurried to think of a reason to say no.

* * *

"I'm going to call the episode *Last of the Gunfighters*," Jay said. "How you're a throwback to an Old West way of doing things, Wyatt Earp but in a contemporary milieu. What do you think, Chief?"

"I always liked Virgil Earp better. Seemed to have more of a conscience."

"Do you see yourself in that way?"

"As having a conscience?"

"As a gunfighter."

He shook his head. "I've never had to draw my service weapon."

"But you served in the Marines. You saw action."

61

Action wasn't the word for it. He felt awkward, self-conscious, aware of being recorded. He tried to think of something clever to say while the truck merged onto I-5, heading south toward Lynden, where Robert Dill lived.

"That era you're talking about," he finally said. "Dodge City, the town tamers. Part of hiring those people was to get them on your side. Keep the bullets flying in the right direction."

Jay made notes. "Do you think Chief Keogh had that in mind when he recommended you?"

"He and I both feel the point of carrying a weapon is not having to use it."

"So why carry at all?"

Ethan shrugged. "Sometimes you have to use it."

"Would it be fair to say the frontier mentality was part of your upbringing?"

"All my life."

He was getting more and more uncomfortable. Not Jay's fault as an interviewer, but the questions didn't have straight-ahead explanations. Some were things he'd been puzzling over for decades. Any answer would seem pat.

"My father named me after Ethan Edwards," he said. "*The Searchers* was his favorite film. Wayne and Ford. Seen it?"

"Don't think so," Jay said.

"Ethan Edwards is a Confederate renegade, a racist who's so driven by hate he can't be part of civilization. That made him a hero to my father."

"An intense legacy," Jay said. "He died when you were fifteen?"

Ethan nodded, only then realizing the mic wasn't picking up his body language. "Yes. Every summer he'd make camp in someplace wild, where he'd never been. Alaska, the Sangre de Cristo mountains. I went with him a few summers when I was eleven, twelve."

"His body was never recovered, is that right?"

Again he found himself nodding, not caring this time.

They'd fought, he and his father. Sometimes it felt they'd been fighting all their lives. Jack Brand assumed his son would go with him that last summer. In fact, he'd ordered Ethan to. Ethan was finished taking his orders. He'd gotten a forestry job instead. His mother backed his decision. As ornery and difficult as his father could be, the man wouldn't balk Agnes Brand. So his father had gone alone, not telling them where.

Three weeks later, a pilot friend told his mother he'd dropped Jack Brand off at a lake in northern Saskatchewan. When the pilot came back on the prearranged day, he'd found the camp still standing, no one in sight. The first search party found nothing. The second, which Ethan and his mother had been part of, was led by two men from the Plains Cree who knew the area. Cutting for sign, the men found tracks, and a small section of raft floating in some reeds. The fresh-cut timber had been lashed together with rope that matched his father's. Jack Brand had likely taken sick, built a raft to cross the lake for help, foundered, and went down to the bottom.

The lake was too deep to drag, and his mother didn't have money to hire a diving team or sonar. As a burial place, Ethan thought his father would approve of the lake.

All he could say to the *Skyline* reporter was, "No, he was never found."

* * *

Robert Dill's home in Royal Coachman park was a double-wide trailer with an overhang and carport. The homes were arranged in a long row, on hard-packed dirt and amid sparse evergreens. Dill's wash line was hung with faded bedsheets, despite the gathering clouds. A small Honda with a dented hood was parked out front.

Before he could ask Jay Swan to wait in the truck, the reporter said, "This is about the dead person found yesterday, right?"

Ethan nodded and pointed at the recorder. Jay switched it off with only a little reluctance.

"This is her father's place," he told the reporter. "I'd appreciate if you'd let me handle this alone. On the way back, I'll tell you what I can."

"Was she murdered?" Jay seemed stunned.

"Think up your questions," he said.

Robert Dill answered the door, a round-shouldered man with a paunch and a jowled, careworn face. He reacted to Ethan's uniform, to his solemn expression.

"Laura," Robert Dill said, in a very small voice.

Ethan shifted a blanket off the couch and took a seat beside the father. He told the man simply that a body had been found, that it was possibly Laura, and an identification from the father would be a great help.

"But there's a chance it's not her, isn't that right?"

"There's a chance," Ethan said.

Dill nodded. "Probably not her."

Robert Dill's wife had passed. The urn sat on top of the small refrigerator. He had a sister in Everett who could come with him for the identification when she finished work. It wasn't a good idea to drive himself.

"Was Laura ever in an accident?" Ethan asked.

"She's real cautious," the father said. "She was in the passenger's seat when her mama crashed. A truck took a corner of the PCH a little too fast, and sideswiped them. Suzie died instantly, but Laura only broke her leg. Ever since, she's been wary of cars."

Ethan nodded, thinking of the broken tibia on Jane Doe. "Does Laura have friends up in Canada?"

"I don't know her friends."

An only child, Laura had gone to school in Lynden, working at an outlet mall until she moved out at twenty-four. That was a year after the accident. The loss of her mother had been tough, and Laura had retreated from her friends, spending time on her own, staying out late and sometimes not coming home till the next day. When her father asked where she was, Laura hadn't said. Neither of them wanted to argue. After a few more broken curfews, Laura packed and left.

From time to time she dropped in to see Robert, the last time around Christmas. Laura gave him the impression of living in Seattle, couch-surfing, waitressing or working retail. She seemed to be doing okay.

"I should have asked more questions," Robert said. "I wanted to ask. I just, I dunno, couldn't."

"Did she seem desperate?"

"Never. Laura can look after herself. Always could."

"Does your daughter carry a purse, bag, anything like that?"

"Pocketbook belonging to her mama. The leather's all cracked to hell, but Laura sewed in a new lining."

"Any other personal items?"

"Just her backpack." Robert smiled. "She's lived out of backpacks since high school. Most recent one was kind of a hazy yellow color."

"Mustard yellow?"

"Could call it that. Why?"

Reading his answer in Ethan's face, Robert Dill began to cry.

10

On the drive back, Ethan's answers were terse, his mind preoccupied with the knowledge that Laura Dill had been murdered, and while he now had a name and a piece of her luggage, that was all he had. The department was still far from finding her killer.

As they pulled into the station parking lot, Jay Swan said, "I won't include her name, Chief, but can you give me a quote for the story at least?"

"We're doing what we can, as fast as we can."

"No offense, but as a sound bite, that kind of stinks. How about I write that 'The new chief assures us justice is winging its way to Blaine'?"

"Sure hope that's true," Ethan said.

* * *

In the department's muster room, he assembled the officers assigned to the Laura Dill homicide. He'd been chief for a day and a half, he realized, but hadn't yet been a leader. In charge, but not taking charge. Not yet.

Each officer ran down their part in the investigation. Brenda Lee hadn't found any passenger who'd spoken with Laura Dill, though one remembered a woman with a yellow backpack in the dining car. The passenger couldn't remember if she'd been alone or with someone.

A sample had been taken from the blood on the backpack and sent to the state toxicologist. The coins inside the pack amounted to thirty-eight cents. If the receipt for $69.62 they'd found beneath the body was from the dining car, the coins were exact change from seventy dollars cash.

The tire tracks had been preserved with plaster. With help from the forensics lab in Bellingham, the treads would hopefully be matched to a brand and model of dirt bike, if that was indeed what they were from.

Heck Ruiz had talked to the principal of Blaine High, and had names of two kids who'd broken windows in the gym. Shooter Kwon and Collin Rusk. "'Smoke pit kids' is how the principal described them," Heck said. "Not bad but prone to mischief. Kwon is the instigator, Rusk is the one who takes it that little bit too far. They were both suspended last year."

Ethan relayed the findings from the autopsy. He also made it clear that Brenda Lee was in charge of the investigation, and would coordinate their efforts. As he said this, he noticed Mal looking at his phone.

"In a couple of hours I'm meeting Laura's father to make an ID," Ethan said. "I'm going to tell him my best people are on this, and we will find who killed her. I'm going to promise him that. Priority number one for this office till that's done."

Overtime would be granted. Auxiliary officers and support staff were at their disposal. They could expect cooperation from other agencies, could come to him with any problems.

"Something else you all should know," he said, deciding in the moment to share with the others. "I received a death threat yesterday."

"How credible?" Mal asked.

"Not really sure I want to test that. Credible enough."

He explained about the elk heart, looking at each of them. Mal nodded and thumbed his phone. Brenda Lee was lost in her work on Laura Dill's timeline. Heck looked surprised, vaguely nauseous.

"Do you think it's maybe connected?" Heck asked. "I mean, the same morning as the murder. Some messed up son of a gun could've done both."

He'd considered it, but hadn't drawn any conclusion. "There's no evidence connecting them, but it's one more person out there making our job harder. Say nothing about this, please, even to your spouses. Nothing about the investigation, either. If that's understood, let's get to it."

*　*　*

At five o'clock Ethan stood behind Robert Dill and his sister Lorrie as Sandra Jacinto opened the curtain in the morgue's observation room. The father wore a long wool coat, the kind with hook and loop fasteners instead of buttons. Beneath that a warmup jacket, and a Harley-Davidson T-shirt below that. He clutched an Irish flat cap in his hands, fingers working around the silk interior.

Lorrie Dill was taller and wider than her brother, wore jeans and a static gray cardigan. Each hand grasped one of her brother's shoulders, as if to hold him up and keep him pointed in the right direction. She said nothing.

Sandra had covered Jane Doe's body with a white sheet, wrapped the top of the head with a towel. No stitches visible. The face was a bluish tint, the expression slack. The eyes were open.

The Dills had already identified a picture of Laura taken before the autopsy. Robert had asked to see her. Ethan had tried to talk him out of it, but the father insisted. "We came all this way. Might as well be sure."

Robert Dill stared at the face and shook his head. For a beat, Ethan thought *not her*, and felt a blast of relief. But then Lorrie Dill touched her brother's arm, and Robert let out a sob.

"It's," he gasped for a breath. "Yes, it's her."

"You're positive?" Ethan asked.

"Yes, sir."

He nodded to Sandra through the window to cover the face. Lorrie wrapped her arms around the grieving father, tilting her own head up as if gravity would help hold back her tears.

*   *   *

In the break room of the station he sat down with the Dills, brought them juice from the vending machine, and made a pot of coffee nobody wanted. Robert Dill looked like a gate battered off its hinges. The father slumped in the chair, answered in a hoarse and lifeless tone. No, he didn't know where his daughter was living. No, he wasn't aware of any enemies she'd made.

Ethan learned a lot about Laura Dill's life, though little that seemed helpful in solving her murder. Robert described her as smart, but an average student; ambitious, but not committed to any one thing. Not particularly secretive, but not someone who volunteered information about herself. They'd put distance between themselves, father and daughter, as a way to not feel the hurt of Laura's mother's absence.

Lorrie rubbed the back of her brother's neck. She dabbed at his cheeks with a napkin when he teared up, and wiped his lower lip. Only when Ethan asked if Laura had a boyfriend did the dead woman's aunt look away from her brother.

Something there, Ethan thought. But it wouldn't emerge now, when Lorrie's focus was managing her brother's grief.

He made Lorrie promise to take Robert home and stay with him tonight. She agreed to meet with Ethan tomorrow morning.

Watching them leave, he couldn't refrain from wondering how he would have fared in Robert Dill's circumstances. The horror of looking at your child in a morgue. There was nothing worse he could think of. Robert Dill lived alone, and obviously regretted the distance in his relationship with his daughter. A distance that would never be closed now. To Ethan, that distance struck home.

* * *

He was still at his desk when the evening patrol came on. The railway company had sent over the footage from the cameras on the train, for both trips Laura Dill had taken. Brenda Lee Page was viewing the footage now.

At six he decided to go home and change before his dinner with the Sinclairs. He paused at Brenda Lee's desk. She was staring at her computer screen, arms slack at her sides. On the screen was a blurry image of a woman in what was called the bistro car, sitting with her back to the camera, two bottles of beer near her arm.

"There's still so much to go through," Brenda Lee said.

"We'll get through it. Don't burn yourself out on the first lap."

"Easy to say, isn't it?"

He pushed a chair out from an empty desk—his former desk—and sat next to her. They'd been colleagues for a decade and a half, and it was difficult to recalibrate their relationship. New responsibilities, new duties to each other.

"Sorry, I'm just preoccupied," Brenda Lee said. "I don't mean it."

"None of this is easy, and it's not supposed to be."

"Doesn't it seem different without Frank to fall back on?" Brenda Lee asked. "I realize that's just cognitive bias on my part. There's no falling back with homicide, is there?"

70

Ethan shook his head. "Not in this department."

He said good night and headed out to his truck. He felt famished, drained. Feet up, a beer and a chicken leg in front of a fire. Music, or maybe highlights from the Seahawks game, or a movie on TCM. The last thing he wanted right now was dinner in a public place with a woman he still cared for—plus her husband.

The moments with Steph Sinclair he treasured had been private. The midnight walks, the meet-ups at the Orca Fin Motel. Midweek vacations they'd stolen. Once he'd become comfortable with the idea that Jazz wasn't coming back, Steph would stay over at his place. Guilt and joy and a thrill of excitement, all seeping into each other.

It had been something special. Then it was over.

Maybe he was fated to be alone for some while. He'd rushed from marriage into a passionate affair, an adulterous affair at that, and now had to pay for it with solitude. He was considering this when he noticed a large pale figure rushing toward him in his periphery.

Without looking up he greeted the figure. "Evening, Cliff."

Cliff Mooney stopped close enough to the truck that Ethan couldn't open the door. The suspended officer wore track pants and a black T-shirt with something spelled out in glitter across the chest. It was raining lightly, beading on Cliff's scalp.

"You said Uncle El and me would have an answer by the end of the day," Cliff said.

"Didn't count on it being this sort of day."

"What's that mean?"

"It means, Cliff, don't push me. It means if you want an answer right now, you won't like it."

Cliff sucked in air, playing up his anger. The large man was used to intimidation working in his favor. The sequined letters on his chest read *Alpha Dog*.

"Two whole months I been waiting," he said. "And all I did was take a damn book."

"If you really think that's all you did, then I've got no use for you."

"So that's it, huh?"

"Go home, Cliff."

The big man nodded, let loose with a kick to the front panel of the Dodge. His boot left a crease in the beige painted metal. The sound kerranged through the empty parking lot.

"You're entitled to one," Ethan said. "You've had it. Now go home."

The former officer pointed at him as he backed up, chest still heaving like he was considering a charge. Ethan dropped his hand, easy, loosed the snap on the holster.

"Just made yourself an enemy, Ethan," Cliff Mooney called. "Got yourself a whole universe of pain coming your way."

As the big man faded into the evening, Ethan had to admit, as far as threats went, it was a good one to leave on.

11

He was running late for dinner with the Sinclairs. First he'd nicked his jaw while shaving, wasting minutes digging around the medicine cabinet for an empty tube of antiseptic ointment. An item for the shopping list, if he ever got around to shopping again. Then the shower had felt so rejuvenating he'd stood under the water for a few more minutes than necessary. The best part of his day, hands down. No demands on him except water and gravity.

Ethan's thoughts kept running to Laura Dill. The contortion of her father's face in loss and pain. The way Laura's aunt had reacted to the mention of a boyfriend. Laura had chosen which details to share with each relative and which to withhold. Was that calculated on her part, or something every person did naturally, choosing which version of themselves to be, depending on the circumstances, fitting themselves to the moment? No different than choosing a suit, which was the task at hand for him.

His wardrobe wasn't extensive, but he hesitated between a black broadcloth coat and a Harris tweed blazer Jazz had brought him back from Scotland. He'd last worn the suit at his aunt's funeral. The tweed had been a favorite look of both Jazz and Steph. That might be an argument to go with the black.

Part of his procrastination was seeing Steph again. Nerves. Except this wasn't a date, it was a performance for Blaine's upper crust. City Councillor Sinclair and wife sit down with the new chief of police, putting to rest any rumors of animosity.

The left breast of the tweed was slightly pouched, a result of wearing it over a shoulder holster. That clinched it. Between the death threat, the run-in with Cliff Mooney, and an unsolved homicide, it wouldn't be smart to be caught unarmed. The tweed, then. It fit snug over the .45.

The rain was pelting the roof of the porch as he locked up. To his left, skulking around the shed, the pale blue eyes of the coyote gleamed at him. He'd need a name for her if they spent any more time together.

Ethan shot his cuffs and smoothed the tweed. "What do you think?" he asked the animal. "We breaking any hearts tonight?"

The coyote didn't volunteer an opinion.

* * *

The Ocean Beach Hotel was the closest thing to luxury within the center of town. The O.B. was the hub of tourist activity in the summer, and each winter Wynn Sinclair sponsored the light display along the boardwalk, leading, of course, to the door of the hotel. A modern building, gridded with glass-fronted balconies, the O.B. reminded Ethan of an old tool chest his father had owned, the kind with clear plastic drawers for screws and washers and other useful things.

The Supper Club adjoined the hotel, a white structure with an octagonal roof like a large gazebo. In warm weather the large double doors were retracted and diners could sit on the patio and look out on Drayton Harbor. The food was Continental, emphasizing local seafood, expensive and good.

Packed tonight, he thought as he stepped inside. He was twelve minutes late. A piano player in a white coat knocked out jazz standards in the corner, all but drowned out by the chatter. Was he imagining that the noise level dropped as he entered?

They were here to see him and Wynn Sinclair, he realized. The councillor had been outspoken in wanting Brenda Lee Page for the chief's job. The diners were seeking a front-row seat for the drama, or at least the strained courtesy of two prominent citizens who hated each other.

Too strong a word, hate. Ethan didn't much like Wynn Sinclair or his vision for the town. Homes were already too expensive for all but the rich, and the job of the police had to be more than keeping poor people off the beaches. He knew things through Steph, personal things about Wynn that didn't endear the councillor to him. Wynn's temper, the corners he cut, affairs he'd carried on. But hate? That took time and energy that were better directed elsewhere.

Did Wynn Sinclair hate him? he wondered, spotting the councillor at the long mirrored bar talking to Arlene Six Crows. Did Wynn know about him and Steph, and if so, did he care? She knew about her husband's infidelities, but did Wynn hold his wife to a different standard than himself, and hate the person she'd chosen for a lover?

He supposed he was about to find out.

Sidling up, he ordered a whiskey and soda and waited for a break in the councillors' conversation. Sinclair and Arlene were smiling, speaking at least partly for the benefit of the room.

"Not a bad idea per se," Wynn said. He was wearing black, a yellow carnation in his lapel. His rocks glass was empty and he jingled the ice at the bartender. "Any investment in real estate, the trick is to make it economically feasible."

"Since when is community an issue for the bean counters?" Arlene had a drink with a parasol in it, untouched, a prop for her conversation. "If it helps Indigenous youth understand where they come from, you're telling me it also needs to turn a profit? Since when does culture count for less than frozen yogurt?"

"Mixed-income, mixed-use space is to the benefit of everyone, Arlene." Wynn noticed Ethan, but the man's expression didn't change. "Hello, Chief. Get you a drink?"

He held up his glass. "All set, thanks. A thousand apologies for being late."

Wynn Sinclair waved his hand as if time itself meant nothing. "I heard you had your hands full with Eldon's nephew."

His confrontation in the parking lot with Cliff Mooney happened barely an hour ago. "Word gets around," he said.

Wynn smiled. "Small towns. For what it's worth, I think you made the right call. If change were comfortable, it wouldn't be change."

"Sure hope the mayor feels the same."

"I've known Eldon thirty years," Arlene said. "If it doesn't float and have a sail attached, it's of no consequence to the man. This is what the uncouth would call a dick waving contest."

Wynn Sinclair agreed. He raised his glass and beat the side of it with a glass straw. "Everyone, your attention? A toast to Blaine's new chief of police. May his reign be long and untroubled."

The room drank and golf-clapped. Ethan nodded politely.

"My beautiful blushing bride is checking something in the kitchen," Wynn said. "I'll tell her our guest is here. Arlene, join us for dinner?"

"Places to go and community centers to build," Arlene said. On her way out, she whispered to Ethan, "Come see me tomorrow when you get the time. And don't let your guard down all the way."

He puzzled over her words, standing alone at the bar. Did she mean Wynn had it out for him? Or was it more of a general caution?

Across the room, Wynn beckoned. Ethan threaded his way between tables, not catching a glimpse of her. And then there she was. Steph Sinclair's hair was up, twisted and chopsticked, above a blue dress that displayed a sweep of collarbone and the strong line of her neck. An intricate tangle of gold hung around her throat. He remembered kissing his way down from there.

They shook hands. He detected a tremor through her palm, felt the warm metal of the bracelet she wore.

"Thanks so much for coming, Chief Brand." Steph's smile was touched with a harried set to the mouth, as if she wasn't entirely able to forget some issue with the kitchen. A smart way to play things and avoid awkwardness, he supposed.

The Sinclairs sat on one side of the table, Ethan on the other with his back to the wall. Oysters, white wine, a salad with arugula and a raspberry vinaigrette. A blackened filet of halibut and another whiskey.

The conversation was pleasant and remained bobbing along the surface. He made an effort to keep from staring at any one thing for too long. They discussed a new shopping complex, renovations to the Historic House, the need for all branches of civic government to "pull the cart in the same direction," as Wynn put it. They drifted to local news. Then crime.

"I'm hearing you've got a murder on your hands," Wynn said.

Ethan wondered if the councillor wasn't hearing too much, if the town was really that small. "I can't say a lot at this stage."

Wynn nodded with understanding. "I've always been curious about something, Ethan, and I'd love a lawman's opinion. Do you suppose murderers are very different from ordinary people?"

"Wynn." Steph's voice carried polite admonishment.

"No, I'm serious," her husband said. "Speaking philosophically, what do you think?"

"Depends," Ethan said.

"On the type of person?"

"On the type of murder."

Steph gave a good-natured sigh. "This isn't the most stimulating topic, gents."

"On the contrary," Wynn said. "I can't think of anything more fascinating. You say it depends on the type of murder. Does that mean there are murders an average person could commit, and some he or she couldn't?"

"You don't have to answer," Steph told him.

Ethan was silent for a moment, thinking of an appropriate response that would also be true. His train of thought was interrupted by a chuckle from Wynn Sinclair.

"In older days this would be a drawing-room question," the councillor said. "The wives would clear the table while we retired with our cigars to sort out the important issues. Thankfully we live in more enlightened times." Nodding at his wife as he said this. "Can I share my own opinion?"

"Please."

"Thank you for indulging me." Wynn finished his drink. He'd had three during the meal, at least two before. Straight scotch, from the look of it. "I think, Ethan, all human beings, and maybe all animals, share a similar heart."

The last word struck him. It was an effort not to react. Ethan nodded as if weighing the matter. He couldn't tell if Wynn Sinclair meant the word to have that effect, but the councillor seemed eager to make his point.

"The heart is a primal, savage thing. And civilization bricks it over with etiquette and customs and social rewards. We punish infractions with laws, public shaming. But all it takes is the removal of a few choice bricks, whether by mistreatment, hardship, mental abuse. Or the ordinary cruelty of the world."

Wynn took a long sip. Enjoying holding the table's attention. Even Steph seemed intrigued.

"Or instruction. Those who are taught to kill. I suppose you'd fall into that category, Ethan, military training and all."

"Wynn." Steph's knife struck the plate with force.

"I don't mean it's all the same, you understand. Only that we're talking about different ways to get at the same barbarous spirit needed to end a life. That's in all of us, I believe, but only some of us have access to it."

Wynn bunched his napkin and deposited it on his plate. He smiled.

"That's my theory, anyway. Does it jibe with your experiences?"

"I'd have to give it more thought," Ethan said.

"You don't have a gut feeling?"

Was Wynn trying to provoke him? Was the man drunk? Or was this genuine curiosity pushing at the edge of politeness? Judging from the way Steph glowered at her husband, he considered this might be part of some private battle between the Sinclairs, and Ethan was only an observer.

"I think I'd approach the question another way," he said after a while. "Respectfully."

"No, I'd love to hear it."

"I think Hawthorne had it right," Ethan said. "Nathaniel, that is. My mother was a fan. Named me after one of his stories, though she let my father think otherwise."

"I'm afraid I don't read much in the way of literature," Wynn said.

"Hawthorne says there's only one unpardonable sin."

"Murder, I suppose," Wynn said.

He shook his head and turned to Steph, who shrugged, not wanting to upstage her husband.

"The unpardonable sin is, let me think just how Hawthorne phrased it. 'The violation of the sanctity of another's heart.'"

The table was silent for a moment. Wynn Sinclair rubbed the bridge of his nose. "I'm not sure how that answers my question, Chief."

"My best guess, it means we're all a little more fragile than we like to admit."

12

"All the time I was in prison, I kept thinking of home," Sally Bishop said. "The counselor told me to draw a picture of what I really wanted most. And you know what I drew?"

Ethan shook his head. Two stories below the ledge of the window, he could see his truck parked up on the curb. It was dark, and G Street was empty. From three stories up, the hood of the Dodge looked like a postcard. Or a target.

"I had this broken down armchair with a really ugly green fabric," Sally said. "It was my grandma's, and when she passed my papa put it in the basement, and I dragged it into my room. All kinds of cigarette burns on the arms, wine stains. One of the springs was a little broken and if you squinched your butt around, you could feel the metal. But I didn't care, I loved sitting in that chair playing records. You like music, Chief?"

He nodded. "George Strait especially. Dolly, of course. I'm partial to Sam Cooke."

"My favorite is Madonna," Sally said. "You like Madonna?"

"She's okay."

"She's the absolute best." Sally relaxed, leaning over the edge. "Her slow ones especially. I'd sit in that chair and listen to 'This Used to Be My Playground,' 'Sooner or Later.' When I got out of prison and went home, first thing I wanted was to sit in my chair, listen to my albums. Just for a few days, before dealing with everything else. But I got home and my room in the basement was empty. Mama had tossed everything out. *Everything*. The whole room was just boxes of her sewing and *National Geographic*s. Like I was never there."

Sally looked down at her dangling bare foot, the toenails bright green.

"Guess that's when I started feeling like this."

A car sped through the blinking intersection below. It was eleven forty. Ethan Brand had taken the call an hour after leaving the Supper Club. He'd been driving, trying to sort out how he felt. Taking the long way home.

Now he was leaning over the ledge, near where Sally Bishop sat dangling her legs, speaking to her calmly and clearly. Sally's neck was turned to him, the rest of her aimed out the window. The breeze off the water was cold. Sally didn't seem to notice she was shivering.

"I just started to feel like it all meant nothing. I still feel like that. Worse, 'cause it's like I'm too late to do anything right, so I lost the chance to get myself set up how I want. Do you know that feeling, Chief?"

"Sure."

"You're not just saying that?"

"No."

Near the end of his meal, he'd gone to the restroom, passing the Supper Club's kitchen. He meant to ask the chef about the elk heart, though venison hadn't been on the menu. At a table on the other side of the pass station sat the Sinclairs' children, Jess and Wynn Junior. Empty plates in front of them, Nintendo Switches and phones out. A seventeen- and a fourteen-year-old, waiting for their parents to finish brandy and dessert.

He'd said hello. Wynn Junior scowled at him. Jess had held his gaze, something like disdain in her young face. Teenage attitude, or did she suspect something about his feelings toward her mother? Blame him for the chill between her parents?

Steph and Wynn's marriage was rocky long before he'd taken Steph on that first midnight stroll. But the point of their dinner tonight had been clear: This was a peace talk, a drawing up of new treaties and relationships. In public, the three of them would be cordial. And in private he'd be nothing to the Sinclairs.

"No, I'm not just saying that," Ethan told Sally Bishop. "Not that I'm above a fib if it got you off the ledge. There's no such thing as an unmixed motive."

He grinned, but Sally didn't return it. "Tell me about you feeling like that," she said.

"Why don't we keep talking about you?" Ethan said. "Your son's five, right?"

"Five and two-thirds. He turns six in August."

"A fun age," he said. "You can take them places, they still need you. I bet in that picture you made for your counselor, your boy was a big part."

Sally nodded. "I wanted to bring him to my room and play Madonna for him. I used to sing to him before, you know."

Sally drew a long breath, making a slurping sound, and stared down. Three stories up, the fall probably wouldn't be fatal unless she landed wrong. It didn't much matter. There were higher heights in Blaine.

"I don't want to talk anymore," Sally Bishop said. "Tell me about how you sometimes feel like this, and what you do about it."

"Tall order."

Ethan stretched an arm out to rest on the ledge, inches from Sally's own hands. He tried to appear lost in thought.

"The most lost I ever felt was when I came out of the corps," he said. "At first I was too keyed up to feel much of anything, the way a car with the gas light on can still go a pace. But after a few weeks, I came to a stop."

"Why?" Sally settled back, leaning inside a bit more than out.

"Lots of reasons," Ethan said. "Lack of purpose, diminished abilities. I didn't have a sense of who I wanted to be. You know?"

Sally nodded.

"I had a couple of friends, Brad Dobbs and Ben Henriquez, who I'd gone through basic with. Ben was our platoon leader, married with a kid on the way. Brad came from this old southern family with sixteen cousins, the whole county named after his great-great-grandmother's people. You mind if I close the window a bit? I'm cold."

She didn't seem to notice, and soon they were sitting on the ledge facing inside. "What happened to them?" Sally said.

He could remember the explosion, the taste of dirt, the feeling of the earth showering down on them. Confusion outweighing pain, and then *only* pain.

"Brad and Ben didn't make it home," Ethan said. "And I did. Me, with no family at the time, no roots but my mother."

"I used to see her at the Super Value before I went away," Sally Bishop said. "Real nice lady. She always had her coupons ready."

Ethan smiled. "Why don't I drive you home?"

"Okay." She hopped down off the ledge.

In the truck, he told her of feeling aimless, like the wrong person had been selected to survive. He spoke generally, leaving out his injury and the solace he'd sought from painkillers. Relating his own story so it would make sense to Sally, who had once stabbed the mother of her son's friend with a pencil crayon.

"How'd you pull out of that feeling?" Sally asked.

"I had help. A friend offered me a job and a reason to get dressed in the morning. I built on that. But it took time, and it wasn't all one direction. I stumbled plenty. Still do."

Sally lived in a clean living house on C Street. Ethan made sure she got to her door, and watched her take her medication.

"Thanks, Chief," Sally said. "Guess I feel better. Still wish I had that chair, though. It would be nice to sit there with Lucian and listen to Madonna."

"There'll be other chairs," Ethan said.

* * *

When his phone rang at three forty in the morning, he was in the middle of a very sexual dream. A memory of a weekend in San Francisco last year, a law enforcement professionals conference Frank Keogh had insisted he attend. Steph had flown down separately. Three days spent mostly in bed or near the water, walking hand in hand in Union Square, dining along the Embarcadero. No hiding of their affection. Ethan hadn't even picked up his name tag for the conference.

The call roused him out of the dream, and he said, more irritably than he meant to, "What?"

The voice was male, soft. Not a voice he recognized. No accent. The words were enunciated clearly.

"Get my message?" the voice said.

"Can it wait till the morning? I don't have the department voice mail number, top of my head."

"I asked, did you get my message."

Immediately he was awake, the silence of the house now constricting and oppressive. "I got it, yeah."

"Then you should leave now."

He tried to open the voice recorder on his phone without ending the call. The voice was calm but threaded with an almost religious intensity. Waves in the background, it sounded like, or it could be static. He didn't recognize the number, though the 360 area code meant the call was local.

"I'm not going anywhere," Ethan said. "You're welcome to come to the station, though. We can hash things out in person."

"You won't leave?"

"I can't."

"Then I'm going to kill you," the voice said.

13

The morning brought a chill, along with a cold spatter of rain. Ethan sensed a similar coldness in the town. Glances from other drivers, greetings that were more formal than friendly. If his thoughts hadn't been circling around the phone call and the soft-spoken person who wanted him dead, he might have wondered why.

On his way to work he'd authorized a trace on the number that had called him, guessing it would turn out to be a disposable phone. He had tried phoning the number back, but it went straight to an anonymous voice mail. By the time the phone company could get around to providing him with the location the call had come from, along with the registration information, the phone itself would probably be nestled at the bottom of Drayton Harbor.

Ethan was having breakfast with Laura Dill's aunt this morning. Inside Lucky's, Mei nodded at him as he took his seat.

"Heya, Chief." The young woman's greeting wasn't quite as exuberant as usual.

Lorrie Dill hadn't arrived yet. Ethan ordered coffee and studied the magnetic chessboard. He made his move, remembering to develop his pieces toward the center of the board. Mei set down his mug and the dish of creams, glanced down, and checkmated him.

"Scholar's Mate," she said. "Not gonna be your day, is it?"

He soon saw why. The only other patron in the café finished her breakfast and set the morning's *Skyline* on the counter. Ethan's face stared back at him from above Jay Swan's byline. *New Police Chief Hunting 'Grisly' Killer, Vows Swift Justice.*

Below the fold was a second article, also by Jay. *Riding With Chief Brand.* The piece started with the line, "Dodge City had Bat Masterson, the Oklahoma Territory had Marshal Bass Reeves, and the Brothers Earp patrolled the mean streets of Tombstone." Quotes from Ethan's interview with Jay were interspersed with a history of law enforcement west of the Mississippi.

There was nothing factually wrong about either article. Jay was a responsible journalist and they'd quoted Ethan accurately and in context. But taken together, the two stories painted a picture of a police force obsessed with gunfighter glory on one hand, and stumped by a fresh homicide on the other.

All he'd done was try to be honest and not give away too many details of the investigation. But if he'd been Laura Dill's father or aunt, and had read today's paper, he would be worried whether the case was being handled with the skill and gravity it deserved.

All because of one interview. Well, lesson learned. Laura Dill was today's focus. He pushed everything else out of his mind, death threats included.

Lorrie Dill arrived at the café at eight thirty, dressed in a black pullover and black corded jeans. She kept her sunglasses on as she entered, pausing to look at the wall-sized black-and-white photo of Chinese gold miners posed at their claim. Handsome hard faces that offered silent testimony to unrelenting hardships, deprivation, and the lure of fortune.

"Thought we were having breakfast," Lorrie said. "This place looks more like a Chinese restaurant."

"Chinese American," Mei said with a polite edge. "We eat breakfast too."

They moved to a table beneath the photo on the wall. "I was listening to your interview on the drive over from Lynden," Lorrie said. "Doesn't sound like you've found out much about who killed my niece. Isn't there some forty-eight hour rule about murders?"

"Homicide cases take as long as they take to get right," Ethan said. "That's why there's no statute of limitations."

Noticing Mei draw closer, Lorrie said to her, "Cup of orange pekoe if you got it."

"You betcha."

When the tea arrived, the dead woman's aunt added two thimbles of half and half, stirring with the string attached to the tea bag.

"My niece is murdered," Lorrie said. "And the same day you're giving interviews."

Ethan didn't bother to correct her. "I apologize. Laura's homicide is our priority. My best people are on this, and the resources of the entire county are behind them."

Lorrie Dill extracted the tea bag from her cup. "Let's just get this over with. Ask what you need to ask."

"What was Laura's home life like?"

"Well, it wasn't all sunshine and puppy farts," Lorrie said. "Robert and Susan loved her, though. After the accident, that was a different household. Robert still hasn't come to grips with it."

"Did Laura have someone to confide in?"

"Me."

Ethan nodded. "When I spoke with Robert yesterday, he said his daughter didn't have a boyfriend. Thought I caught a reaction to the contrary from you."

"This place do eggs?" Lorrie asked.

She ordered an omelet. Ethan ordered his usual and a refill of coffee. He borrowed a pencil from behind the till and rested it on top of his steno pad. He waited for Lorrie to find her voice on the subject of her niece.

"I made a point, after the crash, to be there for Laura. You met my brother. Robert isn't, what's the word, demonstrative. The silence in that home was so thick sometimes you needed a hacksaw. Gloomy."

Lorrie cut a piece of omelet with the edge of the fork but didn't eat it.

"I told myself, Lorrie, she needs you, it's time to step up. So I took her out once a month, special occasions or just whenever. I was her dad's big sister, and I kind of had that role with her, too. Asking what she wanted out of life, helping her if I could. I love Robert, but my brother isn't ambitious."

"And Laura was?"

"In a way, she was the most ambitious person I know."

Lorrie Dill folded the remains of her omelet between two pieces of toast and chewed down the sandwich. Ethan took notes between bites.

"Robert had gotten an insurance settlement from the crash. What he didn't spend on Susan's funeral went to Laura's schooling. Around the time she moved out, she asked her father for the cash. He gave her some of it, I think—I don't know exactly how much. Once she moved to Seattle, I saw less of her."

Ethan didn't ask why. He waited, letting the silence build, until the aunt volunteered to speak.

"My niece was working in a restaurant, busing tables, waitressing. One of the line cooks got it in her head to buy a food truck. She asked Laura to go halves. I worked in a bank, Chief Brand. I know a thing or three about business. I told her the success rate of new restaurants is about as low as a gopher's hidey hole. Long and the short of it, Laura lost everything. She had a few bad months after that."

"Drugs?" he asked.

"I never saw her take anything stronger than light beer."

"But something changed for her."

"Yeah. Laura got mean. Started to act like she was owed. Asked me to ask her dad for the rest of that money. When I said I didn't think that was a good idea, she stopped returning my calls."

Mei took the plates, left their check, and reset the chessboard. She played white, moving the E pawn two squares forward. The restaurant had a half-dozen patrons now. Ethan caught their glances.

"The last time I saw Laura was about a year ago, at Easter," Lorrie Dill said. "She was excited again, focused. Even apologized to me. She said her boyfriend had hooked her up with a new job, for big money, which was going to start soon. Laura was moving in with him."

"What was the job?" Ethan asked.

"Laura didn't say, only that travel was a part of it. She asked me to help her get her passport. She wanted to use my address, but I told her I didn't feel good about that. She used her father's instead."

"Why not the boyfriend's place, if she was living there?"

"Beats me," Lorrie said. "My niece didn't volunteer many details."

"Would you say she made a point of not mentioning what kind of work she was doing?"

Lorrie thought about it, nodded.

"Could it have been criminal?"

"Maybe," she said, quickly adding, "but if you think my niece was some hardened dope dealer—if you're going to write her off, instead of finding who killed her—"

"The very last thing I want to do," Ethan said. "If we know the reason for her trip over the border, we can figure out who else might've known."

"Well, I'd definitely start with that boyfriend," Lorrie Dill said.

"You have a name?"

She shook her head. "I dropped her off at his place on my way home from Robert's. The night of Easter Sunday. Might still have the GPS in my phone."

She called it up, turning the screen so Ethan could see where the pin had been dropped. An intersection northwest of Lynden, at the junction of a logging road and a long private driveway. Ethan recognized the place. The McCandless homestead.

14

"There's no chance in hell Jody McCandless will talk to us," Brenda Lee said.

Ethan maneuvered the truck around a pothole on Giles Road. They were heading southeast, toward the address Lorrie had given him. Blaine's small warehouse and industrial district gave way to second-growth redwoods and small stretches of farmland.

"Jody will talk," Ethan said. "He just won't say anything."

A century ago, soon after the Semiahmoo people were relocated across the border, the McCandless clan settled in Whatcom County. They tried raising livestock, growing apples, corn, but finally gave up and grew nothing. The location of their homestead, close to the Canadian border, made it valuable real estate during Prohibition. When bootlegging dried up, they learned to smuggle other things.

The family was suspected of having a hand in most of the drug markets in Blaine. Bringing in heroin from the Vancouver port, trucking cocaine up from California. As middlemen, the McCandless family could have made quiet fortunes. Joe McCandless, a Vietnam vet, had been cagey enough to stay out of reach of the law. His three children, Seth, Sissy, and Jody, had made very different choices.

Seth McCandless was currently serving a three-year sentence in Clallam Bay for assault. His second conviction, though he'd been suspected in several other crimes. A violent man with a hair-trigger temper, Seth had taken over the family business from his father. Ethan remembered how Seth McCandless had peacocked through the courtroom, right up until the verdict came in. Then Seth had struggled against the bailiffs, cursing at Ethan and everyone else who'd helped put him away.

Seth McCandless was a bruiser, bullnecked, tall, prone to settling problems with his fists. His younger brother Jody was harder to figure. Jody was slight and looked like you could knock him down with a willow branch. That didn't stop him from running his mouth. Jody would talk crap to anyone, even the law. *Especially* the law.

When it came to backing up his words, though, Jody wasn't eager for a fight. Not a fair one. He was suspected in setting two fires, one in a bar where a waitress had disrespected him, the other the family home of a speed dealer who allegedly owed him money. The dealer's mother had suffered second-degree burns. Both victims refused to name Jody as the arsonist.

An informant of Ethan's had explained the difference between the brothers. "Seth McCandless will crack your skull if you piss him off, then go back to doing business with you like it never happened. Anger's like a light switch, on and off. Jody, though, that kid will flap his gums till you tell him to shut up. Then he'll act nice to you. He'll keep on acting nice for years. And then he'll slit your throat."

With Seth in prison, Jody was in charge. The family business was still operating, as far as Ethan knew, though in the last few months he had heard complaints of a dry spell, drug-wise. That meant fewer overdoses, but also more break-ins and property crimes as dealers raised prices. Jody could be out of his depth as a leader. Or maybe he was planning something.

Where did this leave Sissy McCandless, the middle child? Ethan often wondered just that. After earning a business degree from community college, Sissy had bought Breakwater Travel, arranging package vacations for people who didn't want to bargain hunt online. She lived above the shop in a small apartment, visited her family homestead on holidays, and otherwise had little to do with her brothers.

Or so it seemed.

The white sheep, Frank had called her. How likely was it for a family of criminals to have a sister completely out of the criminal life? But then how fair was it to condemn Sissy McCandless for what her brothers had done? If anyone had the right to the benefit of the doubt, it was a young woman trying her best to steer clear of the family business.

The truck bumped along Giles Road. The McCandless homestead had been formed from several smaller properties, only some of which fell within the town limits. As they approached, Ethan saw a FOR SALE sign on one side of the road. A barren field wrapped in barbed wire.

On the other side of the road was the farmhouse itself, three stories of ramshackle weather-stripped wood. The carcasses of old cars and trucks cluttered the yard. The walkway to the house was rotting plywood laid over mud. The officers walked the path carefully.

"How can anyone live like this?" Brenda Lee muttered as they passed a kitchen sink, smashed to pieces on the dead lawn. One of the boards of the front staircase was missing, and coffee cans on the porch held cigarette butts, fast food wrappers, a slingshot, and stones. In front of the door was a mat with a drawing of two cave men standing on either side of a giant cauldron. Inside the pot was a man in a suit, flames rising around him. *Trespassers Welcome to Stay for Dinner*, the mat said.

Brenda Lee beat a fist on the screen. More than a minute passed before they heard coughing and the creak of floorboards from inside. She knocked again, louder.

"Mr. McCandless, please come to the door," she said. "Your car is here, we know you're inside."

Parked near the staircase was a massive, brand-new Ram, its black paint spotless. The homestead didn't look like much, but Jody took pride in his truck. The Ram reminded Ethan of something his mother had once said: "Clean pickups and dirty pickups are owned by different types of people."

"Slide your warrant under the door," a voice said from inside. He couldn't tell if it was Jody, and couldn't help compare it to the voice from the threatening phone call. Both muffled, male, calm.

"We just want to talk," Ethan said.

"So talk through the wood."

"You'd rob us of the pleasure at gazing on your pretty face?"

"Pretty my ass," the voice said. But Jody opened the door, stepping out and closing it before they could peer inside.

Jody McCandless was even rangier than the last time Ethan had seen him. Medium height, long hair a chestnut color and folded into a bun. He wore a silk shirt with the collar unbuttoned, cargo pants in desert camouflage, blue Crocs. On Jody's throat was tattooed a barbed wire M. His brother Seth had the same tattoo on his bicep.

Jody looked from Brenda Lee to Ethan, mean-mugging the officers. He pointed at the porch ceiling, the black bubble affixed below the eaves.

"Just so's you know, this conversation is being recorded on camera," he said. "Speak your piece and leave."

Ethan pointed at the field on the other side of the road. "You're selling part of the farm. That your idea or Seth's?"

"Family reached a consensus." Jody smiled. "You're too late to put in a bid for it, Chief. Not that you could afford it."

"We'd like to know about Laura Dill," Brenda Lee said.

"And who's that?" His exaggerated scowl was hard to read.

"We heard Laura was your girlfriend, and was working with you."

"Who'd you hear all that from?" Jody asked.

"A reputable source," Brenda Lee said.

"Uh-huh. And that reputable source give you any proof to back all that up?"

"Are you saying you don't know if Laura Dill was your girlfriend?"

"They come and go so fast, it's hard to keep track." Jody made a point of scanning Brenda Lee head to toe. "Always room for another, though. You're a bit older than my usual, but an old piano still plays, doesn't it?"

"Watch your mouth," Brenda Lee said.

"No disrespect, Officer." Jody looked between them, amused. "How'd you like working for this guy?" Meaning Ethan. "You started at the cop shop same time as him, didn't you? So why aren't you the new boss?"

"It's an appointment, not a job based on seniority or merit," Brenda Lee said. "Sort of like being the younger brother of a crime boss and having things handed to you."

That struck a nerve. Jody snorted and glared at her, at Ethan, who was wondering if Brenda Lee meant it or was trying to provoke Jody. Probably both, he reckoned.

"I earned my spot, lady," Jody said. "Paid my way in blood."

"Whose?"

Jody's sneer curdled into a smile. He clenched and relaxed his fists.

"My sister says when I get angry, I should take a few breaths. 'Step back from your emotions' is how she puts it. So if you'll excuse me, I'm gonna do that."

"Before you do," Ethan said. "Tell us where you were the day before yesterday."

"Why?"

"The woman you're not sure you know was found dead, stabbed, near the railroad tracks."

Jody wasn't fazed by the news. "Sorry to hear that," he said.

"Your whereabouts?"'

"Here, for the most part."

"Can anyone verify that?" Brenda Lee asked.

"My word ain't good enough for you, beautiful?" Jody placed his hand on his chest as if hurt. "If you'd like to ask me again over dinner?"

"I'd like to kick you between the legs several times," Brenda Lee said.

"You hear that, Chief? Threats." Jody was enjoying himself.

Ethan held up a photo of Laura Dill. "We're pretty sure you know her."

"Not saying I do or don't."

"You own a knife, Jody?"

"Man, who doesn't?"

"We recovered a piece of her luggage."

"So?"

"So if you're lying to us about Laura Dill, we'll find out."

"Well hoo-ray for you, Chief." Jody clapped. "Sounds like you're really putting your stamp on the department, yes sir, proving you're the right dude for the job. You know this lady hates you, right? You can see she wants your job?"

"That's neither here nor there," Ethan said. Jody was adept at spotting a weakness or a sore spot. A skill that probably came in handy dealing with his family. "We're collecting evidence, and a lot of it's pointing in your direction."

"You found a backpack. Whoop de doo."

"I didn't say backpack," Ethan said.

Jody realized his mistake and scowled out of reflex. Angry at himself, at Ethan and Brenda Lee. His fists clenched. His body seemed beyond his control, and for a moment it seemed possible he'd strike out.

But Jody mastered whatever turbulent emotions were at work inside him. "Off my property, please and thanks." The door slammed behind him.

They picked their way carefully down the broken stairs. "You called it," Brenda Lee said. "The little shit told us a lot of nothing."

Ethan took no pleasure in being right.

15

In the soft interview room, Heck Ruiz was talking with Shooter Kwon, one of the students who'd been caught smashing windows. Kwon's parents accompanied him. Once Heck explained that he didn't care about the broken glass, that all he cared about was the body, the Kwon family seemed eager to help.

Yes, Shooter and Collin Rusk had thrown a few rocks down at Mo's Scrapyard. No reason, just bored. They liked to walk the train tracks, smoke cigarettes, and break things. Shooter's parents seemed more concerned about the tobacco than the vandalism, though they offered to pay the Singh family for the repairs.

The boys had seen the body, yes. They hadn't spoken up because of their own petty crime. They didn't get close to the corpse, just saw it and left.

Ethan watched on the closed circuit monitor outside the interview room, a triangle of club sandwich in his hand. Heck inched his chair closer to the teenager. The station had "hard" and "soft" interview rooms. The soft one was furnished with comfortable chairs, Easter colors on the walls, and a beige table at a child's height. Artwork had been taped up, crayon drawings by kids who'd spent time in the room for a variety of reasons, all of them sad.

"I've been your age, dude," Heck said to Shooter. "I know how boys are. No boy is gonna walk by something as freaking cool as a body without at least taking a look. Which is fine, no one's mad, but we gotta know if you touched the crime scene, or if you took anything, or saw anyone around. Could be important."

Heck seemed to have a good rapport with teens. Maybe being younger himself was part of it, but his attitude was also genuine and understanding. You couldn't fake that. Kids picked up on his sincerity.

"We wanted to get closer," Shooter admitted. "But we heard someone coming."

"Along the tracks? On foot?"

"No, like a motor." Shooter rolled his Rs, making a high-pitched revving sound.

"Like a motorcycle?" Heck asked. "Or more like a car?"

"More like a dirt bike."

"So you heard this dirt bike engine, then you ran away."

"Yeah. Kind of."

Heck waited.

"We heard the motor first," Shooter said. "Then we saw the— saw her. And we figured this person might come back, so we left."

"You didn't see anyone, though?" Heck asked.

"No. Just heard."

"When was this?"

"Like maybe seven thirty. Before school started."

Shooter explained that he'd walked to school after that, while Collin Rusk had gone home to get his books. While the teen was explaining what he'd done the rest of the day, Ethan's phone rang. He tossed the remains of his sandwich before answering.

"Mayor Mooney," Jon Gutierrez said before connecting them.

Not a conversation he'd been looking forward to, but an unavoidable one. "Morning, Eldon," he said. "Your nephew probably told you of our conversation last night. I reached a decision, it's final, and I'm sorry."

"That's not why I'm calling, Chief Brand."

The formality in the mayor's voice might mean he was on speaker with others listening in. It wasn't a good sign.

"Council is concerned. We'd appreciate a few minutes of your time."

"Sure," Ethan said. "Is this afternoon all right?"

"We'd prefer right now," Mooney said.

* * *

What a difference a day made. Gone were the smiles and chitchat. The council chamber was quiet, empty save for the seven people seated on the dais. The mayor presided, the others looking to him. Only Arlene Six Crows nodded a hello in his direction.

Projected on the wall was the front page of today's *Skyline*. Ethan understood. He moved to the center of the horseshoe and folded his hands at ease.

"We're more than a little troubled by what we've been reading," Eldon Mooney said. "And listening to. Have you heard Jay Swan's podcast? Allow us to play you an excerpt."

He nodded toward the back, and soon Jay's voice boomed out from the PA system, followed by Ethan's own.

"Would it be fair to say the frontier mentality was part of your upbringing?"

"All my life."

After a minute of the exchange, the mayor signaled to cut the audio. He looked at Ethan expectantly.

"I was discussing a mindset I grew up with," he told the council. "Not one I endorse."

"Are you saying your words were taken out of context?" Mooney said.

"I'm saying that *was* the context."

"Justice."

Before Ethan could respond, the mayor sniffed and turned a page in front of him. An act, Ethan thought. Mooney wasn't wasting time paying him back for firing Cliff. The passive-aggressive way Mooney conducted the meeting was meant to provoke him into anger, hanging himself with his own words. Underneath the mayor's passion for boats and his folksy manner, Eldon Mooney was a political jackal.

As a group, the other councillors seemed neutral on the matter, though Ethan suspected at least one would be happy to see him go. Wynn Sinclair was studying something on his tablet, swiping the screen and not looking up. As if they hadn't shared dinner last night.

"Chief, your beliefs are your own," Mooney said. "And I am aware that you're not a practiced public speaker. However disagreeable some of us might find these statements of yours—we won't go into that now—we're here because of a much more grievous affair."

"An update on the Laura Dill homicide."

"If you please."

He told them of the work the department had done, what they projected to do. That afternoon he'd be sitting down with the Washington State Patrol, Customs, and the RCMP to discuss Laura Dill's trip to Canada.

"How many homicides have your people investigated?" the mayor asked. "Ballpark, of course. A dozen, two dozen, over the last ten years?"

"Two," Ethan said.

"Two dozen?"

"Two cases, Your Honor."

A pause so this could sink in with Mooney's fellow councillors. "And these were what you'd call open and shut cases, were they not?"

"I wouldn't call them that."

"But the perpetrators were caught quickly, within a day or so."

He nodded.

"And the last time the department handled a homicide was when?"

"Two years ago."

"You see our concern, Chief Brand."

Mooney was shaving the dice, making him look inexperienced. That was unfair, but it wasn't completely untrue. Murder wasn't a common occurrence in a town the size of Blaine.

"I get your concern, yes," Ethan said. "Between the sheriffs and WSP, we have access to the support we need. This is our top priority."

"With respect, Chief," Mooney said, "the question isn't one of manpower so much as experience. Leadership, if you will. Can you honestly tell us this case would be handled best under your supervision, rather than by an agency with greater resources?"

There it was, Mooney's ploy to undermine his leadership. Either Ethan admitted his department lacked the ability to handle a case such as this, or he insisted he could solve it, which meant tying his career to finding Laura Dill's killer. All other outcomes would spell failure. *His* failure.

So be it. He cleared his throat.

"In my experience there's no such thing as an open and shut case," he said. "Even if you know who did it, you need to find evidence to prove it, preserve that evidence properly, present it in court, and conduct yourself honorably from first response to last appeal."

"With respect, Chief, I'm not following your point."

"Then I'll spell it out for Your Honor," Ethan said. "Two of what you call open and shut cases are two cases put down. Which means our department has a one hundred percent clearance rate on homicides. Doesn't it?"

"I suppose," Mooney said.

"My aim is to keep it that way. Ms. Dill was found within our jurisdiction, which makes this our case."

"So you're saying the council can count on you to resolve this, Chief Brand?"

The mayor's quizzical expression couldn't hide satisfaction at his own gambit. Ethan met the gaze with a smile and all the confidence he could summon.

"You're damn right, Your Honor."

* * *

Coming out of the Banner Building, his thoughts were back on Jody McCandless, what the smuggler's relationship had been to Laura Dill, and how to get Jody to talk. At first, when Jody had spoken through the door, his voice had been muffled. It wasn't exactly the same as the voice from last night's phone call, but there were similarities. Male, soft, muffled. Lost in thought, Ethan walked smack into Steph Sinclair stepping onto the curb.

His arm snagged hers as she stumbled, holding on as Steph regained her footing. Both of them flustered, shocked at the other's touch. Steph's purse had fallen. He picked it up.

"Beg your pardon," Ethan said. "My mind was on other things."

It wasn't now. Steph was so close he could smell the separate scents of her shampoo and body scrub, lemon and apricot. She was wearing buff-colored slacks and a pale blue angora sweater, and carrying a white raincoat over one arm.

"Your husband's inside," he said.

"Actually, it was you I was coming to see."

"You knew I was here?"

"I saw you go in," Steph said. "Can I walk with you back to the station? There's a favor I'd like to ask."

It was a short walk but strained, both of them excessively formal, playing at being acquaintances, worried an intimate gesture or phrase would give them away. There wasn't anything to give away anymore. It was over. And yet.

"Thank you again for dinner last night," Ethan said. "Please thank your husband for me. I didn't have the chance to tell him."

"It was our pleasure, Chief." Steph remarked about the clear and sunny April day, and after he responded, she said, "I was wondering if you could have a talk with my daughter."

"Pertaining to what?" he asked.

"Jess is struggling a little with school, and with what she wants to do after."

"Considering a career in law enforcement?"

Steph smiled. "Thankfully, no. But she was never this difficult."

"Isn't difficult on par for a seventeen-year-old?"

"Not *this* seventeen-year-old." They crossed the street, passing the Super Value. "Jess has always been engaged with the world. Lately she seems troubled. And when Wynn or I try to press her, she shuts down."

"If you think it'll help, I'll talk with her." Was this the sort of thing people expected a chief of police to do? Or did Steph have another reason to ask him?

They'd broken things off on a walk like this. Snow had been on the ground and Steph Sinclair had been underdressed when she arrived at his place. After they'd made love, she borrowed an old jacket of his for the walk back to the restaurant. And then, as they came in sight of the O.B., she slid it off her shoulders and handed it back.

"I can't be two people anymore," Steph had told him. "I need to make a change."

"So change," he'd said. "Leave Wynn. Bring the kids."

"I can't."

"You don't want to, you mean."

She'd opened her mouth to protest, paused and nodded. "I guess I don't."

He'd accepted it, feeling the pain strike him in the solar plexus. He remembered snow in her hair. They'd kissed, their last kiss, the only kiss shared in public. That had been the end.

And now here they were. Walking together again. The months apart seemed of no consequence. Time melted away with her close.

At the corner of H Street, Steph stopped and touched his shoulder. She reached a hand to his face. Her left hand, the wedding band visible and drawing his eye.

"You have a little piece of fluff in your hair," she said, pretending to pick it out. And as she leaned closer, she whispered, "Jess knows about us."

16

In the late afternoon, sitting in a darkened conference room in the Peace Arch Customs building, waiting as Brenda Lee connected her laptop to the overhead projector, Ethan wondered why Steph wanted him to talk to her daughter. Wouldn't the person who almost wrecked your parents' marriage be the last person you'd want to speak with?

If Jess was distraught, what could he say? And if her knowledge of Steph and Ethan's relationship was affecting her schoolwork, could it be severe enough to make her send death threats?

The voice had sounded male, but what did that mean, anyway? A shade lower in register, but that could be forced. The more he thought on it, the more it *seemed* forced, a higher pitched voice faking a tenor.

If Jess Sinclair had threatened to kill him, he'd have to charge her. What would that do to Steph? And if he covered that up, what would that to do him?

The projector flickered and video footage filled the screen. The others in the room—Lieutenant Moira Sutcliffe from the Washington State Patrol, Deputy Gus Murphy from the Whatcom County Sheriff, a US Customs official, and a staff sergeant from the Mounties—gave the video their attention. A train compartment, double rows of empty seats separated by an aisle. A trim porter walked down, head swiveling, double-checking the car was clean.

"Miguel Royas," Brenda Lee said. "Seven years with Amtrak. He took Laura's ticket but doesn't remember her."

The inspection done, the porter disappeared. Passengers flooded the compartment, entering below the camera, a parade of bald spots, ponytails, and Seahawks caps. Some followed luggage to the storage shelves near the door. Others hoisted bags into the overhead bin. Brenda Lee named each one of them, summarizing their minor interactions with the dead woman.

Laura Dill was the last passenger seated. Her back was to the camera until she reached a quartet of unoccupied seats. She unslung her backpack, tried to muscle it over her head, but could only raise it chin high. A woman in a pantsuit tapped her shoulder, made an offer of assistance. Smiling, Laura shook her head, heaving the pack onto the window seat beside her.

"Charmaine Boon, masseuse from Tukwila," Brenda Lee said. "Her only interaction was to ask if Laura needed a hand."

"A heavy pack," Moira Sutcliffe said. "Could indicate smuggling."

"Customs search her thoroughly?" Gus Murphy asked.

"Hey, don't look at us," the Customs official said. Snickers. Ethan focused on the screen, the dead woman settling into her seat.

Brenda Lee sped through the next hour of footage. Morning light began to filter through the windows. Laura seemed to be napping, or sitting with her thoughts. No book, no electronics.

The heads of the passengers began rotating as the train came to a stop. Two Customs officers boarded and examined passports and IDs.

"Her documents were completely in order," the Customs official said, mildly defensive.

The inspection finished and the train started up again. After a few minutes, Laura Dill stood, lugging her backpack up the aisle, disappearing out of view. Brenda Lee hit pause and clicked open another video file.

"Here's where it gets a little strange," she said.

The new footage showed the same compartment from the opposite end. Brenda Lee paused as a head bobbed partially into view, followed by the edge of a door.

"This is the last footage of Laura, likely entering a washroom. The time is ten past six. The train was due into Bellingham at six twenty, but was running fifteen minutes behind. Laura's body was spotted at seven thirty by two teenagers. Officer Ruiz and Gurvinder Singh found it shortly after eight."

"No better angle on the washroom?" Moira Sutcliffe asked.

"This is what we have." Brenda Lee touched the screen. "Bellingham is coming up. Three passengers off, including Laura if we go by her ticket. There's no footage of her getting off at the station. Seventeen passengers get on."

New faces settled into the seats. A bald man with a rumpled suit wheeled a suitcase toward the aisle, then doubled back and swung the washroom door open, disappearing inside.

"Bob Galvin, unemployed from Bellingham," Brenda Lee said. "Rode the train to Everett to buy a present for his mother. Didn't see Laura at all. According to him, the washroom was unoccupied."

Gus Murphy asked the question everyone was thinking.

"So how did this woman get from the restroom of the train to a field without anyone seeing?"

"The train's cameras aren't meant for continual surveillance. Laura could have left the washroom, stayed in the vestibule between the cameras, and leaped off."

"Or been pushed," Sutcliffe said.

"Or wasn't on board at all," Ethan said.

His comment coincided with Brenda Lee throwing the lights on. He found himself receiving several curious glances from the others.

"You think someone hacked the train's footage?" the Customs official said.

"Or maybe Laura Dill has a secret twin," Murphy said.

Not a twin, Ethan thought. But there was something amiss on that train.

* * *

Driving back, Brenda Lee said she'd make a trip to Vancouver on Monday to show Laura's photo around the train station and hotels. Maybe someone remembered her.

"Do you think she was working as a drug mule?" Brenda Lee asked.

"If she knew Jody McCandless, that's a possibility," Ethan said. "Her face would be hard to pick out of a crowd. That could be an asset in his line of work."

"It would explain why Laura's backpack was empty, too. Not to mention give us a motive."

But there was something about that version of events that didn't fit. A lowly courier wouldn't interact with someone as high up as Jody McCandless, not unless they were moving a significant amount. Even then it would be a stupid risk on Jody's part. And if Laura Dill was moving a large quantity, why take the train instead of a vehicle?

"What if she was bringing something else over the border?" Ethan asked.

"Like what? Money?"

"Cash would be easier to sneak across than drugs."

"Easier for someone to steal, too," Brenda Lee said.

* * *

In the station muster room they assembled the others and went through the day's discoveries. Heck Ruiz had tried to interview Collin Rusk, but the teen's parents weren't cooperating. Brenda Lee had found no passengers on the northbound train who remembered Laura Dill. The cashier in the bistro car remembered a woman with a yellow backpack ordering several drinks, but couldn't recall who she was with.

Ethan told them what Jody McCandless had said—and hadn't said. It was clear the smuggler knew Laura, and likely he knew something about her disappearance.

Mal Keogh had waited to go last, excited, his leg pumping under the desk. Spinning his tablet so the others could see the screen, he showed them a photograph of the clay depression next to the old church. He swiped the screen and the photo was replaced by a close-up of the tread mark left in the earth.

"Let me introduce you to the Trail Wolf," Mal said. "Shooter Kwon heard a high-pitched engine like a dirt bike. But these aren't dirt bike tire treads. Too wide, but not wide enough for a truck."

"An all-terrain vehicle?" Brenda Lee asked.

Mal nodded, peeved that someone had leaped ahead in his presentation. He clicked again. The screen split to show the tread mark next to a photo of a tire with an identical tread.

"The Carlisle Trail Wolf is an off-road ATV tire," Mal said. "My hypothesis is whoever drove it parked in the depression behind the church to keep it out of sight while they burned whatever was in the backpack."

"Not bad, Mal," Heck said. "For a nerd, I mean." The two younger officers bumped fists.

"Very nice," Ethan agreed. "You have a list of recent sales?"

"Working on it. Blaine Muffler and Tire has sold forty-three Trail Wolves in the last two years."

"An odd number," Brenda Lee said.

"Off-road tires take a real beating."

"I'm aware of that, Mal."

Before any further tension could build, Ethan ended the meeting.

* * *

"I'm not saying he isn't a very good forensic investigator," his senior officer said moments later. They were speaking in Ethan's office, just Brenda Lee and himself. His last meeting of the day.

"Mal is used to Frank giving him latitude," Ethan said. "You've worked with a boss's kid before. He's doing good work."

"He's testing my authority," Brenda Lee said.

"Sometimes that's necessary."

"You're taking his side?" She held up her hand before Ethan could reply. "I know it's more complex than that. But I'm frustrated, Ethan. I had tasks for him to do while I was in that meeting, tasks he disobeyed. That extra work falls on me."

He nodded. "That's unfair. I'll see it doesn't happen again."

"Thank you," Brenda Lee said. "Can I bring you anything back from Canada?"

"Evidence would be nice."

* * *

At home he set up a video call, speaking to his kids before bed. A touch football game, a science project. For Easter Mom was taking them to Grandma and Grandpa's. The whole backyard would be turned into a giant egg hunt. Wasn't that super cool?

He missed them terribly. "Good night, Ben. Good night, Brad," he said to the screen.

"Night, Dad."

"Night."

Ethan closed the computer and sat on the porch for a long time, thinking of parents and children, life and death, listening to the distant traffic from the highway.

17

At eight AM on a remarkably clear Sunday morning, a whistle screeched. Thirty-one pairs of boots started forward, marching over train tracks, through undergrowth, on either side of Portal Way. The terrain was too varied to move shoulder to shoulder, but the group stayed in a rough line, scouring the area they passed.

The line was made up of officers and volunteers from several different agencies. Ethan chose to make the walk with the others, stomping through blackberries and a grove of second-growth yew. His ankle smarted as the morning wore on. But he liked the woods, enjoyed the dart of squirrels, the Steller's jays and crows flapping out of the trees as the search party encroached on their territory. A pair of eagles spun above them, taking in the work of this strange task.

On farmlands, they asked permission to cross. A woman leaned against a pickup truck, smoking and watching them cross her field. She waved, enjoying the morning's entertainment.

That reminded him, he owed Arlene Six Crows a visit. Yesterday he'd been so busy with the case and the meetings, he'd forgotten. He would do that today, after the search wrapped up.

To his right, Moira Sutcliffe called out, "Found something."

Mal Keogh blew the whistle again, halting the party. He jogged over to inspect.

"Knife," the lieutenant said. Ethan had gotten to know Moira when she worked at the Whatcom County Jail. She was personable, funny, but clearly didn't see the Blaine PD as the equal of the state troopers.

Mal photographed the knife, bagged it, and held it up. Ethan squinted. A simple clasp blade, the metal tarnished and the wood handle black and chipped. Too stubby to match the wounds in Laura Dill's side.

"Probably been here twenty years," Mal said. The disappointment in his voice traveled along the line of canvassers like a plucked guitar string. The march forward resumed.

By nine they'd combed the area up to Mo's Scrapyard. Ethan noticed the Singhs had already replaced the broken windows in the shop. By ten, the group had snaked all the way to the church. A mile beyond was a rest stop near the highway, where the search ended. Ethan had coffee and breakfast waiting, along with a borrowed school bus to carry the searchers back to where they'd started.

Moira scraped yogurt with a wooden spoon. "Wish we'd had better luck," she said to Ethan. "Least the weather held. How's it feel being honcho numero uno?"

Ethan had stuck with coffee, and was on his fourth cup of the morning. "There's a lot to the job."

"I bet," Moira said. "And they saved you a homicide as a nice little welcome present. First one in a while for Blaine, isn't it?"

"Two years."

"You're too good a cop for a small town force," Moira said. "Not good enough for us, mind you, but almost. You ever want a faster pace, we could probably make an exception for you."

"The offer's appreciated," Ethan said. "So is the help today."

The lieutenant finished her yogurt and looked around the rest stop for a garbage bin. "Got me out of doing chores around the house. Any Sunday morning where I don't have to scrub a toilet? That's a win in my book."

*   *   *

At the station, Mal and Ethan combed through the bags of items recovered from the forest. Mostly junk, beer cans, food wrappers, old bits of clothing. Nothing that screamed out a connection to Laura Dill. The bags reeked of cigarette butts, stale beer, rotten food, and decomposing leaves. Ethan was glad he'd skipped breakfast.

With each item, Mal picked it up, turned it over in gloved hands, and if it seemed promising, subjected it to a glance under the table-mounted magnifying glass. Ethan wrote down a description. *One apple core, brown. Shred of plastic wrap from cigarette package. Clasp knife, blade heavily oxidized.*

Mal paused to snort antihistamine. He tossed a squashed 7-Up can into the sorted pile. "We really should have support staff to do this," he said.

"Small department, small budget." Ethan didn't mind. They had the muster room to themselves. "You can put on music if you want."

"That George Strait stuff you listen to? Pass, Chief."

They finished one bag, started on the second. Most of the canvassers had picked up nothing, but some had scooped up every human-made item they'd spotted. Volunteer help was necessary, and appreciated, though sometimes more work than relief.

A beer can used as an ashtray. A plastic shotgun shell.

"There's a lot of tension between you and Brenda Lee," Ethan said. "I need you two to figure out how to work together."

Mal didn't look up from the pile. "You think my work hasn't been my best?"

"I think you and she need to tailor your approaches to each other. Get on the same page."

"Her page, you mean."

"She's the lead on this."

Mal nodded. "If I did that, would we have the tire print or Laura Dill's backpack?"

"You're doing top-notch work," Ethan said. "So is Brenda Lee. But having two star players on the field means jack shit without teamwork."

Mal examined several more cans and candy wrappers before speaking. "Off the record," he said after a minute, "I don't understand how you're okay with her."

"With Brenda Lee? What do you mean?"

"My father picked you, whatever his reasoning might be. Brenda Lee declared herself a rival candidate for the job. She found some disgruntled councillors to support her and dug up everything she could about my father. And about you."

Ethan hadn't been aware of that last point. Hadn't even considered it. How far did Brenda Lee Page dig? Did she know about his injury? His opioid use? The affair with Steph? Would Brenda Lee have used those things against him if she did?

"Honestly, Chief," Mal said, "I don't know why you trusted her with the most important case we've had in years. If we don't solve this, it reflects on you. Not her. Brenda Lee can always say she didn't have adequate support, and it'll be your word against hers."

They finished the second bag, taped it shut, and placed it in a large evidence box with the other. Mal ripped off the latex gloves and dabbed hand sanitizer on his palms.

"Brenda Lee has ambition," Ethan said, "but she would never sabotage an investigation. Let alone a homicide."

"Sure you want to stake your career on that?" Mal asked.

"I think I already did."

* * *

The canvass had been fruitless, but walking the area again had helped Ethan to better visualize the crime. The use of an ATV made the location seem less random. An isolated stretch of brush in the early morning, set back from the only nearby road. The area had been chosen specifically, either as a point to meet someone jumping off the train, or to stash a getaway vehicle. He felt certain of it.

The victim likely knew her killer, and since Laura Dill knew Jody McCandless, that meant Jody might know who committed the crime. How to get that information out of him, though? It would be difficult—especially if Jody was the one who killed her.

He had to find a way to get Jody to talk.

18

Arlene Six Crows owned a small timber-framed shopping complex near the waterfront. Her law practice was located on the second floor, between a dentist's office and a holistic therapist's clinic, all the shops connected via walkway. On the ground floor was a bakery, a wine shop, and an art gallery specializing in work by Coastal First Nations artists.

Ethan had set out for Arlene's office at two, but recognized her through the window of the gallery. She was standing next to a handsome older couple, a forest of corks and bottles in front of them.

"Come on in, Ethan," Arlene said. "We were trying to decide what to serve at Yvette's opening tonight. You both know Chief Ethan Brand? Timothy and Yvette Lemieux."

Ethan recognized them from the wine shop. Both wore white dress shirts with *BW Wines* stitched on the breast. Tim's hair hung in a long gray braid, Yvette's in silver-black bangs. On the walls of the gallery were pop art images given an Indigenous touch. An Andy Warhol four-color print of Buffy Sainte-Marie; a *Star Wars* helmet with a Salish tribal design; most striking to Ethan was a portrait of Chief Dan George done like Shepard Fairey's Obama poster, with the word LAND replacing HOPE. Ethan recognized him from *The Outlaw Josey Wales.*

"We're stuck in a three-way tie," Yvette said. "I like the merlot, Tim is fond of the pinot, and Arlene prefers this Riesling, which I wouldn't use to clean my brushes with. Would you give us a tiebreaking vote?"

"On-duty drinking is frowned upon," Ethan said.

"Tragic. Will I see you at the opening tonight?"

He'd promised dinner to Sandra Jacinto, but said he'd try to swing by.

Arlene followed him outside, shaking her head in amusement at the couple. "They're good people, but about as close to Indigenous yuppies as you can get. Let's talk in my office."

The woman was tireless. Although they only went up one staircase and over two shops, Arlene managed to greet nine people by name. Her voice was booming and warm, and her laughter was like thunder along the halls. A true extrovert. In court, when Arlene Six Crows turned all of that attention on a person taking the stand, it could feel like an avalanche hurtling down. Ethan knew from experience.

In her private office, the two of them alone, he felt a little of that landslide energy.

"Took you all of three days to make an enemy of Eldon Mooney," Arlene said. "Not that Cliff didn't deserve being handed his walking papers, but your timing could have been a tad better."

"Had to be done," Ethan said. "What did you want to see me about?"

Arlene picked up her phone and texted. "I'm gonna ask a favor, Ethan, and I'm gonna do you one in return. The nice thing is, they're the same favor."

"Should I thank you ahead of time, or wait till I know what these favors are?"

Arlene laughed. "What I like about you, Ethan, you know what you know. If anyone else all but guaranteed they'd solve a murder, I'd think they were full of crap. When you said it yesterday to the council, by gum if I didn't believe you."

Arlene's office walls held her degrees from Tulane and Washington State, along with family photos, a ceremonial dress, and what Ethan now recognized as a painting by Yvette Lemieux. Arlene unwrapped a chocolate egg from the smoked glass bowl on her desk. She popped it into her mouth and chewed slowly.

"Love my Easter sweets," she said. "Especially when they go on sale after the holiday. The flip side of knowing what you know is knowing what you don't. In your case, that's politics. Our mayor's having an easy time boxing you in."

"No argument from me," Ethan said.

"Which is why you're gonna hire Mercy Hayes."

"Who's that?"

Arlene explained that Mercy was from the Lummi Nation south of town. She'd married a man from Atlanta who'd been killed in an automobile accident a year ago. The young widow was staying with friends of Arlene's. She needed a job, and had a two-year-old son to support.

"Mercy was in the navy before college," Arlene said. "She's a good candidate, and your department has never hired an Indigenous officer. With Cliff Mooney no longer taking up space, you're down a set of handcuffs, right? So you can see how this works out."

Credit where it's due, Ethan thought. He owned Arlene the favor, but he sensed this was more than that. She meant exactly what she'd claimed: a solution that would work out to mutual benefit.

If only every solution did.

He agreed to interview Mercy Hayes on Monday, and left the lawyer's office thinking so much of his job was turning out to be meetings, interviews, and appointments for more of the same.

His feet ached from trudging through the brushes, his ankle was starting to swell, and he was nowhere near finding Laura Dill's murderer. But an idea was forming, a way to make Jody McCandless talk.

He walked down D Street, skirting the roundabouts, crossing beneath the underpass. I-5 rumbled overhead. Having a transnational highway slice through the town made foot travel a challenge.

Above A Street was a narrow strip of evergreens, all that separated Blaine from Canada. The world's longest undefended border formed the town's northern boundary.

On C Street, between a food mart and a gas station, was a cluster of shops catering to tourists. In April business was only starting to pick up for tie-dye shirts, gemstones, driftwood carvings, and the like. Snug in the middle of the strip mall was a narrow shop, the window advertising cruises to the Yucatán, discounted flights to Hong Kong, whale watching packages. Breakwater Travel, owned and operated by Sissy McCandless.

The white sheep was alone in her shop. Ethan knocked and entered. Sissy looked up from her computer, pushed her glasses up the bridge of her nose, and studied him with mild surprise.

"I guess I should offer congratulations," Sissy said.

"For what?"

"Your promotion. Did you always want to be a police chief, even as a little kid?"

"I wanted to be a cowboy," Ethan said. "Then I wanted to be Ken Griffey Jr. Mostly a cowboy, though."

"Not a lot of open range left."

Sissy gave an appearance of being twenty years older than Ethan, though she was barely thirty. Part of this was fashion. The travel agency was decorated in red and silver, and her clothing matched, gray sweater with a red vest over top, large-framed red plastic glasses. The rest was how Sissy McCandless carried herself, stooping slightly as she moved. As a child her older brother had pushed her out a second floor window, into her mother's flower bed. Sissy's spine had repaired itself, but her movements showed deliberation and, Ethan thought, some pain. He sympathized.

"What about you?" he asked, taking a client's seat. The silver plastic wasn't sturdy, and he couldn't take his weight off his ankle. "What did you want to be when you grew up?"

Sissy tapped a framed diploma on the wall behind the counter. *Cecilia McCandless has completed her two-year degree in Graphic Design.* "Visual artist was my first choice, until I learned what a visual artist makes. Mostly I didn't care, so long as it was far away from my brothers."

"You talk to them recently?"

"I visit Seth once a month," Sissy said. "Suffice to say, he's not a member of your fan club."

Not for the first time he wondered if Seth McCandless had put someone up to leaving the death threats. "What about your other brother?"

"Jody is a fan of trucks and money and not much else. I have dinner at the homestead every so often. Why?"

"I was hoping you could ask him to talk to me," Ethan said. "I'm investigating the death of a woman who by some accounts was Jody's girlfriend."

"Laura," Sissy said.

"You knew her?"

"I met her at the house once, briefly."

"Jody isn't inclined to talk to the police," he said. "Maybe with a sisterly nudge, he and I could sit down in the same room."

Sissy nodded, not agreeing, but turning the request over in her head.

"What an odd idea you must have of my family," she said. "What makes you think Jody would listen to me—or talk with you, even if he did?"

"It's in his best interest," Ethan said.

"How's that?"

"If he cooperates, he's less of a suspect. If he helps us catch Laura's killer, he's off the hook. And if he did it, telling us demonstrates remorse."

Sissy laughed. "Jody cares about remorse less than he cares about you."

"Is your brother mixed up in this, Sissy?"

The travel agent stared at him. If Jody had done it, would his sister be aware of that fact? If she found out, would she tell the authorities, maybe even turn him in? What did it say about their family if Sissy honestly didn't know which side to take?

"I'll call him and set something up," Sissy said. "But don't get your hopes up, Chief. My brother has a mean streak wider than a six-lane highway. He's looking for any chance to prove himself."

19

The Blue Duck Saloon was the oldest drinking establishment in town, a blood-and-guts honky-tonk on Marine Drive that had been renovated five years ago. The scuffed dance floor remained, but the juke box now played Taylor Swift in addition to The Judds. On weekends a food truck sold tacos in the parking lot, and the strains of a live band carried out into the night.

Sandra Jacinto wore a pink wrap dress under a denim jacket, her hair styled up to make her slightly taller than Ethan. She looked good, she knew it, and she could dance.

"My husband hated places like this," she said as Ethan carried a pair of longnecks to their table. "Loud noise, beer, people having fun. His idea of fun was a steak sandwich at his country club, me hanging out with the wives while he golfed."

A pair of young men in washed denim passed the table, one tipping his Stetson to Sandra.

"Tell me, Ethan," the doctor said. "Is cradle robbing a chargeable offense in Whatcom County?"

Ethan smiled. He was wearing black cords, and the only snap-button shirt he owned. Without the pistol he felt, not naked, but vulnerable. But that was what a date was all about, wasn't it? Vulnerability? It had been a while since he'd been on one.

The doctor took her beer bottle and clinked it against his. "Is it true you haven't seen anyone since Jazz moved out?"

"True enough," he said, unable to keep from thinking of Steph, but also aware of the woman in front of him, the sharp toe of her boot tracing down the arch of his good foot.

"When I left my husband, I gave myself a month," Sandra said. "Thirty days to weep and moan and feel absolutely rotten about being single. Two days in, I realized something. I *like* being single. Dating a cute guy, having fun, then starting work Monday morning with no strings." She held up her bottle. "To the perfect life. Someone's gotta live it."

The band was solid, the steel player exceptional, and they danced to a few songs he recognized. It was fun. Sandra was fun. She was honest in looking for a good time, with no complications, and what was wrong with that? They liked each other, and there was chemistry there.

"Lab reports come in yet for Laura Dill?" he asked between dances as they took their seats.

Sandra waved a silver-tipped finger at him. "You're not ruining a nice night with work, are you? That's the problem with cops and doctors. No such thing as off the clock. Firemen never have that problem."

"I'll endeavor to be more like one," he said.

"But since you asked, yes, the tox came in. Ms. Dill had no amount of drugs in her system, no alcohol, not even THC. Her stomach contents were all but digested, which means she had an early dinner. Chicken fajitas, if that helps."

The band started a slow one and Sandra pulled him back to the floor. He recognized the tune, "Carried Away" by George Strait. A favorite of his, one that he and Jazz had often danced to. His ex, when they met, had been so sure she hated country music.

"Any luck with your heart?" Sandra asked.

He realized she meant the elk heart. "Had a phone call from the same person. Another threat."

"Someone must really hate you," she said, tightening her arms around his neck. "If I'm going to seduce you, I better work fast."

When he went to fetch more drinks she stole up to the bar, standing behind him, so when he turned she was pressed close to him. He was aware of her perfume. He held out one of the beers, but the doctor ignored it. Instead she kissed him.

"Let's make this our last drink," Sandra said. "I'll just freshen up."

He waited at the bar, nursing his beer. The Blue Duck was getting crowded. Heck Ruiz and his wife were at a table near the front, and Ethan saw others he recognized. Including a familiar head of thinning yellow hair.

Cliff Mooney was shouldering his way across the dance floor, the former officer wearing slacks and another glittery T-shirt stretched to its breaking point. He moved with a drunken roll to his step, a mixture of rage and lack of coordination. Cliff bumped a couple, knocking the man into a nearby table, and didn't slow down. So tanked you could set him on fire and he wouldn't notice till he sobered up.

"Outside now," Cliff nearly shouted.

"You're drunk, and I'm off duty."

"Good, 'cause we got business, you and me, 'thout you hiding behind your badge. Outside. *Now*."

The band was still playing, but now people were looking over, their conversations drying up. Fights weren't uncommon in the Blue Duck, but people wanted to see what their new chief would do.

"Cliff, I'm not trained to hurt people with my fists," Ethan said. "Why don't you let me buy you a beer?"

"I'm pulling your punk card. Calling your ass out."

He called Ethan a few other things, before stomping out through the back doors, past the cluster of smokers, into the hard-packed dirt parking lot.

Ethan waited until he could see Sandra returning from the restroom. He held up a hand, back in one sec. Then followed Cliff through the door.

The cold air was welcome after the heat and sweat of the bar. He'd parked his truck at the midpoint of the lot, where the lights from the blue and yellow neon sign didn't reach. Cliff Mooney was pacing there. Empty handed, which was a relief. He ran at Ethan, eager to lob his fists at the man who'd fired him.

Ethan waited until the big man committed to his swing, put his hands up as if to ward off Cliff's blow, sidestepped, and snapped a front kick with his repaired foot into the peroneal nerve. Cliff's left knee buckled and he flopped forward. The big man lunged up, roaring, racing into a right elbow that broke his nose.

To his credit, Cliff stayed on his feet. Ethan tagged his chin with a left, and when Cliff's arms flailed, trying to protect all of his ruined face at once, Ethan dug a fierce right into the big man's rib cage with enough behind it to drop Cliff in the dirt.

Chest heaving, Ethan opened the tailgate of his truck and sat down, watching Cliff writhe. Any anger he'd felt at his night being wrecked was fading. The kick had worsened the ache in his ankle, but hadn't dislodged the heel plate. For his part, Cliff was still breathing, though with difficulty.

"I told you I'm not trained to hurt people," Ethan said to the injured man. "Everything I know about fighting hand-to-hand involves killing. Let me help you up."

He got the big man into the bed of the truck, made sure Cliff's airway wasn't blocked. The lineup for the food truck had quickly turned into an audience. He headed past them, back inside, and asked the bartender for a bag of ice. Sandra approached as he was waiting.

"What's going on out there?" the doctor asked. "Did you get into a fight?"

"A little set-to with Cliff Mooney." He took a bar napkin and tried to wipe some of the blood off his hand. "I'm going to drive Cliff to the hospital. I understand if that's the end of our date. But if you don't mind a little detour, and the sight of blood, we could maybe grab an ice cream after."

"I see blood every day, Ethan, though usually not from a live subject." The doctor smiled and shook her head. "You are not a boring date."

20

Someone was standing on his porch.

He knew from the silence of the house, from the way he'd woken up immediately, had instinctively taken up his service weapon. Call it a sixth sense. He knew without really knowing. The squeal of the plank outside only confirmed it.

Ethan slid from the bed soundlessly. His feet moved single file through the hall to the kitchen, avoiding the pressure points of the hardwood floor. What time was it—three? He'd parted from Sandra around midnight.

Stepping into a pair of gumboots, he edged open the kitchen door and descended onto the path of concrete hexagons that led around the side of the house. First a note and a heart, then a phone call. What would be next in the campaign—fire?

His neighbor to the west had a high trellis, which draped a long curtain of shadow over the walkway between houses. The light from the street didn't reach this far back. Moonlight was sufficient for him to pick his way. He was protected by the darkness as he neared the corner, moving silently.

Before he broke he heard the staccato beat of footsteps across the porch. The shuffle of grass. A solitary figure running frantic, all out.

Rounding the corner Ethan broke into a lopsided run. Without the heel plate, his left foot came down on the ball or instep, throwing off his gait and sending shooting pain through the ankle. Ahead he could only see the waving grass of the field, a figure moving hunched over, disappearing over the rise.

He stepped carefully over the fence, fingers outside of the Smith & Wesson's trigger guard. He stumbled, plunged ahead. No sign of the trespasser in front of him. He was following noise.

Cresting the hill, he could see houses and housing developments. Kickerville Drive was quiet this time of morning. Not a light on. Below him, the hill fanned out into yards with chain and picket fences, laurel hedges, a tree with a tire swing.

Aware he was silhouetted against the hill, Ethan crouched and scanned, looking for movement, disturbances. He saw nothing. A street asleep.

It began to rain.

Heading back, he saw what had spooked the intruder. A pair of brilliant blue coins regarded him from a gap in the fence. The coyote paced along the east side of the house. As Ethan neared her, she trotted off, unconcerned with him.

Wearing boxer briefs and boots, carrying a pistol, with a sore elbow from the fight, and a hickey on his throat and two deep scratches on his shoulder blade, he felt foolish and exposed and tired.

"Two of us and one of them," he admonished the animal, who continued skulking away. "And look at us."

* * *

No sense in trying to regain admission to the land of sleep. Ethan made coffee and showered, then headed to the station. There was paperwork to double-check, overtime to approve. A message from Brenda Lee Page saying she'd stayed over in Vancouver and wouldn't be back until the afternoon. Brenda Lee implied she'd found something, and also made it clear she expected to be reimbursed for the hotel.

Sitting at his desk, Ethan tried to square the friendly tone of Brenda Lee's message with the information Mal had given him. Was the job of chief so important to her that she'd hire an investigator to dig up dirt on her colleagues? And just what, if anything, had been turned up?

Whatever she discovered couldn't have amounted to much, he reasoned. His opioid use had been excessive but short-lived. His relationship with Steph—his affair, though he hated the judgment in the word—was hardly a crime. That left the injury. More specifically, concealing the injury, lying about it. Like Watergate, the act itself was less of a problem than the cover-up.

In hindsight, maybe he should have declared it to Frank. Shown him the extent, how it didn't stop him from getting around. There were all sorts of stories of differently abled people working productively in law enforcement, overcoming limitations, being inspiring. At twenty-eight, he hadn't wanted to be inspiring. He'd wanted to do the job and be treated like anyone else.

There were worse secrets to harbor. And there was no evidence that his senior officer knew.

At seven the phone company forwarded the information from the threatening call. The number had been activated with a prepaid calling card. The call had pinged off the cell tower near the marina, which probably meant the phone was on its way out with the tide. Still, Ethan walked down to the last location the phone had been used.

Word had spread of the parking lot fight. If people had been a little colder to him since the newspaper articles, now they seemed friendlier. Nick Greco, who ran the Java Hut, even congratulated him. "Really showed that Mooney kid something, Ethan." The half dozen people who'd been lined up for tacos would swell to become a hundred eyewitnesses, all telling exaggerated versions. Everyone loves a tough guy.

The marina was empty. A cold wind rolled off the harbor. Joggers crisscrossed the shore on the residential end of Semiahmoo Bay. Skiffs and cabin cruisers lay in neat rows ahead of him. To his left, the old salmon cannery and the office buildings built in the late 1800s. Gulls stirred and settled as he passed.

No sign of the phone, of course. A father and son passed him carrying crab traps.

This was the toughest part of an investigation. Questions, doubts, leads fizzling to dead ends, or worse, into a dark night of possibilities with no evidence to light the way. Either you gutted through it until a new piece of evidence presented itself, or the case ended up in bank boxes on a shelf in the evidence room.

He wouldn't let that happen to Laura Dill. In the case of the death threats against him, it would mean living day to day with the knowledge an unknown enemy wanted him dead. Both were unacceptable to him.

Ethan hated to admit there was an ugly sliver of himself that had wanted the job of chief, the same sliver that had reveled in putting Cliff Mooney in the hospital. Someone had to be chief, and why not him?

Well, he'd got the job. He was chief now, with all the problems that entailed, and all the threats, and nothing riding on it except justice and his own survival.

21

In the afternoon, with Brenda Lee Page still in Canada and Heck Ruiz off, the department was short staffed. Ethan himself responded to a domestic disturbance from Bay Road.

Deke and Lorraine Rusk both worked for Black Rock Logistics. Their ramshackle house had been the site of more than a few call-outs. Usually the Rusks' fights involved shouting, alcohol, and several smashed items. Deke Rusk was particularly fond of breaking mirrors.

When Ethan showed up, Deke was pacing the yard, a trickle of blood from his left ear soaking his gray undershirt. His underarms boasted tattoos and a farmer tan. Lorraine could be seen through the living room window, pawing aside the blinds to hurl insults at her husband.

"Worthless broke-ass know-nothing no-account jerk," she called.

Deke said to Ethan, "Tell that woman all I want is, be able to spend *my* money how *I* decide."

"How's your ear?" Ethan asked.

Deke felt it, looked at the red on his fingers, and said, "That's assault, right? I want to swear out a formal complaint on my wife for injury to my person."

Ethan took the front stairs, knocked. Collin Rusk opened the door. Taller than his father, hair shaggy, the teen stared at Ethan mistrustfully and barred entry to the house.

"How are you holding up?" he asked the kid.

Collin shrugged. Sullen anger, embarrassment, fear of the authorities meddling with his family—the kid felt all those things, but he'd also been through this enough times to know how the scenario would play out. Desensitized to the violence. That was about the saddest thing Ethan could think of.

From the living room, Lorraine said, "Tell Deke, he wants to bounce insurance payments when I especially put the money in our joint account for that purpose, next time he can bounce his ass out of here for good."

"Yap, yap, yap," called her husband, now sitting cross-legged on the lawn.

"And also, Officer, I don't want him saying I did that to his ear. That was Deke's own fault for making me mad enough to throw that vase."

Ethan took statements and cooled each party out. The Rusks' domestic arguments always seemed to be financial, though their house had been inherited from Lorraine's aunt, and they both earned a decent wage. Debt was a hole that helped dig itself. The brand new cars in their driveway didn't help, nor did the takeout boxes piled by the front door. Living beyond your means was a tough habit to break, and being broke led to chasing that feeling with booze or whatever else put your money troubles out of mind.

By the time he left, Deke was upstairs sleeping, and Lorraine had promised to see a debt counselor. It was a sincere promise, he thought, though one she likely wouldn't keep.

Ethan asked Collin to walk him out.

"I didn't see who threw the vase," the kid said without prompting. Whether it was true or not, Ethan couldn't say and didn't much care. As a kid he'd done the same, defending his parents against authorities and strangers. You couldn't expect anyone else to understand.

"It's a school day," he said.

Collin shrugged.

"What's your best subject at school?" he asked.

"I dunno," the teen said. "Shop, I guess. Why?"

"You like engines and machinery?"

"I guess."

"My father was a plumber," Ethan said. "He was a lot of things, a sonofabitch among them, but he was also a guy who could fix anything that involved running water."

"So?"

"So if you've got a trade, a skill, and if it's something you don't mind doing, you got a fighting shot at a happier life than you have now."

"Nothing wrong with my life," Collin said.

"Not saying there is."

Ethan stepped off the porch, opened the door of his truck, but didn't get inside.

"If I could swing it so you'd pay off that window you broke at the scrapyard by working there after school, would that be something you'd be interested in?"

A shrug was what he expected, and what he got. But the kid's eyes lit up, calculating the possibility of a job against the embarrassment of facing the people he'd wronged. Or taking a favor from a cop.

"If that's such good advice," the kid asked, "how come you didn't learn a trade?"

"Wisdom came to me later in life," Ethan said. Not sharing the real answer. *I did learn a trade, kid. It just took the United States Marine Corps to teach it to me.*

* * *

Brenda Lee Page's trip to Vancouver netted new information. Laura Dill had stayed two nights at a bed and breakfast, paid for using a pay-as-you-go credit card. The owner, an elderly woman with a house near the beach, remembered Laura as "a little mousy and standoffish. Kept to herself and didn't like my eggs."

The morning after checking in, Laura asked the owner to call her a cab. The owner remembered Laura's conversation with the driver, "Only because the girl was so darn obnoxious."

Reported secondhand to Brenda Lee, and thirdhand to Ethan in his office, Laura had asked the taxi driver to take her to the Royal Bank. The driver had said "Which one?" and Laura had repeated the bank's name. The driver had explained that there were several branches, and did she want the closest one, or the main branch? "The main," Laura had told him, as if he should have known.

As Brenda Lee found out, the dead woman had a safe deposit box at the main branch. To get it opened, the request would have to go through layers of international bureaucracy. But the branch manager had taken pity on Brenda Lee and checked. Yes, Ms. Dill accessed the box on the day she was in the city.

"Laura walked out of the bank with more than she walked in," Brenda Lee said. "The manager had to help carry her backpack to the cab. Same mustard color, he recalls. When she walked into his office it was empty, or at least very light. He remembers because she sat it on the chair next to her."

"So she cleaned out whatever was in the box," Ethan said.

"And she was bringing it back the morning she was killed."

"We must have missed something on the footage from the train," Ethan said. "Did she talk to anyone? Did someone take an interest in her?"

"Not that I could see, Chief."

"She do anything else in Canada?"

"Went to a drug store, but I don't know for what. Toothpaste, probably."

"Why not take the bus or drive? She could have crossed there and back in one day."

"Maybe the train seemed less conspicuous," Brenda Lee said.

An idea was coming to him, slowly forming out of observations and stray thoughts.

"The whole trip, her backpack is stowed above her?"

"That's right."

"And she took it with her when she went to the toilet?"

"It's not unusual," Brenda Lee said. "Tampons, makeup, skin cream—I know a woman who travels with her own soap. Laura could have even been smoking a cigarette in there."

"The pack was heavy enough she needed help with it," Ethan said. "If she brought it with her into the restroom, either she didn't want it out of her sight—"

"—or she knew she was getting off the train." Brenda Lee nodded. "I'll look over the footage again. Any progress with your threats?"

"Cell phone location on the call, but there was nothing there." He didn't mention the early morning trespasser. "Maybe I should hire a PI. Ever use one?"

"Can't say that I have," Brenda Lee said. Her expression was unreadable. He let the matter go.

22

Ethan's interview with Mercy Hayes was conducted with her son Davy waiting outside his office, on a chair beneath the circulation board. The woman had spent her enlisted years at Naval Base Kitsap. Marriage and pregnancy followed. Since her husband's accident, Mercy had been working at the Nooksack Casino as a third-string security guard, picking up shifts here and there. The pay was fine, but she would prefer a job closer to home.

Mercy sat hunched forward in her chair as if it was the first time in days she'd been off her feet. Something in her frame reminded Ethan of rugby players, a rough-and-tumble athleticism.

"You ever play rugby?" he asked.

"Lacrosse," Mercy said. "State champions in high school. Why?"

"This can be a rough job."

Mercy nodded. "The rough part I can handle."

There seemed to be an unspoken hesitation, a problem she was grappling with. Mercy looked around his office, which still bore more traces of Frank Keogh's personality than his own. He hadn't had time to redecorate.

"I'm real grateful to Arlene for setting this up," Mercy Hayes said. "And you for seeing me. And no offense or anything."

"Please speak your mind."

"The thought of arresting someone for littering . . . helping a landlord put folks in the street who can't pay their rent . . . Would I have to do things like that?"

"Sometimes."

"I don't know if I can do that, sir."

Ethan nodded. "I wish I could say all laws are fair and every situation has a tidy resolution. There are ugly aspects to this job, Ms. Hayes. Decisions you'll make that are unpleasant, even if they're the best you can do. You'll get desensitized, question who you've become, how your heart got so hardened. Your friends won't understand."

"Sounds like a tough job."

"It's several tough jobs," Ethan said. "I don't think any one person can do all the things we expect from cops. My former boss used to say 'Law and order only go together on TV.' The justice system grinds on people. Often the best you can do is keep people out of the gears."

He thought of Jess Sinclair, who knew about her mother's affair. He still hadn't made the time to talk with her. He thought of Collin Rusk. And he thought of all the people their age he hadn't been able to help. Young people still figuring out who they were, weighed down by choices their parents had made. If the job had any point at all, it was to protect them.

He walked Mercy Hayes and her son outside the station.

"Something else Frank used to say, which I found made a lot of sense: 'You want to find anything worth looking for, you need to look beyond yourself.' Given your background, your service, I expect you understand things about the world the average citizen doesn't. There's a lot of hard choices to make in this line of work. I expect you'd make good ones more often than not."

"Does that mean I have the job?" Mercy asked.

"If you're sure you want it."

They shook hands. Mercy picked up Davy, who waved at him. Ethan waved back.

"Being frank, there are things I'd push to change," Mercy said. "But yes, Chief Brand, I think I want it very much."

*   *   *

At five he walked down to the Supper Club, hoping to find Jess Sinclair helping out in her mother's restaurant. The day had felt exactly how he'd described to Mercy Hayes—a grind. At least the gears seemed to be grinding in the right direction.

Sissy McCandless had phoned to say her brother would see him tomorrow, if Ethan came out to the homestead again. "Jody says he'll try and fit you in around noon," Sissy said, conveying her brother's satisfaction at making the chief of police wait on him. "You alone."

Laura Dill had probably been bringing money across the border. Maybe Jody knew who had killed her. The McCandless family had enemies and rivals to spare.

Could Jody have done the killing himself, or hired it done? Ethan couldn't think of a motive, unless it had been romantic. Maybe Laura was seeing someone in Canada? He doubted it.

The smell of pot assailed him from the alley behind the O.B. A pair of teens went bug-eyed as they spotted him. One tried to pocket a vape pen without him seeing. The kid was short for his age, dressed in black cargo pants and a long-sleeved Nirvana *In Utero* shirt. Wynn Sinclair Junior, he recognized.

"Give it here, son."

"Not your son."

But Wynn Junior reluctantly handed over the pen. Normally he would warn the kids of the dangers of marijuana consumption, call their parents. Maybe he didn't because this was Steph's child, or maybe on account of the day he'd had.

"Is your sister inside?" he asked.

"Don't think so."

"Any idea where she could be?"

The kid only glared at the ground.

Ethan nodded, awkward at the encounter. If things had turned out differently, if Steph had left Wynn and taken her children with her, this small teenager with the vintage shirt could have been his stepson.

Life was strange.

"Take it easy," he told the kids.

The Supper Club was full of early diners, but he didn't see any of the Sinclair family. The smell of fish and garlic woke up his stomach. He let the maître d' lead him through the dining room, heading for a table close to the kitchen.

A solitary diner sat with his back to the wall, a man wearing a white suit. Thin, with a sharp nose, longish hair dyed a yellow so pale it almost matched his clothes. The man in white was eating linguine alle vongole, coiling the noodles and clams around his fork and slurping loudly. He wore fashionable sunglasses. As Ethan got closer he noticed that the man's hair receded sharply along the left temple, a result of some wound, and the side of his face had a coarse, scarred appearance.

The man in white set down his fork and shook red pepper flakes onto his plate. He took a sip of wine and resumed eating. With the sunglasses on, the man might have been looking anywhere. A knot in Ethan's stomach quashed his hunger pangs.

That sixth sense again. It told him that behind the shades, the man was watching him. A momentary pause in chewing, a slackening of the jaw, told Ethan the man was surprised to see him in the restaurant. Surprised, but not worried.

He'd never seen the man in white before, but knew he was dangerous, that he'd killed people before. Enough people that killing sat easily with the man. An atmosphere around him of matter-of-fact violence.

Ethan walked over to introduce himself.

23

The man in the white suit made a show of looking up from his dish, pretending to notice Ethan looking at him, and staring back with polite confusion.

"*Scusi*," the man said. "You want something?"

"How's your meal?" Ethan asked. "Clams aren't really my thing. Oysters, though."

The man in white studied him, noodles hanging between his teeth. Then with a loud slurp he continued eating, eyes dropping to his plate. Ignoring Ethan, who pulled out the other chair and sat down.

The suit was well-tailored. If the man wore a shoulder holster under the breast, the cut of the fabric and the flared lapels hid it expertly. Ethan kept his chair at an angle from the table, hip turned so he could clear his own weapon if the man in white drew. Around them the restaurant chatter continued, sounds of glass and cutlery, calls for the bill.

The maître d' looked between them, trying to grasp the situation. "I have a private table near the window," he said. "Beautiful view."

"I'm comfy here, thanks." Ethan put a hand on the man's plate and dragged it to the center of the table, causing the man to drop flecks of parsley and red pepper on the tablecloth. Now the man looked up.

"What you want?"

Ethan took a slice of bread out of the basket and sopped olive oil and balsamic vinegar. He chewed while the man in white watched him.

"What's your name?" he asked.

The man kept silent.

"If you don't feel free to talk here, I'll have to ask you to come down to the station with me."

"I am under arrest?" The man's voice was soft, a trace of gravel in the throat.

"No arrest," Ethan said. "Not yet."

"Why am I asked to the station, then?"

"Thought you might find your voice with a change of scenery."

The man seemed unsure whether he was serious. Two scarred fingers began pulling his plate back towards him. Ethan reached to hold the plate in place. Just long enough to elicit another flash of irritation.

"You talk," the man said.

"What's your name and why are you in my town?"

"The town is yours?"

"I'm its."

The man chewed, talking between mouthfuls. "You have a, *che si dice*, opinion of yourself. A high opinion."

"Pretty high," Ethan said. "You didn't tell me your name."

No answer.

"You have a permit for a concealed weapon?"

"I don't carry."

"Not sure I believe that."

The chewing stopped. For a long moment the two of them sat and said nothing. The man in white set down the fork in his left hand. Southpaw, Ethan thought. The hand moved to the breast of his jacket, a short move, accomplished smoothly. In a straight draw, it would be close.

But the man extracted a wallet, setting it down on the table. He picked up his utensil again.

"I am here for watching of the whales." He pointed with his fork toward the hotel. "I'm staying here. Vacation."

"Can you prove it?"

He tapped the wallet. Blonde leather, cut for European bills. Inside was a security professionals license in the name of Nazareno Fulci, a wad of fifties and hundreds, and a ticket for the Pacific Wildlife Extravaganza, a Zodiac cruise leaving from the harbor in two days.

"Nazareno," Ethan said. "That's a ten dollar handle."

"A what?"

"It's a nice name."

Nazareno Fulci pulled out two bills to cover his meal, replacing the wallet in his breast pocket. The surgically repaired tissue on the side of his head gleamed pink under the Supper Club's chandeliers. "You live close?"

"Close enough."

"Maybe I will visit you there."

"Don't think you'll have the time," Ethan said.

"Are you telling me to leave town?"

"And wishing you a speedy goodbye."

"What if I don't wish to leave?"

The sunglasses had dropped down the bridge of the man's nose, exposing small brown eyes, the left ringed with scar tissue.

It would be damn close.

A tapping of metal on glass prevented him from finding out. At the bar, Wynn and Steph Sinclair stood holding flutes of champagne. The restaurant's wait staff were traveling around the room bringing bottles and glasses to each table.

"Your attention, folks, please and thanks," Wynn said. He was wearing a tuxedo, beaming at the crowd. Steph wore her red and white checked dress with her hair down, a double string of pearls around her throat. Her smile seemed less than her husband's, but that might have only been wishful thinking on Ethan's part. She noticed him. The smile didn't change.

"It's nearly been eighteen years since the wonderful day when this pretty gal became my wife," Wynn said. "Along the way she's given me two wonderful children, the best times of my life, and a few hellacious disagreements here and there."

Chuckles from the crowd. Cheers.

"Steph and I have decided to renew our vows," Wynn said. "A little ceremony down by the water, followed by a reception here. You are all invited."

Ethan applauded along with everyone else. Steph leaned into her husband, who called for everyone to raise their glasses.

"So please join us this coming Sunday, and let's toast the happiness of this wonderful gal who's brought me so much joy."

A champagne flute was somehow in his hand, and he was drinking to their health and happiness. Wynn and Steph Sinclair kissed and the crowd of diners wished them the absolute best of everything. Including Ethan.

When he looked back, the man in white was gone.

24

At a quarter past six, the southbound passenger train made a stop in Blaine for the first time in over forty years. Passengers waited as Ethan, Mal Keogh, and Brenda Lee Page boarded and swept up the aisles of the compartments, through the bistro car, the quiet car, the bicycle storage and baggage bins, and finally the off-limits areas for the crew.

The stop was a courtesy, arranged by the rail line. The officers weren't looking for evidence so much as an understanding of how someone could disappear.

Most passenger cars connected with the entrances flush against each other, creating a tunnel passengers could move through. Locked doors prevented movement through the front cars, where there were exposed couplings, areas where a person could jump. Mal did just that, landing with a *chuff* on the gravel.

The stabbing was hard to visualize. Ethan leaned forward and had Brenda Lee approach him from behind. She delivered two stab wounds to his side with an invisible knife. He fell forward, hand on the door so he wouldn't drop completely.

A train moving at high speed, an injured person trying to escape. Maybe Laura Dill had leaped, not realizing she had already been stabbed. But if so, where was the blood? Had she lugged her backpack with her to wherever she'd jumped from? Why had no one seen her?

The train cars varied in age, some a quarter century old. If Laura hadn't opened the washroom door too wide, she could have moved from the passenger car to the nearest exposed coupling, and with the door unlocked, have leaped from there. Theoretically, at least.

A harried official watched the officers role play victim and attacker with impatience. As soon as they climbed down, the official radioed to the engineer. The train started moving.

"Thoughts?" Ethan asked as they walked back to the station.

"I suppose it's possible the victim made her way off the train without leaving a trace," Brenda Lee said.

Mal was shaking his head before she'd finished. "She'd have left some trace behind—footage, prints, blood spatter, something."

"I'm aware of Locard's Principle, Mal. I'm saying it is possible that it happened."

Ethan instinctively looked over at the hotel, wondering if the man in white was awake yet, watching them from the window of his room. "For the sake of argument, say it did. What happened to the backpack?"

"Either she carried it with her or her assailant did," Brenda Lee said.

"This assailant, who I guess must also be invisible, mind you, straps on Laura's pack and chases her down narrow train corridors while wielding a knife? You believe that?"

"I didn't say invisible. You have a better theory?"

Rain dampened their foreheads and shoulders. Mal and Brenda Lee had begun walking ahead, spurred by their argument, outpacing him. Ethan followed, enjoying the sensation of the cold water on his face.

"While you were looking at the doors, I was checking out windows," Mal said. "Each car has however many passenger windows, some that even open. Washroom, too. There are also access panels in the ceiling and floor."

"A spelunking killer," Brenda Lee said. "Now who's straining credulity?"

"My point is, there are ways off the train where the cameras wouldn't see. An open access panel, a broken window—"

"You don't think I searched for broken windows when I was on the train days ago?"

"Do I think you examined every single window both outside and in? No, Brenda Lee, I don't—"

"If you were so concerned about my thoroughness, you could have participated instead of gallivanting—"

"Right, finding tire treads is gallivanting—"

As they approached the police station, Ethan broke, crossing the street, continuing past the building.

"You forget where you are, Chief?" Mal called.

"You two finish your squabbling. I have something to do."

A block away he allowed his pace to slacken. He hadn't handled that perfectly. Choosing sides wouldn't help, but chastising them both would do nothing to build morale and department cohesion. Mal Keogh was his mentor's son, a Black officer, a keen investigator, and at times borderline insubordinate. Brenda Lee Page, on the other hand, outranked Mal, was no less an asset, yet her by-the-book frankness and inability to compromise weren't inspiring cooperation—and as a woman in authority, having her position undermined was unfair to her. Ethan himself couldn't pretend to be above the fray, either. He was letting this fester by forcing them to work together. But what else could he do—send the two off on a team-building exercise while in the middle of a homicide case? Blaine had few officers experienced enough to handle such a case. He was stuck with a problem he couldn't wrap his head around.

Funny, he'd always seen himself as a good officer and something of a rebel. Mostly he had followed Frank's lead, though there had been times when he disagreed, even disobeyed. Now, in the role of supervisor, he was finding out the headaches that caused.

Damned if you did and if you didn't. He headed to the high school, determined to accomplish something of value before noon.

* * *

On the grounds of Blaine High School was a miniature version of the Peace Arch statue. *Brethren Dwelling Together in Unity* etched above the arch. The school he'd once attended had been torn down, a brand new commons built in its place. The black and orange colors of the Borderites sports teams hung from the walls, along with photos of previous classes.

His mother's class photo was on the wall near the front desk. Agnes Devereaux had been a pretty young woman, her dark hair in bangs, high planed cheekbones. Back before marriage to Jack Brand. Ethan had inherited his looks and temperament from her, and was grateful for both. He'd also picked up an interest in poetry he'd never been able to square with his other hobbies. Ethan missed her.

He wasn't sure if his father had even gone to high school, let alone graduated. That was a part of him, too. He'd learned a lot from his father, and as much from his father's absence.

The guidance counselor, Mrs. Trask, led him into her office. He explained that Mo's Scrapyard had agreed to hire Collin Rusk on a one-month trial basis, minimum wage, after school and weekends. Ethan had guaranteed Collin's work. Mrs. Trask thought the part-time job was a great idea. "He's a bit of a troubled soul," she said.

"Aren't we all."

Ethan waited in her office while she fetched Collin. There were reports of low-level gang activity at the school, and the typical gossip among students and teachers. Better not to have Collin seen cozying up to a police officer.

The kid listened to the offer, shrugged, said thanks, not exactly overwhelmed with gratitude for the job. No matter. Either it would work out or it wouldn't.

His first task fulfilled, he asked Mrs. Trask to send in Jessica Sinclair.

"You have a job for her, too?" The guidance counselor sounded surprised. "Jess has a pretty full plate of extracurriculars."

"Just need a private word," he said.

Ms. Trask checked her computer, learned Jess was in gym right now, and left. A few minutes later, an out of breath Jess Sinclair stepped in, wearing a sweat suit with GO BORDERITES! down the right leg. She saw him, scowled, and tried to play her expression off as disinterest. Just another adult.

"What do you want?" she asked.

"A word."

"And you want to have it here?" Jess had picked up a bit of her mother's sass, an amusement at the world's stupidity. She resembled Wynn more in the face, though her dark umber hair was a match for Steph's. Jess would be a popular kid.

"I had other business here," Ethan said.

"So this is like an afterthought. Work me into your schedule."

"It's a busy schedule."

"I don't have anything to say to you," Jess said. She picked at the seam on the chair's arm. Ethan noticed her nails were chewed. After a minute or so, Jess added, "This is so weird."

"For me, too."

"Your picture is down in the science wing," she said. "Your hair looks really dumb. Were you a nerd or something?"

"The style at the time," Ethan said. "I was okay at history and English. Made the wrestling team, but we didn't have money to go to the meets. What about you?"

"Soccer, badminton, A.P. math, A.P. history, debate." She shrugged. "So you and my mom, huh?"

"She's worried about you."

"Please don't give me that 'just say no' lecture," Jess said. "I smoke pot sometimes, like super occasionally. Mom's the one who should—never mind." He waited, but Jess didn't want to say more about that.

"Your parents have had some difficult times."

"Because of you?"

The question threw him. "Because relationships are complicated. Your mother made a difficult choice. She thinks it's the right one for herself and her family. I can't hold that against her."

"I hate them," Jess said. "This stupid vow ceremony they're planning."

"Not how I'd choose to spend a Sunday, either."

"Do you love my mom?"

A challenge in the question and in Jess's eyes. He remembered Steph asking if he loved her. Telling her yes. "How do you know?" Proving it to her with his hands and mouth.

Now he found himself having to translate those feelings in a way Steph's daughter could understand. Lying would be easier on them both. But he imagined Steph had asked him to have this conversation with Jess knowing he wouldn't lie. She was seventeen and deserved the truth from adults.

"Yes," he said. "I love her."

"You two slept together."

He didn't deny it. Jess scowled, hurt by the answer, by what it said about the people she loved.

"So how does it work?" the teen said. "Your wife and kids leave, so you just decide to take someone else's?"

"It started with both of us upset, talking out our hurt with each other, finding we had feelings."

"Right."

"I hope you'll forgive your mother, or at least try and see where she's coming from. And don't punish yourself as a way to punish her."

Jess's fingers pulled a thread from the arm. "I heard them arguing one time," she said. "About you. And now they're acting like everything is all okay."

"Sometimes we act that way in the hope it makes it true."

"Does it?"

"Sometimes," Ethan said. "Does your brother know?"

"I don't think so. Junior still thinks Dad's a hero. It'll really hurt him when he finds out he's just another rich asshole."

Ethan said nothing, worried he'd agree too enthusiastically, or she'd catch him in a lie.

"Is that it?" Jess said.

"Yeah, that's it." As she stood up he said, "I've been getting some threatening notes, phone calls and the like. You wouldn't know anything about that, would you?"

Jess smiled. "No," she said. "I don't know anything about that. Swear."

He left the school wondering if he believed her.

25

Ethan had never seen a pair of designer overalls before, couldn't imagine an occasion to wear them, but that was Jody McCandless's outfit for their meeting. Almost all he was wearing, other than unlaced combat boots. The overalls had roses and cattle skulls stitched onto the legs. A queen of hearts decorated the bib. Jody had only one strap buckled, his reedy chest and tattoos exposed to the gray afternoon sun.

Jody was standing at the end of his drive when Ethan pulled up. The smuggler waved and darted across Giles Road, only making a show of looking both ways once he was on the other side. Grinning, having himself a good time. Ethan left the truck and followed him.

"Thanks for showing some flex with the schedule, Chief," Jody said. "I accepted an offer for this." He gestured at the long stretch of empty field on this side of the road. "Hate to sell off a slice of the homestead, but the offer was just too good. Seven figures, you know."

"Hard to pass up," Ethan said. "Especially when your other business isn't going so well."

Jody didn't rise to the bait. "Buyer's on his way. We can talk till then."

Ethan didn't waste time, though he wondered what Jody was up to. Why meet here and now? Jody's grin, his confidence, was worrisome.

"Who killed Laura Dill?" he asked.

Jody held up his hands. "Don't got a clue."

"She was working for you, living at the house."

"That a fact?" Jody's shrug made the tattoo on his neck move. "She helped out some, in exchange for room and board."

"Helped out how?"

"This and that."

"What did Laura leave behind? Clothing, papers?"

"Not much."

"Toothbrush?"

"Used mine."

"Tampons?"

The land deal had Jody in a good mood. He wasn't flustered, even when he didn't have an answer prepared. "Laura carried around everything in her pack," he said, making a point to add, "That's how I knew what you were talking about when you said 'luggage.' The girl traveled light."

"Could I take a look at her room?"

"Well, Chief, that's technically *my* room," Jody said. "I'm a sticker for my privacy."

"Stickler." Ethan pointed at the house. "So there's nothing of Laura's in there at all?"

"I'll make a real thorough search and get back to you on that."

"You drive an ATV?" Ethan asked.

"No, but I *ride* one sometimes." Paying him back for *stickler*.

"You know what type of tires it has?"

That piqued Jody's interest. "Whatever the best are."

"You don't know the make?"

"Can't say I do 'cause I don't."

"That's all right," Ethan said. "We can check."

Jody was calling, "Now hold on a sec," but Ethan had already crossed the road again, heading around the side of the house, to a blue tarped object behind the fragments of broken porcelain.

"Now I didn't say you could touch my stuff," Jody said.

"I don't need to touch it." Ethan saw at the back, the tarp wasn't laced down. Water pooled in the creases above the tire well. An ATV all right. One muddy Trail Wolf visible.

"When did you ride this last?" he asked Jody McCandless, who folded down the tarp to cover the tire, dumping one of the puddles onto his own boots. Jody swore.

"I don't ride during the winter," he said. "Snowmobile season."

"The mud on the tires looks fresh."

"Hell no. Not from me." But Jody looked. The ATV was sitting on relatively dry earth, which drank up the water he'd spilled, but the wheels had a crust of beige around the rims, and more mud caked between the treads. Ethan wasn't a soil expert, but it looked similar to the clay from the depression near the church. Before Jody could stop him, he'd snapped a photo.

"I never invited you onto my property," Jody said. "This isn't admissionable."

"Are you asking me to leave?"

Across the street, a black Cherokee was pulling in front of the locked gate on the sold property.

"You know a guy named Nazareno Fulci?" Ethan asked.

"Nope. Why?"

"He's in town."

"I don't live in town." The smuggler's confidence was coming back. "After this sale, all our family holdings are outside the town limits. Which means you got no jurisdiction, doesn't it?"

"How much money was Laura Dill bringing to you when she died?" Ethan asked.

A woman was getting out of the driver's side of the Jeep. Ethan recognized her as a real estate agent from town. She was pointing something out to her passenger, still hidden behind the tinted windows. Jody crossed the road once more, waving at the woman in the truck.

"Someone's after you," Ethan said, knowing this was his last play. "Or at least after your money. How much did Laura have stashed in that safe deposit box for you? Hundred grand?"

Jody's easy gait stuttered with the mention. He kept walking. Ethan could almost hear him counting to ten.

"Anger management won't change the fact someone killed her and took your money."

The realtor looked up as they approached, greeting Jody with practiced warmth. The smuggler pulled her into a hug, and she scrunched her face as he kissed her cheek. The passenger door of the Jeep opened.

"Chief, I'd like to introduce you to the dude buying my acreage," Jody said. "But I guess you two already know each other."

"How you doing, Ethan," Frank Keogh said.

* * *

In Lucky's, over bowls of egg drop soup, Frank explained how the deal had come up.

"My partners are looking to expand, and that means new fields. The McCandless land hasn't been worked in years, so it's fertile. Soil pH is just right. The yield should be fantastic."

"You're not worried you'll find a few body parts in there?" Ethan asked.

"I did business with Jody. It's not like I'm *in* business with the man."

"I guess that's a distinction."

"If it wasn't me, son, it would be somebody else."

159

Ethan wished it was. Frank wasn't just a friend but the former chief—and Ethan was Frank's successor, chosen by him for the job. If Frank Keogh was involved in this . . . He pushed the thought from his mind.

"You heard about Cliff Mooney?" he asked.

"That you fired him, or that you whupped his ass?"

"Was it a mistake?"

Frank set his bowl aside, dabbed his mouth with a napkin. "Firing him? Probably was. Some mistakes, though, are plain unavoidable."

"You avoided making that one."

"No, I just passed it along to you."

He wanted Frank's advice—on the Laura Dill case, on the death threats, on sorting out the personnel issues in the department. On what to do about the man in white who'd showed up in town. He wasn't sure if Frank knew that the mayor was publicly calling into question their judgment.

But there was no advice, other than to muddle through. No way out but forward. And Frank was no longer his boss—or above suspicion.

26

On Brenda Lee Page's computer screen, Laura Dill lugged her heavy backpack up the aisle of the train car numbered B7. In another window, the dead woman passed underneath the camera, the washroom door swinging open and shut. Brenda Lee dragged the footage forward at high speed. Nothing happened. The restroom door didn't move.

"Maybe she fell in," Heck Ruiz said.

Heck, Ethan, and Brenda Lee watched as the luggage area filled with passengers, who pulled their cases down and crowded near the exit, blocking the camera's view of the door.

"I've watched this at least two dozen times," Brenda Lee said. "I assumed Laura slipped out around now. But it struck me this morning, what if she was still inside at this point?"

"That'd be a very long pee," Heck said.

"Now watch."

The crowd filed off the train at Bellingham Station. More travelers got on. Shortly after the train resumed moving, Bob Galvin wheeled his suitcase to the washroom and entered. Three minutes later he came out.

"Man's all business," Ethan said.

The door closed. The train stopped moving, another train whipping by outside the window. Brenda Lee nudged the feed forward minute by minute. After about an hour, the door opened from inside.

The woman who stepped out didn't resemble Laura Dill. Identical in build, yellow curls piled on her head, the woman wore a navy blue suit jacket with skirt, and clutched the handle of a small leather carry-on bag.

"Holy crow," Heck said.

They watched the blonde woman leave the train at Edmonds, Bob Galvin behind her. They didn't acknowledge each other.

"Galvin must have given her the wig and change of clothes," Brenda Lee said. "Laura probably fit the backpack inside his case. The footage from Edmonds Station shows them getting into a cab together."

She clicked one of several dozen browsers. The three watched the blonde woman and Galvin do just that, stepping off the train, walking past the covered waiting areas, out through the station to the parking lot.

"Where did they go from there?" Ethan asked.

"I'm waiting on a call from the cab company. Hopefully they can tell us. But in any case, we know where she ended up."

The timing of things seemed wrong. The train arrived in Edmonds at half past eight. Edmonds was at least a ninety-minute drive south of Blaine. At that time Ethan had been standing over the body of Laura Dill.

Assuming the footage hadn't been doctored, there were only two possibilities. Either the body had been misidentified, or the woman on the train wasn't Laura Dill. Had someone taken her passport, or copied it somehow? And how exactly did the dead woman end up with a receipt from the train's dining car?

Nothing made sense, though in a way things were simplified. They now had an accomplice, a man who brought Laura or her imposter a disguise. Maybe Bob Galvin had betrayed and killed Laura. Ethan asked Brenda Lee what she knew about him.

"I only spoke to Galvin once, and his answers were all perfunctory. He didn't remember seeing Laura on the trip. Never heard her name. He lives in Bellingham, and said was traveling to buy a present for his mother."

"Let's pay him a visit," Ethan said.

Mal Keogh had been given the task of following up on the tires. Jody McCandless was on the list of names of people who had purchased Trail Wolves in the last two years. The photo Ethan had taken of Jody's ATV filled a corner of Mal's screen. He was on the phone, and didn't look up as Ethan and Brenda Lee passed.

"Why do we keep taking your truck?" Brenda Lee asked as they started south toward the city of Bellingham. It was four o'clock, edging into rush hour. Traffic on I-5 was heavy but still moving.

"You're going to laugh," Ethan said.

"I never laugh. That's a joke, by the way."

"Thanks for telling me. The reason is, it's familiar." To make the point, he patted the cracked brown vinyl of the steering wheel. "So much right now is new or different, the truck's a comfort."

"Or a crutch."

"Crutches have their use," he said.

"I wouldn't know."

Ethan glanced over at the officer. Another joke, a boast about self-reliance, or a knowing dig at his injury? Had he simply gone paranoid? Fifteen years of working alongside Brenda Lee Page, and she was still capable of mystifying him.

He changed tack. "Frank bought that tract of land from Jody McCandless. Jody had fun springing that fact on me."

"I guess it doesn't surprise me," Brenda Lee said. "There's only so much arable land within the town limits."

"You investigated Frank pretty thoroughly when you were campaigning for his job."

She registered surprise that Ethan knew, but shrugged. "I had to. If I was going to break into the old boys' club, I needed to know everything I could about what goes on in that club."

"You hired an investigator."

"A college kid to do some internet research."

"On me as well."

She made a point of looking at him, making sure he looked away first. Not hard when he had to keep his eye on the road.

"Information is currency, and so is authority. I was very up-front with the council in wanting as much of both as possible."

"Wouldn't it be ironic," Ethan said, "if that's what cost you the job?"

Brenda Lee cranked the window down an inch. "I suppose. But there's no guarantee you'll always be chief, is there?"

Ethan wanted to ask what she meant by that, but they'd arrived in Bellingham. Bob Galvin's home was a one-story rancher in a small cul-de-sac of similar houses, built for the families of army personnel but now privately owned. Galvin's house had brilliant green siding and a brand new Lexus parked at the curb.

"Not the ride of a man out of work," Ethan said.

At the touch of Brenda Lee's knuckles, the door to the house swung inward. They both caught the smell at the same time. A foul, overripe, rotten-sweet stench. Brenda Lee called Galvin's name. No answer.

Galvin reclined in an easy chair in the living room, facing the television, wearing boxer shorts and a sleeveless undershirt. Hair thick on his shoulders and chest. A clear plastic bag had been cinched tight over his head. One of Galvin's hands hung off the side of the chair, the wrist bent backwards unnaturally.

Ethan felt for a pulse, but Galvin was beyond anyone's help. The eyes beneath the plastic were milky and full of dread. Galvin had thrashed and clawed to remain in the world, had failed, and had taken his secrets with him.

*　*　*

Lieutenant Moira Sutcliffe arrived on the scene with coffee, which Ethan forced himself to drink. An hour had elapsed. He and Brenda Lee watched as the forensic team combed the front porch of the house, one of the technicians filming a walk-through, another examining the front door.

"What else can you tell me about the late Mr. Galvin?" Moira said.

Brenda Lee uncapped her coffee and blew across its surface. "I spoke with him on the phone, albeit briefly. He claimed not to know our victim. He was taking the train to Edmonds for the day."

"So this is connected to your case."

"Almost certainly."

The lieutenant turned to Ethan. "Jurisdictionally, this is getting messy. Which means we're looking at the dreaded joint task force, unless you want to give me the other body too."

"You're welcome to what we have on it."

"But you want to keep running with the ball."

Ethan nodded.

"Fine with me." Moira gestured with her cup at the house. "Now about our Mr. Galvin, my guess is two perps. One to hold him down while the other used the bag to suffocate him. Why not use a gun?"

"Small houses, lots of neighbors," Ethan said. "Probably wanted to keep it quiet."

"Nasty business all around."

One of the techs approached Moira and they spoke for a moment, leaving Ethan and Brenda Lee to drink their coffee. They were here more as a courtesy than to offer assistance. The state patrol was a smoothly run machine, integrating with Bellingham PD and the forensics unit efficiently. Ethan couldn't help but contrast that with his own department. A senior officer angling for his job, another who only grudgingly worked with his superior. One happy family.

Moira turned back to them. "If one of you wants to take a gander inside the house, we have a spare bunny suit for you."

Ethan went, only because the white Tyvek suit fit him better. With gloves and a hood, he reentered the house. He spent a few minutes examining the corpse, not finding anything of value, then headed into Bob Galvin's bedroom. One of the techs was coiling the cables of the dead man's computer.

He didn't know what he was looking for exactly. Some link to Laura Dill, something that identified the imposter, or maybe something financial. Why had Galvin helped the woman? Who wanted him dead?

What Ethan found were tickets, crumpled and dropped into the wastebasket. A round trip from Bellingham to Edmonds on the same day. Only the southbound ticket had been used.

Both train fares had been paid for in cash. An itemized receipt was nestled in the basket, a ten percent discount applied to the tickets. Ethan studied the receipt. Why the discount? Veterans received one sometimes, though looking around Galvin's apartment at the inhalers and cigarette butts, the dead man didn't seem the military type. Who else? Senior citizens got discounts, as did students, but Galvin didn't fit either group. Railroad employees, the bereaved . . . travel agents.

Ethan rummaged through the basket, and found a glossy silver and red envelope stamped with the logo of Breakwater Travel. Jody McCandless's sister had done business with Bob Galvin. The two dead people were connected to the same family. Ethan didn't know the extent of that connection, but it was something to go on, something to test.

27

By the time they got back to town, Breakwater Travel was closed for the day. The lights were off in the upstairs apartment as well. Ethan went home, deciding he'd confront Sissy McCandless in the morning.

He spent the last two hours of fading light working on his property. It calmed him to rake up the blossoms from the cherry tree in the back yard, straighten the stakes for the beans. He'd do wax beans this year, romaine lettuce, red Russian garlic, zucchini because it did well no matter how inattentive he was. Maybe a few herbs. No tomatoes, they didn't like the soil. No pumpkins, either, since the kids wouldn't be here for Halloween.

Flowers? Jazz's rose bush had fared poorly since she left, but was still alive. Maybe it was time to pull it up. Or admit that he, Ethan Brand, a former marine and current police chief, was quite fond of roses himself.

Throwing himself into the yard work allowed the case to percolate. Laura Dill's homicide had involved planning and precision, a coordination between her killer, Bob Galvin, and the woman impersonating her. Galvin was now dead himself, possibly suffocated by his accomplices. Somehow Jody McCandless was involved. Maybe Jody's sister, too. Add a man named

Nazareno Fulci who seemed to radiate violence, and what did you have—a conspiracy? Or just a mess?

There were far simpler ways to kill someone. Explosives, for instance. An improvised land mine made of fertilizer and human waste and glass. One minute a person was on patrol with their team, half-distracted by radio chatter and hunger and heat and the thought of his upcoming leave. The corporal suggests a spot they cleared days ago, a spot that looks untouched. The point man checks but he's grumbling about getting stuck with the egg and cheese MREs again, asking if anyone will trade hard candies for M&Ms.

A foot on a pressure plate. A whiff of gasoline and shit and the world upends.

Corporal Ben Henriquez, whose wife had entered one of his photos in *Smithsonian*'s photo contest and won the runner-up prize. PFC Bradley Dobbs, who told Ethan that a year after coming out to his family, his mother had finally written to him. Lives that *needed* to move on ahead, worthy lives, far worthier than his own.

Scientifically, taking a life was an easy thing to accomplish. Figuring out how to live, that took daily improvisation.

The front yard needed a fence with a proper gate. Some landscaping and grass seed, too. He kneeled down to pull weeds. Noticed someone watching him from the street. Ethan freed the hand rake from the soil before looking up.

Collin Rusk hesitated, then started up the drive, coming around to lean his skateboard against the front tire of the Dodge. From where Collin stood he was hidden from the street.

"I saw the girl," Collin said. "I mean the dead girl. I mean before."

"You saw Laura Dill?"

Collin nodded. "There's this old stump near the tracks where sometimes kids leave beers and stuff. I was waiting for Shooter and kind of trying to remember where it was, and I heard that ATV go by. She was on the back, riding double with some guy."

"And this was when?" Ethan asked.

"Like earlier the same day. Seven o'clock or something, I dunno. Before Shooter got there."

"You saw Laura Dill the morning she died? Who was she with?"

"I was crouched down and didn't see the guy. Just her and her backpack."

"You sure it was her?"

He shrugged. "Looked like her."

"Why tell me this?"

Another instinctive raise of the shoulders. "I guess 'cause you got me that job."

Ethan stood and nodded. "Thank you."

He was about to ask the kid to come with him to the station, tell him again in detail as he wrote it down. But with a flip of the ankle, Collin Rusk dropped his skateboard and pushed off, disappearing into the evening.

Ethan went inside, thinking this was confirmation. Laura Dill wasn't on the train.

* * *

His recurring dream was of a shipwreck. The aftermath of a shipwreck to be precise. Rolling into a black shore at night on ash gray waves. The details changed from dream to dream—a moon, a lighthouse. Sometimes he was in the water, holding on to a piece of rudder or mast. Sometimes he was in a lifeboat.

What was consistent was the feeling, the water drawing him on toward a dangerous and unknown land. A feeling of being alone and yet surrounded by others. As if all he had to do was turn his head and he'd see a ragged armada of men and women adrift on boards or clinging to the gunwales of boats. All of them being carried toward something they would never reach.

Ethan didn't put much stock in what dreams meant. The feeling needed no interpretation. Borne on the waves, carried to new danger. The story of life.

Tonight, though, the unease of the dream quickly faded. The air grew warm and stung of salt. He was on the deck of a yacht in the Adriatic, making love to Steph Sinclair. The ship anchored somewhere off the Adriatic coast. Her hair wet from the sea, strands on his face, her arms locked tight around his shoulders. Afterwards they'd hold each other, their backs on the smooth, polished teak, rocking with the waves.

He woke up to see Steph sitting on the edge of his bed. Her white raincoat on, a dreamy smile playing on her face. Steph's hand brushed his cheek and down to his chest, fingers cold.

"Still dreaming?" he murmured.

She giggled. "You or me?"

As she leaned to kiss him she slipped, her elbow jabbing him in the throat. Laughing as she nestled her weight on top of him. Beads of rain on the coat absorbed by his chin.

"I'm getting married soon, and I'm already married," she said. "How do you like that?"

"What are you here for, Steph?"

"If that isn't obvious, Mr. Police Chief Sir, then you're not much of a detective, are you?"

Steph's hand moved down beneath the blanket, patting him more like someone trying to remember which pocket she'd left her keys in.

Ethan took hold of her hands, stilling them. Steph tensed and relaxed, then kissed him. Despite the booze and pills she'd taken, the desperate circumstances she found herself in, Ethan responded to it, invited it, wanting her. He kissed her back fiercely.

"Mmm," she said. Her body rested over his and he realized Steph was naked beneath the coat. "You know something, Ethan? I love you."

"No, you don't," he said.

"But I do. Didn't even know what that meant before you. Just a good little society wife. Two point whatever kids and a ten year lease on the car."

Delicately and slowly, Ethan extricated himself, pulling away despite parts of himself very much not wanting to.

"In the morning when you're sober, you'll realize this was a mistake," he said. "You have a husband you love and two kids."

"I love you. Can't you hear me? I know what I feel. And I know you love me too."

"Yeah," he said.

In her left pocket he found the house key he'd given her, along with a vial of prescription antidepressants. Mixed with wine, that would explain how this happened. He didn't want to care whether her feelings were genuine or brought on by chemistry. He'd be happy not to know. Happier still to join her, chase a couple of these with some rye. There was a bottle of Crown Royal in the cupboard. Forget about the dead man he'd seen this afternoon, all the others it brought back. They could warm each other in his bed. It was tempting.

Instead, he took off her shoes and wrapped her in his blanket. Holding her. Steph didn't resist. Soon she was snoring softly.

It was three twenty. He looked through the kitchen window and saw her Jaguar parked diagonally to his truck. His house was set back far enough not to invite looks from the neighbors.

He dressed and thought about how best to handle this. He couldn't do it alone. Ethan phoned Wynn Sinclair, told him what the score was, hung up, and made coffee.

28

Some people seemed to go to bed well-groomed. Steph's husband arrived less than twenty minutes after his call, bestubbled but otherwise looking as smart as he always did. Wynn and Ethan nodded at each other and worked silently. Steph stirred as they helped her to the passenger's seat of Wynn's Lexus.

"What's wrong?" Jess's voice was similar to her mother's.

Neither of them answered.

Ethan followed in the Jaguar, up to the Sinclair home, an acreage about the same size as Ethan's but overlooking the bay, and most of it filled with house. Lights snapped on along the avenue with the precision of motion sensors. No one was awake. Ethan carried her as Wynn got the door.

He'd never been inside the house before. Carrying Steph across the high vaulted foyer, he followed Wynn to a downstairs guest room, set her on the bed. Steph promptly went back to sleep.

As he walked back through the foyer, admiring the seascapes and abstracts on the walls, Ethan saw Jess Sinclair at the top of the grand staircase. The teen was in her sleepwear, arms across her chest. Worried.

"What's going on?" she asked.

Wynn shushed her and whispered, "Your mother had a little accident. No harm done. She's in bed now sleeping it off. Everything's fine."

"Can I see her?"

"Go to sleep, Jess."

"I want to see her."

"Wouldn't hurt to have someone keep watch," Ethan suggested.

Wynn seemed irked by the suggestion, but nodded. Jess padded down the stairs, visibly grateful to be included.

"Jess is so much more aware of the tension in the house than her brother," Wynn said. "I worry about her. About them both. Let me drive you back."

"I don't mind the walk," Ethan said.

"I insist."

The two drove back in a silence as awkward as Ethan had experienced. What could either say? In Wynn's place his emotions would be in turmoil. But Wynn Sinclair kept his eyes on the road.

When Kickerville Drive came in sight, Ethan said, "Just so you and I are clear, nothing happened tonight before you got here."

Wynn nodded, pulling in next to the Dodge. "I appreciate you saying that."

"It's the truth."

"Calling me was the best thing to do. Steph has done this before. I worry she—"

He couldn't finish the sentence. No tears came, but he closed his eyes and shuddered. The car idled, and Wynn's hands left the wheel. They bent into fists which he drove into his temple.

"I just wish I knew what to do," Wynn said.

Ethan's hand left the handle of the door. "Do you want a drink, maybe just to sit for a minute?"

"Thank you."

Inside his house, Wynn sat on the couch next to him. Ethan poured coffee, lacing Wynn's with rye. For someone always so composed, up close Wynn Sinclair wore a haunted, unraveled expression. He stared at the floorboards, hunched forward. Words came, directed less at Ethan then the universe itself.

"I don't come from people who are particularly good at conveying their emotions. We Sinclairs tend to bottle things up. Especially the men. The number of times my father said he loved me, was proud of me . . . but I knew he felt that. The way Steph must know how much I love her. Mustn't she?"

Ethan couldn't say.

"Show me a couple married for as long as we have, who don't have problems, miscommunications—infidelities. Not judging her. Or excusing myself. But I *love* her, Ethan. Her hair and her smell and the way she is with the kids, her sense of humor, the bony ridge of her wrist. She's my ideal. My rock. Always has been. I know Steph's family didn't run in the same social circles as mine, and my mother wasn't thrilled by our marriage. But I was, I am, and I never looked down on Steph. She raised me up. Made me, or remade me. Without her I would be . . . inconsequential."

"Good word," Ethan said, just to say something.

Wynn Sinclair drank his coffee and gestured to the pot. Ethan refilled it, adding a shorter pull of rye this time.

"After Sunday, things will be different," Wynn said. "There's an awful amount of pressure on Steph because of this. You're coming to the ceremony, aren't you?"

Of all the ways to spend a day, watching the woman he loved renew her marriage vows to her husband wasn't top of his list. "If you're sure you both want me there," he said.

"We do. We insist. A renewal is exactly what it means, and what it will be. The past left behind, a new start."

Wynn drank quickly, unfazed by the booze or the heat of the coffee. He set down his mug and stood up. "Thank you for everything, Ethan. We're fortunate to have you as our friend."

Ethan shook his head, thinking *friend* wasn't the word he'd use.

At the door, Wynn said, "You won't repeat any of this, of course, or speak about what happened."

"Goes without saying."

Wynn smiled. "Good. If you did, I'd have to kill you."

"Is that a threat?"

Ethan watched Steph Sinclair's husband struggle into his coat, smooth the fine black hairs along his temple.

"Hardly," Wynn said eventually. "I'm a coward in most ways. Good night, Chief."

The sun was coming up. Ethan watched him drive away.

29

No sense in trying to go back to sleep. He was at the station early, with the goal for the day to confront Sissy McCandless about the tickets she'd booked for Bob Galvin. He wanted to be at the travel agency when it opened at nine, perhaps a bit earlier. But the morning had other plans.

On Ethan's desk was a note from Mayor Eldon Mooney, requesting an update on the Laura Dill homicide. Ethan was to be in the council chamber promptly at ten, ready to defend the work he'd done and the decisions he'd made. Ethan wasn't surprised, though the timing was less than ideal.

Moira Sutcliffe had forwarded a preliminary report. Robert Jon Galvin, 43. A former assistant manager at a big box electronics store, Galvin had been unemployed for the past year and a half. Friends described him as easygoing, a big kid who never grew up, a little gullible, kind when he was sober.

A former coworker explained that Galvin had lost his job after showing up at work drunk and refusing to go home. A screaming match with the store manager in the cell phone aisle didn't help his employment prospects. Galvin had no children or spouse, no steady girlfriend. His closest relative was his mother, who lived in Tucson. He carried debts of about eleven thousand dollars. The house he lived in was his mother's; every month, Galvin sent her a nominal rent.

The autopsy would be performed later this afternoon in Bellingham. Sandra Jacinto was handling it. Another decision to make: go himself or send Brenda Lee? He hadn't seen Sandra since the night of their date. Moira would likely be there, and Sandra might not want to broadcast that her work and personal life bled into each other. But then, if he didn't go, the doctor might think he was avoiding her.

What was the protocol for a no-strings relationship? Nothing could ever be simple.

Looking over the stolen vehicle sheet from last night, the name *McCandless* jumped out at him. Last evening, Jody McCandless had reported the theft of a Kawasaki all-terrain vehicle, black with custom flame decals on the side, to the Whatcom County sheriff's office. The ATV had been stolen from the McCandless property. Jody hadn't seen who took it, but he heard the motor start up. Regrettably, he'd left the key in the ignition.

Any evidence related to the ATV could be argued away as having been left or contaminated by the thief. Jody was proving to be smarter than his older brother, more forward-looking. Unless they found the murder weapon or something equally incriminating, there would be little physical evidence to connect Jody to the crime.

Which meant the case depended on witnesses. The Laura Dill impersonator was one, Sissy McCandless the other. Between them, he'd need to learn something that could connect the homicides to Jody.

Of course, that was assuming Jody was the culprit. Was it possible he was the intended target instead? Laura Dill was his girlfriend and worked for him. Maybe a rival had eliminated her to weaken Jody's organization, to steal his money, or to pay him back for some grievance.

And maybe Jody had nothing to do with any of it.

Ethan had time to stop by Sissy's place of business before his appointment at City Hall. On his way to the truck, Jon Gutierrez asked if he had a minute.

"A very quick minute," Ethan said. "What's up?"

"My husband Warren—you met him at the Christmas party—he got us a kitten last year. Sparky." The civilian administrator held up the framed photo on his desk showing himself and a handsome man around the same age, on either side of a mackerel tabby. "Warren and I are responsible cat dads, so naturally we made an appointment to have Sparky spayed, which they can't do until she's six months old. Before her operation, there was an incident at home involving the garage door opener—Warren says it was malfunctioning, but personally I think he was just negligent."

Realizing his answer had been everything but quick, Jon made a speeding-up gesture with his hands.

"Long story short, our Sparky now has six healthy kittens of her own. Warren has an uncle who worked at an animal shelter, and knowing how they operate, Warren refuses to—"

"You want to put up a poster in the break room?" Ethan guessed.

Jon nodded vigorously. "If that's all right."

"Of course. I've got to go."

"Uh, Chief?"

Hand on the front door handle, Ethan grimaced and searched for patience.

"Nothing," Jon said. "Only, I know you live alone out at the house now."

Ethan understood. "I'll think about it."

"There's one with snow paws and a cute little wishbone on her forehead. We could hold her in reserve for you?"

Chuckling to himself as he drove toward the beach, Ethan considered the offer. The companionship would be appreciated. But he already had a pet—well, a familiar animal around the property. He hadn't seen the coyote last night. Was it strange to worry about a wild creature? Maybe a person couldn't help who they worried for.

* * *

The sign on the door of Breakwater Travel said CLOSED, but Sissy McCandless was inside the office. Ethan tapped on the glass. Sissy let him in, her expression calm. Classical music was playing.

"I like to start the day with a little Glenn Gould," Sissy said. "My roommate in college turned me on to him. Reminds me there are more important things than packaging airfare and hotels—what's this?"

Ethan had placed a photo of Bob Galvin's tickets and receipt on the counter. Sissy adjusted her glasses and peered down.

"These are from my shop," she said. "Why do you have them?"

"They belonged to a dead man."

"Belonged . . ." Sissy scrutinized the name again. Recognized it.

Waiting her out was important. Sissy arranged papers next to the computer, straightened the miniature flags in the stand on the counter. She rotated her shoulders and readjusted her ponytail. Her index finger and thumb played with her name tag.

"I don't know him," Sissy finally said.

"That's an awful lot of fidgeting for someone you don't know."

"You said he was dead. The topic of death makes me nervous."

"Hopefully you can steady your nerves long enough to explain why you gave Mr. Galvin a discount. Was he a loyal customer?"

"No, I only saw him the once."

Ethan grinned. "So you do recall something about the man."

"Let me think. He was horseshoe bald, dressed pretty nice. He smelled of cigarettes and beer. I remember thinking he dressed more like a wine drinker, the suit and all. Something about him was strange. Does any of that help?"

"It might. Did Galvin come in here alone?"

Sissy closed her eyes, showing that she gave the question thought. "I can't remember," she said. "I think alone, but maybe someone was waiting in the car."

By turning around, Ethan had a clear view of the parking spots in front of the travel agency. The dent on the Dodge left by Cliff Mooney was more noticeable than he'd thought. He turned back to Sissy McCandless.

"How about Laura Dill?" he asked. "The dead woman ever come in here?"

"No, like I said, I just saw her the once at the house."

"How about someone who looked like her?"

"A woman around thirty with brown hair?" Sissy asked. "Yes, I believe one or two customers might fit that description. Or three. Or three thousand."

He ignored the sarcasm. "Anyone recently? Maybe taking a train trip to Vancouver?"

Sissy sighed, but clicked at the keyboard. "Most of my business involves vacation packages," she said. "The rail and bus companies get the bulk of their business through their websites."

"You gave Galvin a discount."

"I have to, just to compete. Margins in this business are slim." In a quiet, conspiratorial voice Sissy added, "Know what customers love more than discounts? The *idea* of discounts. They love to feel they got preferential treatment, put one over on the schmucks behind the till. The discount is factored into my markup."

"Slick," Ethan said.

"A girl has to compete twice as hard."

"I think Galvin worked for your brother, along with a woman who looked like Laura Dill enough to pretend to be her. You ever see a woman around Jody that looked something like his girlfriend?"

Sissy nodded, smiling. "My brother does have a type. He used to see a girl named Carey or Corey or something, Casey maybe. A bit younger than Laura, a bit better with makeup. But the first time I met Laura I assumed she was Cassie—that's it, Cassie Maxwell."

Ethan wrote the name down, grateful for the lead, but thinking Sissy was still holding something back. "Know where I could reach this Cassie?"

"Sorry, no."

"Did Jody ever send any business your way?"

Sissy nodded. "I sold him a trip to Hawaii two years ago. The big island. He thought it was called Hannah Montana."

"Thanks for your help, Sissy." Ethan checked the clock on the wall. He had to appear at Mooney's little show trial in fifteen minutes. "If you think of anything else."

"No offense," Sissy said, "and I'm not trying to drum up business, but you look like you could use a vacation."

"Maybe once this is all over," Ethan said, wondering if Sissy McCandless would offer him the same discount she'd given the dead man.

30

Wynn Sinclair was absent from the morning session. The other city councillors were arranged on the dais when Ethan entered. He waited twenty-eight minutes for other business to conclude. Finally the mayor summoned him to stand before the horseshoe. Eldon Mooney looked ready to rain down thunder and tarnation.

"This town—this *community*—entrusted you to shelter—no, *shield* us from danger, and to uphold, both symbolically and as an example for others, to captain our ship on the stormy seas of law and order—"

Jay Swan sat in the middle row, taking notes and looking amused. They nodded at Ethan, rolled their eyes as Mooney blustered on.

". . . Rumors of a back alley altercation, which we won't get into now, and then yesterday a second homicide, a—a *wave* of criminality breaking upon our fair shore, enough to lead some of us to wonder whether the right hand is on the tiller. What do you say to that, Chief Brand?"

"To what?" Ethan asked.

"What do you mean what?"

"In Your Honor's analogy, am I on the boat holding the tiller, or on the shore?"

A snicker of laughter from the corners of the council chamber. On the dais, Arlene Six Crows buried her grin behind her hands.

"Do not make light of this," the mayor said. "I asked what your department is doing to solve these crimes and fulfill your mandate."

"We're putting evidence together, coordinating with the WSP, Bellingham PD, the sheriffs."

"Do you have a suspect?"

"We do."

"In custody?"

"Usually we put a case together before we make an arrest," Ethan said.

Eldon Mooney had the home field advantage, and would give himself the last word. He clearly relished it. His posture conveyed disappointment, frustration, and a simmering anger, all kept in check by mayoral dignity. It was a grand performance.

"I suggest you get busy doing just that," Mooney said. "Council wants an update tomorrow morning. Prepare a report detailing exactly what steps you've taken. Failure to find justice for this woman is not an acceptable alternative."

"Agreed, Your Honor," Ethan said.

"Get busy."

As he passed up the aisle, Jay fell in behind him, following him out to the corridor. "A word, Chief?"

He hadn't spoken to Jay since the interview. The reporter had a portable recorder with a large microphone, and they aimed it at him while keeping pace. The two of them walked outside.

"Do you feel Mayor Mooney's criticism of your investigation is unfair?"

"He and I want the same thing."

"How are the two murders connected?"

"Can't comment on that."

Jay wheeled around him as he walked, nimbly getting their mic in front of Ethan, walking backwards down the steps. "Do you feel you were disrespected in there, Chief?"

That was one term for it. "Ass-chewing" would be his own formulation. Ethan shook his head.

"Nature of the job," he said. "I have a lot more to do."

First of all, to find Cassie Maxwell.

* * *

On the far side of the harbor, a pair of four-story condominiums had gone up on a parcel of land next to an RV campsite. A breezeway connected the two buildings. Cassie Maxwell and her roommate rented a ground floor suite, off the books and against strata rules.

Welcome to the Birch Bay Arms, proclaimed the sign. *Another unique living environment brought to you by W. Sinclair Developments.*

Cassie's roommate was home. Roxanne Pike invited him into the suite. The smell of cooking lamb filled the small, cluttered apartment. Photos on the fridge, a heap of recycling and wine bottles on the kitchen floor. Ethan accepted a jam jar of water.

"Sorry for the smell," Roxanne said. "I waitress nights, and if I don't cook something during the day I end up having a bag of chips for dinner. Cassie says lamb smells like feet, but I don't mind the smell."

Roxanne brushed black hair out of her eyes. She wore pajama bottoms and a heavy metal T-shirt with a rip in the sleeve. Ethan wasn't sure if she'd just woken up or was en route to bed.

"Cassie's a good roommate, but it's coming up on the first. Plus she owes me forty dollars from last month for groceries and the pizza we split."

"Any idea where she is?"

"Nuh-uh."

"She seeing anyone?"

"Not since Jody." Roxanne's expression told him she didn't hold Jody McCandless in high esteem.

"Have you seen him around lately?"

"Sure, at work," Roxanne said. "Every time he gets a new outfit he comes into the Blue Duck. You'd think a guy who throws money around would be a better tipper."

"What about a fellow named Bob Galvin?"

The name brought a smile to Roxanne Pike. "Double G Bob. That's double gin, half tonic. Now there's a guy knows how to tip. I used to serve him all the time, but he hasn't been in for a while. Least not on my shifts."

"Cassie know him?"

"They worked together at Circuit World or whatever it's called. He used to be her boss before he got fired."

When Ethan asked to see Cassie's room, Roxanne showed him. Barely larger than a walk-in closet, the bed filling most of the space. A trash bag served as a clothing hamper, halter tops and tees and a Grizzlies jersey hanging from the blades of the ceiling fan.

"Anything missing?" he asked.

"Cassie isn't exactly a neat freak."

Her toothbrush and birth control were still in the washroom cupboard. She didn't own a suitcase. A pair of hiking boots were the only thing Roxanne could think of that weren't in the room.

"What does Cassie do for money?" Ethan asked.

"Good question," Roxanne said. "When she was with Jody she had cash to burn. Sometimes she'd hand me three months' rent, all bills, knowing I was gonna dip into it and pay her back. Cassie didn't mind."

"When she left Jody, that stopped happening?" Ethan asked.

"Dried up completely. Then she got the Circuit World job. It's been pretty steady since then, but for a while I was carrying her."

"Do you think Cassie was doing any sort of work for her boyfriend?"

"Work like what?"

"Making trips over the border, maybe?"

Roxanne refilled their water, letting the tap run. Dishes were piled up around the sink. On the small table, the parts of a blender were laid out on a tea towel. She sank back onto the couch.

"Well, she did take a lot of trips with him, but I never thought—'scuse me."

A knocking on the door. Roxanne stood up to answer. Ethan looked around at the thrift store furnishings, the couch with the sagging springs. The sleeves of a few records were thumbtacked to the wall for decoration. David Bowie, Pat Benatar. An aloe plant took in sunlight from the window, its leaves leaning into the glass.

Cassie Maxwell had extricated herself from Jody McCandless, romantically and it seemed financially. That couldn't have been easy, knowing Jody's temper, his influence, and what he was capable of. How did Cassie end up embroiled in murder? Did she know what she was doing?

The photo on the fridge showed Roxanne and Cassie holding up blue cocktails with umbrellas and pineapple wedges in them. Cassie was roughly the same height as Laura, maybe a little heavier. Her lipstick and eye shadow were bold, and in the photo she had an electric blue streak in her blonde hair. Her cheekbones were more prominent than Laura's, her mouth thinner, but with dye and no makeup, Cassie could have passed for Laura Dill.

At the door, Roxanne Pike had been speaking to someone in low tones. Her voice was rising. "No, I *told* you, I don't *know*."

"You are her friend," an accented voice said.

"I'm her roommate."

"Let me come in. We'll talk. Maybe I find her for you."

The voice belonged to Nazareno Fulci. His hand pushed Roxanne backwards. He wore a white polo shirt and a cream-colored Borsalino with a dark band. A suit coat draped over his arm. He shouldered his way past Roxanne. As he did, Ethan stood and let his hand slip to the butt of his pistol. He had the pleasure of watching Nazareno's expression go from confident menace to confusion. Ethan watched the arm covered by the coat.

"Not sure if you're familiar with our local customs," he said, "but it's rude not to take your hat off inside."

Nazareno didn't move or speak. The muscles in his elbow tensed, the coat bobbing a little.

"You know each other?" Roxanne asked.

"Forcing your way into someone's home is also frowned upon," Ethan told the man. "Why don't we talk outside?"

"Far as I'm concerned, you can both do me a huge favor and get the hell out of here," Roxanne said.

Ethan nodded. "We'll do that. Thank you for your time, Ms. Pike."

The man in white said nothing, but tipped the brim of his hat to the roommate.

They walked single file along the breezeway, the bay to their backs, Ethan letting Nazareno go first.

"Seems we're here on the same business," Ethan said. "Looking for the same person."

"I was just going to ask where the beach is."

"Three steps out the front of your hotel. You couldn't find it?"

"I get lost," the man in white said.

"You should," Ethan said.

Nazareno was amused. "You want me to leave? Like a cowboy film, uh? 'Town ain't big enough for the both of us, pardner.' Like that?"

"That's a pretty convincing American accent," Ethan said.

"I have business here. I leave when I finish."

"Like I said, we're here on the same business."

Nazareno Fulci's rental car was parked one space over from the Dodge. The man in white unlocked it. Ethan watched him set his coat on the passenger's seat without disturbing whatever was underneath it. Neatly done. Nazareno started the ignition and lowered the window.

"You're wrong about our business," he told Ethan. "It's not the same at all."

Ethan watched the rental car circle the parking lot before turning onto Birch Bay Drive, back toward the center of town.

31

"**E**mergency meeting," Ethan called.

Mal, Heck, and Brenda Lee left their desks and joined him in the muster room. Ethan had printed color copies of Cassie Maxwell's driver's license photo. He handed each officer a copy of the picture, pinning the last one to the bulletin board next to Jon's kitten poster.

"Priority one is to find Cassie Maxwell before anyone else. If you have informants, favors to call in, places you know where a young woman might stay, check them. Priority two is protect Cassie's roommate Roxanne, and keep an eye on their apartment in case Cassie comes back. Heck, that's your job. Priority three is to dig up what we can on Nazareno Fulci, who's currently staying at the O.B. Mal, I'd like you to do that."

"Who is this guy?" Mal asked.

"A killer who's looking for Cassie, same as us. Beyond that, I don't know."

Mal shook his head. "And I get this wonderful assignment why?"

"You're thorough and have a pleasing telephone voice. Any other questions?"

"Only how to spell Nazareno."

As they filed out, Ethan asked Brenda Lee whether she wanted to view Galvin's autopsy or talk with Cassie's former coworkers.

"I spent an hour once in Circuit World trying to exchange a printer," Brenda Lee said. "The dead are probably more fun. And no, that's not a joke."

* * *

Cassie's coworkers agreed she was a cheerful employee who always remembered birthdays, was happy to swap shifts, and kept Advil and Tums in her purse for the odd emergency. She liked the outdoors, liked people, but was also okay being alone. Her family lived in Tennessee, but Cassie didn't have much to do with them. None of her coworkers had ever met Cassie's boyfriend.

When Bob Galvin showed up at work drunk, Cassie would do her best to get Galvin out of the store before the manager noticed him. After Bob was fired, Cassie kept in touch, and she'd often tell her coworkers that Bob was doing okay.

Ethan tried the bars and restaurants around the store, and then backtracked to Birch Bay Drive to cover the places near her apartment. His search ended at the Blue Duck, where some of the late afternoon patrons remembered Cassie coming in, either to hang out with her roommate Roxanne, or on the arm of Jody McCandless.

In many cases the first thing he heard was, "I just told this to the other officer." The state patrol had more bodies to put on the case, and while he was grateful for the help, it irked him not being the first to question Cassie's friends. Moira's people were more interested in Bob Galvin, so there was fresh ground for him to cover. But it was always easier to be first.

A couple of afternoon drinkers mentioned "Jody and his girl," but couldn't say for certain whether "the girl" was Cassie Maxwell or Laura Dill. The resemblance between the two women seemed to be only cosmetic. From what he'd learned, Laura was smart, introverted, and ambitious, while Cassie seemed boisterous and outgoing. He felt the two women deserved better than to be mistaken for each other.

The afternoon continued with no new leads. And still there was the day-to-day work of the department to handle. A car broken into near the beach. A court order violation on Haida Way. Traffic stops. Narcotics. A verbal domestic near the golf course. Malicious mischief on Sunset Drive.

Ethan ended his shift at the hospital after taking into custody a college kid who'd flipped his mother's Mustang. The car had come off the highway, hit an embankment, made two full rotations and landed upside down, leaving the kid trapped in the wreck. The top was pancaked flat. The fire department had used the jaws of life to cut the kid free. An ugly scene, but he had walked away virtually unscathed: a couple of bruises and some glass in his hair. The kid blew a point two three blood alcohol level, so it was the station for him, after a medical check.

While waiting outside the ER, Ethan asked after Cliff Mooney. The mayor's nephew had walked out of the hospital a day ago— on crutches, but walking. The nurse remembered Cliff had been rude, but claimed his injuries were due to a fall.

Ethan brought the Mustang driver to the station, booked him for DUI and reckless endangerment, locked him in the tank to sober up. He drove to Cliff Mooney's mother's house on Harborview Road. He found Cliff on the porch, shelling prawns into an ice cream pail. The former officer's leg was in a cast.

"Some nerve showing up here," Cliff said. "You gonna beg me not to tell my uncle what you done?"

"Hadn't occurred to me," Ethan said.

"Then what's your reason?"

He took the steps and leaned against the railing, facing Cliff. "What do you have planned for the rest of your life?"

Cliff squinted at him, confusion and belligerence at odds in his expression. "The hell is that to you?"

"You're not an old man, Cliff. There's a lot of things you could do."

"'Cept be a cop, according to you."

"You're not suited for it," Ethan said. "But if you want to help people, or you like working outside, there are other ways to earn a living."

"You think I want a career talk from you?" Cliff threw down the pail. "I should sue you. Get me a settlement. Never have to work again."

"That's your prerogative."

"You didn't write me up, did you?"

Ethan shook his head.

"Why not?"

"Maybe because you didn't pull a weapon on me. Or because I'm still finding my footing with this job. But mostly, Cliff, the reason was, I have to live with you in this town. Which means giving you the same breaks as anyone else, hoping you'll figure a way to move on from this, not make ruining your life into full-time work."

"Still think you made the wrong call," Cliff said. "Pretty square of you not to charge me, though."

"Think we can coexist?" Ethan asked.

The former officer resumed shelling prawns, leaving a mess of exoskeletons at his feet. "I'm coexisting just fine already. New job waiting for me when I'm healed up."

That was news. "Which outfit?"

"Not sure it's your business," Cliff Mooney said. "But Black Rock. They need all the security staff they can get."

Cliff Mooney working for Wynn Sinclair. Ethan was disappointed in them both, but not surprised.

He drove past the Sinclair house on Osprey Road. By day it was beautiful, a shamrock green with wood accents, the gardens bursting with late April blooms. The bay gleamed silver beyond the house. He had carried Steph through an iron gate, up the shaded path to the big front door. Returning her to her family.

Order to chaos and back to order again. He put the truck in gear, asking himself why chaos seemed so much more appealing.

32

Dinner was a po'boy from the Drayton Harbor Oyster Company. Ethan ate in the truck, parked with a view of the water. Heavy drops of rain burst on the windshield like overripe berries. Eventually they grew so numerous the bursts overlapped, connected, forming a sheet of water over the glass.

He'd called homeless shelters in Bellingham and Lynden looking for Cassie Maxwell. Her family in Memphis hadn't heard from her. For all he knew, Cassie could be living in Jody McCandless's house right now, the old girlfriend replacing the new.

Strip everything away from this crime, and what was it about? There were only so many possibilities. Money. Power. Revenge. Control. Security. And sex, of course. Motives bled into each other, just like Laura's roles of courier and live-in girlfriend.

Say Jody has amassed a small fortune on the other side of the border. Say he's placed this in a safe deposit box under Laura Dill's name. And say others in his organization know about the money.

Who wanted the money bad enough to kill for it? Laura, Cassie, Galvin, Nazareno. Don't forget Jody himself. Were there others?

Ethan bought another sandwich, watching the sun decline over the water, silhouetting the Canadian town of White Rock.

The thief has a dilemma on their hands. How to get Jody's money? Solution: convince Cassie Maxwell to make the trip. With her hair dyed to match Laura's, a few of Laura's clothes, and only a backpack to bring with her, what customs agent or border guard would look twice? No weapons, no drugs, no problem.

But complications ensue, as complications are wont to. Who's in on the robbery? Who can be trusted? And who's capable of a double-cross? Everyone, Ethan reasoned. Money was a sore temptation, and once a person was committed to thieving, why not take it all? What was one more body, anyway?

Galvin had been eliminated once his purpose had been served. Whoever his accomplice had been—or accomplices plural—likely they had also killed Laura.

As a theory it held, knitting together the two killings and the impersonation. There were still pieces missing, but the shape of the puzzle was discernible, the edge pieces seemed to form a border.

So who had the money now? Had Galvin's killers taken it, or was there a chance Cassie had disappeared with it? A bag of cash would help a person vanish. Maybe, learning her friend had been suffocated, Cassie hid herself, guessing she was next. A reasonable guess, Ethan feared. The killer wouldn't stop until the money was in hand and all threats neutralized.

Ethan scrapped the remains of his sandwich and drove home, thinking that the evidence needed to prove this wasn't there. Not yet anyway. Cassie Maxwell would perhaps be able to steer him toward evidence. A case like this was built carefully, brick by brick—

The shot sounded no louder than a blown tire. Ethan's heel struck the brake pedal and he threw himself sideways on the seat.

A minute ticked by in fractions of seconds. The only illumination was from street lamps and the running lights of the Dodge. A block from his home, the houses were small and set close together. He killed the engine, halted the march of the windshield wipers. He looked out into the silent evening.

Ethan booted open the passenger door, dropping out to the pavement. He raised up slowly, gun drawn, scanning for movement. Seeing nothing, he inspected the truck, found a neat perforation in the tailgate. Small caliber from the look of it. The shot had come from the laneway between two houses. Someone had waited there for him, knew his truck by sight. Ethan dropped the tailgate, heard the slug rattling around inside.

The small lane had chain-link on either side and curved to the left, leading to a side street. He walked to the street and back, aiming a flashlight at the ground. No shell casing, no trace of the shooter. His shirt collar was soaked. The adrenaline of being waylaid and shot at subsided. What was left was curiosity and anger.

33

A cold morning, heavy rain. Everyone and everything moved sluggishly. Ethan ordered his usual breakfast at Lucky's but found he had no stomach for it. He studied the chessboard, trying to figure out how he was losing. Three moves in and already down a knight.

At the counter next to him, a pair of truckers were discussing the Laura Dill case. "Open and shut," one said, stirring her coffee with a fork. "Case like this, it's the boyfriend every time."

"Or a homeless person," the other said. "Never know what they're really up to."

"I knew a friend, his brother was murdered, they never solved it, but there was a homeless guy seen near his house, so y'know, do the math on that."

Once they left, Mei flitted over with the coffeepot. "You don't look so hot," she said.

Ethan moved his pawn up to attack the bishop, but Mei simply captured the pawn, leaving him with the same diagonal threat.

"You know what your problem is, Chief?" she said.

"Everyone else seems to know."

"You don't got any tactics."

"I'm developing the pieces to the center like you said—"

"That's *strategy*," Mei said. "Tactics is thinking past the next move, three or four moves ahead. Making stuff happen. See?"

He didn't see, not until two moves later when the game was over. He reset the board as Mei took the order of an out-of-town couple who sat near the door. When she came back, she moved a white pawn toward the center.

"Strategy is the basic ideas, like controlling the center, attacking the F7 square, that kind of thing. Tactics is more specific. Say I want to capture your queen. I move the knight here on my next turn, and then if you move your C pawn to capture it, your queen is left open. See?"

"How do I stop that?" Ethan asked.

"You got to see what I'm going for and defend against it. But when you do, I'm gonna change up. That's tactics."

"What if you just let me win? Go easy on me, how about that?"

Mei laughed. "I've *been* going easy," she said.

* * *

Mal Keogh had put together a file on Nazareno Fulci. Born in a village in Lombardy, Nazareno had served as a paratrooper in the Italian army, part of the "Lightning" brigade. He'd been in Afghanistan around the same time as Ethan, part of the NATO force. Mal had found a news story about his court martial.

The Italian headline translated as "Murder on the Battlefield." Sergeant Fulci had killed one of his soldiers with a knife. There were conflicting stories about the cause—one member of the platoon said the dead soldier had been caught stealing, while another claimed Nazareno was the thief, and his victim had confronted him about it. The charges disappeared, but Nazareno found himself drummed out of the service.

Since then, the former soldier had worked as a security consultant for a company in Dubai. No family, no online presence to speak of. Nazareno Fulci was a ghost, trained to kill, living quietly.

"His address is a P.O. box in Milan," Mal said. "He's been in the States for two weeks. Passport is good. That's about all I could find."

"Let's say I wanted to hire someone like him," Ethan said. "How would I go about doing that?"

"Well, you'd need more money than you probably have. I'd guess he operates on a referral system—a friend of a friend, someone he's done business with before."

"It would be done online," Brenda Lee said. "Some sort of chatroom."

Mal nodded. "And there might even be a legitimate contract—consultant, bodyguard, something like that."

"How could we find his employer?"

"Putting him under surveillance would be one way. If we have evidence he's involved, a judge would sign off on a wiretap."

"All we have is suspicion right now," Ethan said. "What else?"

"Look for someone who does business in those circles. Maybe someone who's been to Italy."

"What else?"

"Prison," Mal said. "A lot of networking gets done in there."

He thought of Seth McCandless. Jody's older brother could have hired Nazareno, or brokered a deal. A trip to Clallam Bay to talk with Seth might be smart.

Brenda Lee Page had nothing new to report from the autopsy. Bob Galvin had been suffocated with the plastic bag, held down in the chair by two people. Ethan envisioned Nazareno Fulci and Jody McCandless doing this, but it could have been someone else.

"Dr. Jacinto wanted me to pass you her best," Brenda Lee said.

Mal grinned. "You seeing the coroner?"

"Medical examiner," Ethan said.

The two officers laughed at him. If that was what it took to get Brenda Lee Page and Mal Keogh on the same page, well, so be it.

Still no location for Cassie Maxwell. Her picture had gone out to other agencies that morning. Ethan hoped she was alive.

"We need someone in Jody's organization," he said. "Let's pull his KAs and see who we turn up."

The list of Jody's known associates was short. He'd worked under his brother for years, insulating Seth from most of the family's criminal dealings, though not from the crimes Seth himself committed out of rage. When Seth was convicted, Jody hadn't promoted anyone to fill his old position. He was either keeping a low profile or unsure of what to do. The fact was, Blaine PD didn't have current information on the McCandless organization.

The two names attached to Jody's file were Titus Block and Sky Nelson. Both had gone to school with Jody. Block had washed out of the wrestling team after tearing his quadriceps, had been arrested for possession with intent, and sometimes served as extra muscle for Seth. Block worked at a gas station now. Sky Nelson had opened a karate school, but had used his skills on a student, earning him a suspended sentence for assault, and costing him the business. He dealt out of the Blue Duck on weekends, allegedly. Both still lived in town.

Ethan and Brenda Lee visited Titus Block first, stopping at the gas station, waiting until the pumps were free. Block, a short Black man wearing a collared shirt with the company logo on his chest, had little to say. He hadn't seen Jody in months. Had never met Laura Dill. Block thought Cassie Maxwell was stuck up and ditzy, and had no idea where she could be now.

"Who's Jody's number two?" Ethan asked.

"No clue," Block said. "I don't hang out with the dude anymore."

"You're not selling drugs for him?"

Block pulled the collar of his shirt. "You think if I was, I'd be wearing this?"

* * *

Sky Nelson made deliveries for the Super Value. He was out on delivery now. Ethan and Brenda Lee waited outside the supermarket for him to return.

Ethan told Brenda Lee about last night's gunshot. Shocked, she asked why he didn't report it.

"I took it as a threat rather than a genuine attempt on my life," he said. "If Nazareno had been holding the weapon, he wouldn't have fired once, and wouldn't have missed."

"So you're not doing anything about it?" Brenda Lee asked. "Someone should be with you for protection."

"Most of the time there is."

"Not at home."

"We have two homicides and a town that gets more than its share of day-to-day grief. I can't spare the manpower."

"You're not taking it seriously," Brenda Lee said.

Ethan watched as Sally Bishop pushed a long snaking train of shopping carts out the sliding doors of the Super Value, securing them in the parking lot cart corral. Sally looked at him, nodded, and went back inside.

"It's not that I don't think it's serious," Ethan said. "I could handle this officially, write it up, have it printed in the *Skyline* with the week's statistics. The person doing this might read about it, maybe even get scared off. I wouldn't catch them, though."

"But is it smart to let this escalate?"

"Maybe not smart," he said. "This person is upset, and their tactics are getting reckless. I nearly caught them the other night. And now the bullet. That tells me they're hurting, and they're acting out."

"Or they want you dead so badly the consequences don't matter."

"That's an unpleasant possibility," Ethan admitted. "There's the van."

A gangly tattooed white man parked flush against the side of the building, climbed down from the delivery van, and went inside. Sky Nelson, he presumed. Ethan handed his keys to Brenda Lee and told her he'd find his way back to the station. A one-on-one approach might work better.

When Nelson emerged from the market, carrying a blue tub full of cereal boxes, cans, and milk cartons, Ethan was waiting for him in the passenger's seat of the van.

"I'd appreciate a ride," Ethan said.

"I don't want any trouble. I'm just making deliveries."

"Good, we can talk as you make your rounds."

Nelson self-consciously started the truck, took it a street over, checked his address, and then doubled back. "You're making me nervous."

"If I worked for Jody McCandless, I wouldn't want to be seen cozying up to the police, either."

"I don't—" Nelson began.

Ethan waved off his answer. "Don't bother, I'm not after you. I just want to know about Jody's organization. Who's his second in command?"

"No clue."

"Who would know?"

Nelson brought the van to a stop at the entrance to Kispiox Road. A pair of golden retrievers were running off leash in the fenced-in grass. Their owner was reading a newspaper on his porch, wearing a green rain slicker.

It was a waiting game, seeing who would talk first. Ethan crossed his arms and made himself comfortable. Nelson repeated his answers, got flustered, started and stopped the ignition.

"Jody's into some new stuff. Using new guys. That's all I know."

"Who are these new guys?"

"Dunno."

"What kind of stuff?"

"Seriously, man." Nelson held up his hands. "All I know is what everybody hears, which is probably just gossip."

"I like gossip," Ethan said.

After another uncomfortable moment, Sky Nelson's defenses collapsed. Ethan could almost see it happen. The shoulders went slack, as much with relief as defeat.

"Jody's more of a broker now. Not dealing himself, but putting people on both sides of the border together."

Ethan nodded. "What else?"

"Maybe his brother's still got a hand in running things. Like I said, just gossip."

Nelson asked if he could go now, if they were done. Ethan barely heard him. He walked back to the station in the rain, thinking over what he'd learned. Seth McCandless still in charge. New personnel. How could those possibilities result in Laura Dill's murder? All he really knew about Seth was the man's hatred for him. Maybe he'd even underestimated that.

He had to see Seth immediately.

34

"Splain something to me, Officer," Seth McCandless said. "There's a million ways I could spend my Friday afternoon. Why in blue hell would I spend it talking to you?"

A strong smell of ozone and saltwater filled the air. After yesterday's downpour, the morning sky had been scraped free of clouds. But above and to the west of the Clallam Bay Corrections Center's exercise yard, Ethan could see layers of silver on approach.

Seth cleared his nostrils and hopped onto a picnic table. He'd lost hair and gained muscle since the trial. His beard was now streaked with graphite, his arms heavy with tattoos. He leaned back. "You got something to ask, get to it."

"How do you keep busy these days?"

Seth grinned, showing his fillings. "Man, how *don't* I? The mind is a palace, if you want it to be. Know anything about circuitry?"

"Not a bit," Ethan said.

"I do. Studying to be an electrician. Or a mechanic. I haven't decided."

"Both viable careers."

"Yeah, who'd of guessed."

Seth McCandless looked at his surroundings. Both of them were keenly aware of the armed patrol, the cameras, the guard at the gate of the high chain fence.

"Funny that my grades are actually better in a place like this," Seth said.

"Often the case with mature students."

"Helps that I don't got my old man slapping me every time I mess up my times table," Seth said. "Prison shrink says a lot of my anger stems from issues of self-worth, on account of him tuning me up. Born into violence is what she thinks, though she has a ten dollar term for it. *Acclimated*, I think."

"Good word. When's the last time you talked to your brother?"

Seth looked at Ethan as if understanding had just dawned on him, like he could now see through Ethan's pretense for the visit. "What's Jody done?"

"Was hoping you could tell me."

"I doubt that," Seth said. "You know, or you suspect, and you want me to confirm it. Not sure why I'd tell you jack shit about my family."

"You just said they victimized you. Strike a blow back. Tell me what Jody's doing with his money these days."

"Legitimate agricultural enterprise, 'less you know different."

"He sold off part of the homestead."

Ethan watched as Seth's expression went from disbelief to anger to indifference. He hadn't known.

"Yeah, well, I'm sure he's got reasons for it."

"He said it was a family decision. Ever heard the name Nazareno Fulci?"

Seth hadn't. "Sounds like an explorer or something."

"A gunman. There a reason for your brother to hire one?"

"Protection, maybe. Case you go after him like you did me."

Ethan let that go. "One of Jody's girlfriends died, and another's missing."

Seth examined the bottom of his shoe.

"There's a rumor you're running things from in here," Ethan said.

"Good to hear. Means things are running right, doesn't it?"

"Two dead and a backpack full of money missing. That what you consider right?"

Seth flinched, then went back to checking his sole. Trying to play unconcerned. Ethan could almost see Seth's mind at work, asking questions, wondering what his brother had been up to.

Time for Ethan to make his pitch.

"Someone has it out for your brother, Seth. An inside job, someone he knows. Maybe Sky Nelson, maybe Titus Block. Hell, maybe even your sister. This person took his money, killed someone close to him. My guess, Jody's next on the list."

It was a distortion of what he really thought, but within possibility. Jody's brother didn't seem bothered by the thought.

"Jody's tough," Seth said.

"So is a cheap steak, but neither one is bulletproof. Now, I know you're not the type who cooperates with the police, and I wouldn't ask you to. Except your brother is the target, and anything you tell me will help Jody stay alive."

Seth snickered, shook his head. "Nice try, Officer. You don't know my brother. Nobody thinks he can scrap, on account of his size. But I seen him shoot a bear at our dad's cabin, point blank, the thing running right at him. Jody don't back down. Backing down's not in the McCandless blood."

The prisoner slapped his chest over his heart, as if to say the same blood ran through him. The interview was over.

As he waited for the guard to open the door, Ethan asked, "You know anyone who'd send me death threats, Seth?"

"Not a soul," Seth said. "But if they pull it off, Officer, I'll be sure to send flowers. A big old bouquet."

*   *   *

The drive from Clallam Bay back to Blaine took four and a half hours. Practically a full day spent on one lead. Despite that, Ethan felt better. He hadn't expected Seth McCandless to talk—the interview was about body language. Seth didn't know what was going on back home. He might not be concerned for his brother, but Seth was angry about the land sale, surprised about the robbery. Not the reactions of a person running things.

Seth had mentioned a family cabin. Maybe it didn't exist anymore, but it was something to go on.

After Seth was put away, the McCandless operation had no longer been a priority for Frank Keogh. And now Frank was making land deals with Jody McCandless. Were those facts at all connected? Did Frank lay off the family in his last months as chief, knowing he'd be buying real estate from them? Or was this all coincidence? A small town, a limited amount of land for sale. Ethan just couldn't know. That hurt him, not being sure he could trust his friend and mentor. As chief, he was finding trust in short supply.

At the station he changed out of his uniform. He had Thai food at a new place near Arlene Six Crows' strip mall. To end the day, he walked on the beach, letting his thoughts drift as he ambulated.

What Jody McCandless was doing amounted to isolation and protection. As a mid-level crook working for his brother, having ties to couriers like Laura Dill was part of the job. But the job had changed. Now Jody was boss, and he needed to draw boundaries, insulate himself from the day-to-day operation.

"A middleman," Sky Nelson called him. How many couriers like Laura worked for Jody? How much money did he have stashed away, in Canada or anyplace else?

The land deal, the robbery, the murder—everything Jody had done scratched away some chain of evidence leading to himself. The longer the investigation went on, the harder it would be for Ethan to establish Jody's involvement.

That said, there was opportunity now. The urgency Jody felt to find Cassie Maxwell, the need to eliminate Bob Galvin, meant that either Jody was involved or he'd hired Nazareno to take care of things for him. Likely both—the two of them had probably killed Galvin together. When your brother is in prison, and your organization is rebuilding itself, who can you trust other than yourself?

In a way, Ethan appreciated the dilemma Jody was in.

Ahead of him, the lights of the marina glowed against the twilight. He recognized Eldon Mooney's sailboat, the *Sassy Bess*. A party on the deck, music and chatter. Ethan headed in the opposite direction.

His problems and Jody's problems were nothing alike. Of course Jody had to worry about trust: he was breaking the law. Ethan had no reason to suspect the people he worked with. When had Frank, or Brenda Lee, or any of them, not done their job as well as they could? When had they not supported him? Of course an ambitious, experienced officer would want the top job. Of course a retiring chief wouldn't start an investigation he couldn't see through. Ethan was being unfair to them.

That unfairness extended to his family, too. Jazz hadn't left for the sake of leaving: What had attracted him to her so many years ago was her courage, the way she sought out knowledge and firsthand experience, reached beyond herself. Jazz had embraced small-town life, being a stay-at-home mom for a time. She'd worked to finish her thesis in between making lunches and driving to soccer games. Ethan was the one who'd decided Blaine was home.

He remembered his wife working nights on her dissertation, splitting concentration between family and books on the theory of translation. Jazz would sometimes crash out hours before he put the kids to bed. Ethan had enjoyed those nights, the only one awake in the house. He'd felt like he was guarding something precious.

Now his family lived on the other side of the continent. There had been signs all along Jazz was outgrowing him. No use resenting that now.

On the bay, a blue heron flew parallel to the water. Ethan allowed himself to watch for a while.

He turned away from the water to another favorite sight: the town just after sundown, cars cruising slowly along Peace Portal Way. The rest of Blaine rose beyond the waterfront. Lives being lived, most of them in relative comfort.

Along the marina he saw a figure approaching him. Steph Sinclair. She wore the hood up on a red rain jacket, though it wasn't raining. Ethan stood still, listening to her heels on the planks as she closed the distance.

"Nice evening," he said.

"I'm not interrupting, am I?"

He shook his head. "Just having a long talk with myself about trust."

"I need to apologize for what happened at your place," Steph said. Her voice was strong, warm. Any shame at what happened was dampened by resignation, some feeling neither of them could express.

"Not necessary."

"For me it is. My doctor switched my prescription, so it shouldn't happen again. If I gave you the wrong impression, I'm sorry."

"Are you feeling okay now?"

Steph looked at the water for a moment. The wind unsettled a strand of her hair, which she tucked back into the hood. "I don't even know how to answer that," she said. "I have a family I love very much. I think I'm doing the right thing."

"You mean the ceremony," Ethan said.

"Wynn says he's willing to change. What he's asked is reasonable. He loves me. And I do love him."

Steph laughed, a wounded sound.

"You'd think it would be simple. Love, marriage, family, all flowing one to the next. Yet look at me, Ethan. Look at us."

Us, a word he hadn't thought he'd hear again from Steph Sinclair. A connection neither of them could stamp out.

"My understanding," he said, "poor as it may be, was you decided to stay with your husband."

"Yes. But you never told me how you felt about that."

"It's not my decision."

"If it was?"

"Then I'd tell you to leave Wynn tonight, pack a bag, and come with me. Home."

"That simple, huh?"

"Or don't even bother with the bag."

"And what about the kids?"

"They're old enough to know the heart's a strange thing," Ethan said. "Jess and Wynn Junior would rather see you happy, with someone who loves you, than walking through a bullshit marriage to a bullshit guy. Apologies for the language, but you asked how I felt. I want you and I can't change that and I don't much want to."

The words seemed to catch both of them by surprise, tumbling out, a flood of longing and hurt. Thankfully they were alone and no one else heard him. A long silence followed, the beat of the surf.

"Thank you, Ethan," Steph said. "I think I just needed to hear it from you."

"Doesn't change anything, though, does it?"

Instead of an answer, she headed back toward the Supper Club, leaving Ethan to puzzle over her response. It wasn't what he'd expected or hoped for. His place in Steph's life, he was beginning to realize, was as the Road Not Taken. The honest love she'd sacrificed for Wynn and the children. Runner-up for her heart.

Ethan walked home.

35

The conference room of the Bellingham Police Department was larger and better furnished than the one in Blaine. The walls and desks were of polished red wood, the chairs a sight more comfortable. Coffee and Krispy Kremes were in ample supply. Ethan and Brenda Lee Page sat at the conference table with Sergeant Gail Rao of the Bellingham PD, Deputy Gus Murphy, and Assistant District Attorney Hayley Hokuto. Moira Sutcliffe conducted the meeting with a minimum of small talk.

"In plain language, folks," Moira said, "one person held Bob Galvin down while the other strangled him with a plastic bag. The late Mr. Galvin left us very little to go on. A few barroom altercations, a shouting match at Circuit World, and a mother who was supporting him. Three grand in debt spread over two credit cards. No obvious suspects from his personal life. Galvin's involvement in the train switcheroo, his connection to the murder in Blaine, are the best leads we have. So how do we develop them?"

"Find Cassie Maxwell," Ethan said. "Everything else comes second to that."

"A chat with her would be nice," Moira said. "We have calls to our colleagues in Memphis, where her folks live. We're monitoring her bank cards, keeping tabs on social media. Cassie has been quiet for a week now. Off the radar."

"Is Ms. Maxwell a suspect?" Hokuto asked. The ADA had her laptop open, taking notes without looking down at the screen.

"We won't know the extent of her involvement until we talk to her," Moira said. "Right now, we think it best to treat Ms. Maxwell as a person of interest."

"There's a man staying in the Ocean Beach Hotel who was at her apartment the same time I was," Ethan said. He shared what he knew about Nazareno Fulci. As he did, he saw the deputy sheriff scribbling something in his notebook.

After the meeting, Ethan and Brenda Lee cornered Murphy and asked what he'd been writing.

"Just a hunch," the deputy said. "I picked up a guy for a homicide, maybe two, three years ago. Transported him to Spokane. Found out later the charges didn't stick."

"What makes you think it might be the same person?" Brenda Lee asked.

"What Ethan said about his manner. I've transported dozens of killers, all types. The weight of what they've done, where they're headed, you can see it in their faces. Especially on a five-and-a-half-hour ride. Some are remorseful, others pissed they got caught. Most are fretting about who'll be in holding with them, what their wife's doing while they're inside. All that shows on the face, the body language."

Murphy was a tall white man with a dirty blonde handlebar moustache. His fingers smoothed the bristles on each side of his upper lip.

"This guy seemed the most stone cold of them all. Not bothered by any of it. I don't mean just the crime, I mean the guy didn't care about the whole machinery of justice. Like he knew he'd go free." The deputy nodded to emphasize that last point. "Like he was just killing time."

* * *

Joe McCandless had left his three children a cabin somewhere in Washington State. Mal Keogh had spent the morning pulling the McCandless patriarch's records, looking at titles and deeds, trying to find a copy of Joe's will. All Mal could say for certain was the cabin wasn't close to Blaine.

"The place has to be in a different county, Chief," Mal told him. "What're the odds Cassie Maxwell is there?"

"Call it a hunch," Ethan said.

For some reason the cabin felt like a priority to him. Seth had slipped up in mentioning it. A perfect place to disappear for a week. Cassie Maxwell knew Jody, so it was likely she knew about the cabin. And if it was isolated, so much the better—Cassie hadn't been online recently, which could mean she was staying somewhere without access to the internet.

Hiding out on a property owned by the person looking for you was audacious. Maybe Jody had told her to hide there after the job was done. But if so, why would Nazareno be looking for her in town? Was Nazareno working for someone besides Jody? Something didn't fit. All the more reason to get to the cabin.

It was rare for Ethan to think of his father in positive terms, but now, leaving the station and uncertain how to proceed, he found himself wishing he could consult with the man who raised him. Jack Brand was a lot of things, as Ethan had told Collin Rusk. But among them, his father knew the wilderness.

Joe McCandless had been a popular citizen, well-liked, in addition to being a crook. His sons had been coasting on that goodwill long after Joe's death. Joe had also served in Vietnam, unlike Ethan's own father. An angle worth pursuing.

The Legion Hall was just opening when Ethan walked in. A modest off-white building, the insides were paneled with wood and featured brick archways. The man behind the cluttered bar was Teddy Vance. Tall, Black, and gray-haired, Teddy had operated a tank during Desert Storm, retiring as a lieutenant colonel. Teddy often wrote letters to the *Skyline* about the Veterans Day parade route, or the need for better services for vets. Ethan liked him.

Tapping the veteran designation on his license, Ethan asked for a beer.

"Draft or bottle?"

"I'm easy."

Teddy drew a Coors and placed the mug in front of him. At eleven AM, the only other people in the hall were a pair of elderly men at a table near the television. They were watching curling with the sound way up.

"Not a sport in my book," Teddy said. "You got a broom in your hand, you're doing housework."

Ethan didn't have an opinion on the game, but asked if Teddy remembered Joe McCandless ever coming in.

"That takes me back. Yeah, Joe used to hold court by the cigarette machine. A loudmouth, real cocky, and I don't think I ever saw him pay for a round."

"This is a long shot," Ethan said, "but Joe owned a cabin. I'm trying to find out where it is. He ever mention that to you?"

"Not to me personally." Teddy opened a drawer, pulled out the remote for the television, and muted the sound. He spoke up, voice carrying across the empty hall. "Fellas, either of you know where the McCandless family cabin is?"

"Big Joe McCandless?" one of the men said.

"The very same."

The two conferred for a moment. They could have been brothers, though one had white hair and a port wine mark on his face, the other a jet black pompadour that had come from either a bottle or a toupee shop.

"We remember Big Joe," the pompadour said.

"Sure do."

"Remembering is thirsty work, though."

"Sure is."

"Where'd you serve, fella?"

Ethan joined them and signaled Teddy for a round. The pompadour's name was Roth; the white haired man was Orr.

"Second Marines Light Armored," Ethan said. "July of oh seven to November twenty ten."

"That'd be Operation Enduring Freedom?"

Ethan nodded. "Not sure how well it's endured. You gents?"

"140th Antiaircraft," Roth said. Jutting a thumb at Orr, he added, "He was in the 10th Field Artillery."

"But don't feel too intimidated," Orr said. "A jarhead can still sit with us real soldiers."

"Long as he's buying."

"Happy to." And he was. Ethan hadn't been in a Legion for years. Too busy with family and policework, and before that, too ashamed. But he liked the atmosphere, the quiet. He liked hearing the old stories.

"I'm looking for a cabin owned by Joe McCandless," he said. "Passed on to his son Jody. Did he ever talk about that?"

"Did he ever stop should be your question," Roth said. "The fastest deer you ever saw! A steelhead so big it took him all day to reel in!"

"Big Joe told his share of whoppers," Orr agreed.

"But did he say exactly where the cabin was?"

"Lake Chelan, I'm pretty sure. Another thing he'd brag on, how difficult it was to get there."

"I never understood why a fella would brag about that."

"Just who he was, I guess."

"Where on Lake Chelan?" Ethan asked.

"Hold your horses, guy. It was the upper part of the lake, because he'd brag on how in order to get there you needed to drive for hours, then take a boat. No roads to the cabin. What's that town called?"

"Stehekin," Roth said. "More of a landing than a town."

"Right. Big Joe would say the average fella had to travel all day, but not him. He'd hire a float plane, drop him on the north side of the lake."

Ethan added the name to his phone, looking at Stehekin on a map. Joe McCandless hadn't lied about the difficulty. To get to the small community required a highway drive around Mount Goode and North Cascades National Park, then a ferry ride up Lake Chelan. Cassie Maxwell would be hard pressed to find a more isolated hiding spot.

Heavy rains were forecast for the night, lasting well into the afternoon. Blaine to Chelan was a six hour drive. The ferry wouldn't run until the next morning.

"Don't suppose either of you know who Joe used to hire as a pilot?" he asked the vets.

Orr and Roth both laughed at him. "Thought you grew up around here," Orr said.

"Had kind of a sheltered childhood."

Roth pointed at Ethan, speaking to his drinking buddy. "Jack Brand's boy."

"Explains it."

"Mother was one of the Devereaux girls."

"How'd Jack ever manage that?"

"Man was never short on gumption."

Before Ethan could interrupt, Orr said to him, "Rodney Duke used to be thick as thieves with Big Joe."

"This Rodney still fly?" Ethan asked.

"Hard to fly when you've been dead going on six years," Roth said.

The lead gone, Ethan thanked them and paid for another round. A few more drinkers were at the bar now, but Teddy Vance motioned him over. Ethan waited while Teddy opened a bag of Lay's for a customer and rang up the bill.

"Overheard you ask about a pilot," Teddy said. "My wife Maxine runs a charter. She can make that trip. Could use the business, too."

"I appreciate that," Ethan said. "First I should probably try to find whoever took over from this Rodney Duke. They might know the exact location of the cabin."

"Might at that." Teddy smiled. "Maxine is Rodney's daughter."

*　*　*

Maxine Duke kept her plane in a hangar at the Bellingham airport. Not only did she still have her father's old flight logs, but had flown with him once to Stehekin to drop off Joe McCandless and his oldest son. Over the phone, Maxine sounded slightly tipsy, her words slurred. She told Ethan they'd leave at first light.

He phoned Brenda Lee Page to tell her his plans. They would need to study a satellite map of Lake Chelan and try to pinpoint the likely area where the McCandless cabin would be.

"I want to come along with you," Brenda Lee said.

"Odds are we'd both be wasting our time."

"I don't think so." His senior investigator hesitated, then added, "I think you're in danger, Ethan."

Teddy had let him use the phone in the Legion office. He could look through the blinds and see the dent in the Dodge, the bullet hole. Proof that Brenda Lee was speaking the truth. Danger was following him. It wouldn't hurt to bring backup.

"Any idea where the danger is coming from?" he asked.

"Not the threats."

"Then what are we talking about?"

Brenda Lee's answer surprised him. "The mayor. He's asking about your medical records. He thinks you're hiding an injury that would disqualify you from being chief."

Thrown, Ethan tried to keep his voice even. "Why would Mooney think that?"

"I don't know how the rumor started, but he phoned me at home to ask if I'd heard it. I said I had, but didn't know if it was true." Brenda Lee sighed. "Maybe I shouldn't have said anything. I'm sorry."

"Nothing to be sorry for," he said. "See you tomorrow at dawn."

He thanked Teddy for the use of the office and headed to his truck. Outside, he stood beneath the overhang, waiting for his eyes to adjust. A woman next to him was smoking, expelling tobacco vapor into the afternoon rain.

Politics and friendship, family and power. Four subjects that often seemed interconnected. Day by day, Ethan was learning how little he understood about any of them.

36

Maxine Duke was a short white woman of about fifty, who seemed cured in tobacco smoke and draft beer. She wore jeans and a denim jacket, a Mariners cap, her frizzy brown hair secured in a ponytail. From the way Maxine quaffed coffee and downed aspirin, Ethan suspected she was dealing with a hangover, a lack of sleep, or both.

He and Brenda Lee followed the pilot past the hangars, to the tie-down field on the outskirts of Bellingham Airport. The sun was up. Rain pelted their department-issue slickers.

"Ladies and gentlemen, prepare to behold the astonishing," Maxine said. "It's my pleasure to introduce to you the terror of the sky and the scourge of the waves, the one and only *Sea Pig.*"

She waved her hand at a single-prop Cessna, painted pink and gold at least once in its three-decade life span. Maxine kicked the blocks away from the amphibious skids.

"You're sure the weather's not a hindrance to flying?" Brenda Lee asked.

"This ain't weather." Maxine helped them into the back seat of the plane. Her gear bag, charts, and a travel mug cluttered the front bench. "You want to talk weather, one time I took the *Pig* through a freak storm, wildfire season, flying on instruments alone. Had to drop right through the smoke. Barely got the old girl on the water."

"Comforting," Brenda Lee said.

"Any idea where the McCandless cabin is?" Ethan asked the pilot.

"I might recognize the direction when we get there. No guarantee, though. All set?"

Ethan had brought nothing other than his copy of *Middlemarch*, Brenda Lee a small travel bag that she clutched on her lap. The plane wobbled over the grass to the end of the runway. Ethan wanted to ask Maxine about her trip with Joe McCandless, but the engine drowned out further conversation.

Soon they were racing up into a morning sky the color of buttercream. The trees shrank to bristles on a thick green carpet. All too fast they were surrounded by mountains, the *Sea Pig* passing over the white peak of Mount Baker, more peaks coming at them.

Brenda Lee took calming breaths and looked at her feet. Ethan read a few pages of his novel but couldn't concentrate. Was this a tactical mistake, the department's two most senior officers leaving town to chase down a lead? Maybe he should have delegated this. But it felt too dangerous—*was* too dangerous—to assign to someone else. The others had tasks to perform. Like a film director, like a coach, being chief meant you were both the most and least necessary person on the team.

The *Sea Pig* dipped and banked lower, skimming a narrow stretch of placid blue water. Lake Chelan, he recognized. The rain was lighter here. He could see the town of Stehekin now, a few rustic buildings of wood, a stone-and-glass lodge house, boardwalk, and jetty. Other structures, campgrounds, cabins, stretched around the lake or were built into the parched hillsides.

There was no cell service here, no amenities. Not even a road. According to the Park Service website, Lake Chelan was the third deepest lake in the United States. The name meant "the way through" in the language of the Coast Salish peoples. A way through was exactly what Ethan was looking for—a way through the investigation that had started with Laura Dill's murder. That investigation had brought him here.

The plane bounced on the lake and rolled, and Brenda Lee grabbed his arm. Maxine motored to the end of the jetty, hopped down, and tied off the plane. Ethan and Brenda Lee struggled out from the back seat.

"Door to door in thirty minutes or it's free," the pilot said. "How long you want me to wait around?"

"Depends how quickly we can find the cabin," Ethan said. "Anything coming back?"

Maxine pointed at the trail cut into the hill to the northeast. "Somewhere along there. I remember Joe and his kid taking that general direction. Kid was rude to my dad, I remember that."

Brenda Lee had circled the most likely locations, both of which were along Company Creek. The trail Maxine pointed out would intersect with the creek a few miles down the trail.

"We have a bit of a hike ahead of us," Ethan said. "Can you wait for us at the lodge?"

"It'll cost you," Maxine said.

He knew that already. The question was how much.

*　*　*

An illustrated map on the wall of the visitors center showed dotted lines leading off from Stehekin. Hiking trails. Residences and cottages weren't included on the map. The town, if you could call it that, was both secluded and concentrated around the dock. The daily ferry route connected Stehekin to larger towns at the southern end of the lake. During the summer the campgrounds and marina would be full, but in late April, visitors were rare.

Not rare enough, though, that anyone remembered Cassie Maxwell. If they did they weren't speaking to two out-of-town officers. The woman at the bike rental desk gave them a westerly wave to indicate the same direction Maxine had pointed out. That was all the help they received.

"I like this place," Brenda Lee said as they started up one of the trailheads. The side of the mountain was thick with Douglas fir. Horse and deer tracks dotted the trail. She'd worn thermal leggings and hiking boots over her uniform slacks. "I could see Terry and me coming back in the summer. Maybe staying at the resort."

Ethan had followed trails like this as a kid, in all seasons, though never staying at resorts. Accompanying his father deep into untraveled wilderness, he'd built lean-tos, foraged, made camp with only a pocket knife or hatchet. Jack Brand had wanted his son toughened up, ready for anything the natural world could pitch at him. Ethan supposed he should be grateful for that.

"I want to apologize again," Brenda Lee said. "I shouldn't have spoken to the mayor. Your medical history is nobody's business."

"Thank you."

After a short distance, she added, "I imagine if it were true, a hike like this would be quite painful."

She wasn't wrong. The uphill gradient set the heel plate at a sharper angle than was comfortable. Tramping over wet dirt, stepping over rivulets running down the hillside, caused shooting pains up the nerves of the ankle. He gritted his teeth.

"We can stop for a minute," Brenda Lee said.

They did, sharing a gulp of water from her pack. He caught her eyes moving to his right boot.

"Something you want to ask me?" he said.

"No," she said. "I, well—I already know about your injury."

"The investigator you hired turned it up, huh?"

Brenda Lee shook her head. "I told you that was just to run a background check."

"Then how?"

"Ethan, I've worked with you for fifteen years. You've been cautious, and it hasn't affected your performance. But there are times it's obvious you're in pain."

"And you didn't use that against me to get Frank's job?"

"That wouldn't have been right," Brenda Lee said. "I deserved it on my merits, not your deficiencies."

He laughed. "That's the most Brenda Lee logic I've ever heard."

"Thank you. Should we continue?"

They followed the horse trail upwards for another half hour, drifting northwest along the Stehekin River, into the backwoods. They passed gravel drives leading to A-frames and campsites. Company Creek came in view. On the bank of the small waterway were two cabins, and what looked like a third in the trees behind a rusted Gulfstream trailer. A dirt road driveway cut down toward the closest cabin, barred by a rusty gate. A sign. *PRIVATE PROP-ERTY. TRESPASSERS SHOT. SURVIVORS RE-SHOT.*

"I'm guessing it's that one," Ethan said. "The McCandless family has a thing about trespassers."

They legged over the gate and moved down the drive. Smoke trailed from the chimney of the cabin, diffusing into the rain. A large woodpile was stacked beneath a lean-to a few yards from the side of the cabin. No windows along the side.

Ethan and Brenda Lee cut across the path in single file, the woodpile shielding their approach. They circled around. The screened-in back porch looked out on the creek. The shore was grassy, the current surprisingly swift.

As they closed on the front door, the screen banged open. A rangy barefoot woman in drawstring pants and a blue cotton shirt emerged, pointing a double-barreled shotgun at them.

"Maybe y'all can't read," Cassie Maxwell said.

37

Beside him, Brenda Lee took a sharp sip of air. The creek was at their back, curving behind the cabin. Crows battled in the nearby trees.

He noticed more during moments like this. The rust and pitting on the barrels of the antique coach gun. The frayed left sleeve of Cassie Maxwell's shirt. Her feet were large, nails painted a dark blue. A tattoo of a long-stemmed rose up her right calf.

Rain pelted his shoulders and hood. Beneath the slicker, his hand found the grip of the pistol. Clearing it would involve flipping up the tail of the coat. A two part process.

Brenda Lee held a hand out to the woman with the shotgun. "Miss Maxwell, we're officers from Blaine."

"It says that on your raincoat," Cassie said.

"Do you know why we're here?"

"Take me to prison for something I ain't even done."

Cassie shifted foot to foot, shivered. The shotgun was heavy. The resemblance to Laura Dill was strongest in the face. Ethan hadn't seen Laura when she was alive, but there was a wildness in Cassie's eyes, caution and confidence, that was unique to her.

"That's not the reason," Brenda Lee said. "We're aware of what happened on the train, what you did in Canada. I've spoken to the bank manager."

"Wasn't none of it my idea."

"I know." Brenda Lee wiped water from her glasses. "Can we come inside and talk?"

"I didn't kill no one."

"We believe that."

"Go on and drop your guns."

Cassie Maxwell had held the barrel at the midpoint between them, but now swiveled it from Ethan to Brenda Lee.

"You want to talk, drop your guns and come in and we'll talk. Otherwise get going."

"We can't let you disarm us," Ethan said.

"You're hiding out, Cassie," Brenda Lee said. "You're afraid of someone. We can help."

"I'm afraid what I'll do, your gun ain't on the ground in five seconds."

Would the young woman shoot? Hair matted to her face, restless from the cold and the weight of the weapon. She didn't seem to feel she had a plethora of options. Neither did they. Ethan doubted Cassie Maxwell would pull the double triggers on the ancient shotgun. But the longer the muzzle remained pointed in their direction, the less certain of that he was. Desperate people do foolish things.

"How about this?" Brenda Lee made a show of unzipping her slicker and unsnapping the holster. "How about I give my pistol to Ethan here, you lower your shotgun, and the two of us go inside and talk. Just you and me inside with no weaponry. Would that be satisfactory?"

Cassie was nodding before her face took on a suspicious cast. "So Two Gun Pete over there can break a window and shoot me? Hell no. I ain't dumb, lady."

"Then we'll reverse it," Brenda Lee said. "I'll stay out here with the guns."

"And you won't try nothing?"

Brenda Lee held up open hands. "Miss Maxwell, I'm a mother of three. You remind me of my oldest. I want us all to come through this unscathed. Talk to Ethan for five minutes, and if you don't like what he says, we'll leave."

Cassie let the barrel drop, her shoulders slumping gratefully. She nodded. "Five minutes."

Ethan handed the pistol to Brenda Lee, muttering, "Mother of three, huh?"

"Counting two dogs and a husband."

Cassie held the door. "You coming or ain't you?"

*　*　*

Inside, Cassie fed tinder into the mouth of a potbellied stove. "Split the logs myself," she said. "Jody pays a buddy with a chainsaw to top up the woodpile. Anything to get out of honest labor, that's Jody."

She said this good-naturedly, propping the shotgun with the barrel leaning on the windowsill. The cabin had been insulated and wallpapered, built with one long kitchen and living room, a pair of bedrooms with a small washroom between them. Outside Ethan had seen a well and cistern. Joe McCandless had built the cabin properly—or taken possession from someone who had.

With the fire stoked, Cassie sat down in the rocking chair, motioning to the overturned apple crate next to the card table. Ethan sat, extending his leg to take weight off the ankle. If it came to it, he could push off with the other leg, throwing himself toward the shotgun with a good chance of beating Cassie to it.

Through the thin curtains, he saw Brenda Lee stroll toward the lean-to, flicking water off her hood.

"I love it here," Cassie said. "First time Jody took me I felt like I used to back home, when my daddy and me would go fishing in the Smokies. Want some coffee?"

"Wouldn't turn it down," Ethan said. "You know why we're here?"

"The murder, I expect."

Cassie dumped a few scoops of Maxwell House into a scored metal coffeepot. She filled it with water from the tap.

"I ain't have a clue that was gonna happen," she said. "The girl getting killed and all that. Was weird, her looking so similar. Like it was me dead."

"Do you know who killed her?"

"Nuh-uh."

"What about your friend Bob Galvin?"

She nodded. "That's why I'm up here."

"Who killed Bob?"

"I didn't 'zactly wait around to get introduced," she said. "Just saw him with Jody from across the street. Medium height, kinda skinny, dressed in a white suit, not white but like eggshell or something. And wearing one of those Michael Jackson hats."

"What were they doing?"

Cassie didn't answer right away. She scratched the instep of a dirty foot. Grabbed a second cup from the wash basin, then a third. "Guess the lady outside'll want one too, huh?"

"She might appreciate coming inside even more," Ethan said. The rain wasn't heavy but it wasn't letting up, either. When Cassie didn't respond to his suggestion, he said, "Tell me about the man in white."

"Not much to tell. Guy scares me."

"Does he work for Jody?"

"They got business together, I could see that much."

"Which of them hired you to empty Laura's safe deposit box?"

Cassie shook her head. "Nuh-uh. I ain't incriminating myself."

He tried to make his voice firm but not cold. A good parent's voice. "Do you think we flew here to charge you with theft, or using a fake ID? We're here because of Bob Galvin and Laura Dill."

The coffeepot belched, the grounds and water hissing into steam on the top of the stove. Cassie wrapped her hand with a dishcloth. She lifted the pot, let the grounds settle, and poured out three mugs.

"All I did was cross the border," Cassie said. "Pick up what Jody asked me to. It's his money, anyway. That damn girl refused to make the trip. What else could he do? Bank box was in her name."

"Jody paid you to do this?"

"Two grand. Plus five hundred to Bob for bringing me regular clothes on the train, and helping me with the money."

"Why the costume change?"

Cassie shrugged. "Jody said people were watching."

"People?"

Another shrug. Cassie didn't know.

"How much was in the pack?" Ethan asked.

"A lot. Fifty grand, maybe?"

"You didn't count it?"

"You mule for Jody, his rule is, don't look at nothing. That way, they ask you how much, you ain't gotta lie."

"Did you know what would happen to Laura?"

A vigorous headshake. "Cross my heart, stick a needle in my eye, I had no clue about none of that."

As Cassie explained, she and Bob Galvin had left Edmonds and returned to his home in Bellingham. They'd had a few drinks and hung out. She liked Bob, not like-liked, but as a buddy, as someone to talk to. "Good comp'ny," she said. "Jody was s'posed to meet us at Bob's, pick up the case, and give us our money. Only he said we had to wait a couple days, on account he was being watched. We just hung out at Bob's, had pizza and PBR, played some Nintendo. Sure enough, couple days later, Jody shows up, only he's got the man in the hat with him."

She'd been out buying beer and was on her way back to Galvin's house. At the cross street she saw Jody and Nazareno drive up and force their way inside. She'd made the decision to run.

"I dated Jody off and on for four years," Cassie said. "I never seen that guy before, but I seen lots of that type. Know what I mean?"

Ethan nodded, he did.

"There's dangerous, and then there's mean and dangerous. The ones that enjoy it a little bit. Jody's only mean if you get on his bad side, and he ain't mean like that. This dude in the hat put his arm around Bob's neck, made him step inside with him like they were buddies. The way he grinned, I could just *tell*, I wanted to live I had to run."

Cassie added a heaping tablespoon of sugar to each cup. She stirred with the same spoon. Ethan took a sip. For campfire coffee, it wasn't bad.

"Why hide out here?" he asked. "If this man works for Jody, what makes you think it's safe?"

"I wasn't planning on staying forever," Cassie said. "Just seemed a good place to hide for a few days while things cool out. Jody's not mean all the way through. He likes me, and I'm no threat to him."

Ethan nodded, thinking the woman was woefully underestimating Jody McCandless. She wasn't the first. He took up Brenda Lee's mug. "Back in a sec."

"I'll be watching from the window."

He carried the coffee outside, wondering just how well Cassie Maxwell knew her former boyfriend. Some people were drawn to gangsters, to violence itself. Like celebrity, it could distort your perception. For Jody McCandless, showing a girlfriend one side of himself, hiding the other, more cold-blooded side, would be second nature.

But maybe Cassie knew what Jody was capable of better than Ethan did. Maybe even better than Jody himself. Hard to say.

Brenda Lee had been sitting on a stack of wood beneath the lean-to. As Ethan brought out her coffee she stood and crossed the soggy ground.

"I hope the two of you are comfortable in there," she said.

Ethan was thinking of a reply when the instinct struck, a mallet knocking into his chest. The cause was a glimpse of movement in his peripheral vision, an unnatural wave of the bushes at the base of the hill to their left. A glimmer of white. He dove, the coffee arcing as he dropped the mug, hearing the shot as his knees hit the mud.

Brenda Lee was falling, too. Good, he thought, she'd anticipated the shot. Then he saw the blood.

38

Everything moved too damned slowly—Ethan himself most of all. As Brenda Lee tried to push herself to her feet, he secured an arm under hers, lifted, pulling her and turning so they both rose, stepped, and stumbled together. They fell, this time with the woodpile between them and the hillside where the shot seemed to come from.

There was blood on Brenda Lee's right hip. He clamped her hands to it, ripping his slicker over his head, bunching it to stanch the wound. That done, he took Brenda Lee's service weapon from its holster. He couldn't see his own.

The distance from the brush on the hillside was maybe two football fields. Two hundred yards was a reasonably difficult target to hit. Whoever was aiming at them—and Ethan had an idea—was a marksman.

"I think I'm hurt," Brenda Lee said.

"Yeah."

He heard the screech of the window being opened. Cassie Maxwell's voice yelled, "Hell's going on out there?" In response, another shot echoed, smashing glass. The shotgun cannoned its response.

From the woodpile to the side of the cabin was maybe twenty feet, double that to move around the front to the door. They'd be exposed all that distance. But the screened-in porch at the back—they could get inside the cabin from there. Assuming getting inside would be smart. With his officer hurt, it was the best bad option.

Ethan tried to remember where his pistol had ended up. Brenda Lee must have set it down on the woodpile where it wouldn't get wet. No use to him now. Crouching, he stepped to the edge of the lean-to, sighted on the bushes using Brenda Lee's gun. Aimed high and fired. Not expecting to hit anything, but at least make the shooter tentative.

"We're gonna run, next time I fire," Ethan said. "Can you move?"

She was in pain, but her eyes tracked him. "I don't think so."

"Okay. Can you stand?"

"Let's see." With a grunt, Brenda Lee pulled herself up, leaning into the wood. Her hand still clamped the slicker to her side. She grimaced, but managed to stay upright.

"On three I'm going to fire three times," Ethan said. "We'll take our chances after that. One. Two. All right."

On "Three" he squeezed off two rounds, the reply immediate, a rifle shot that struck the wood in front of him. Instead of firing the third shot he transferred the gun to his left, looped an arm around Brenda Lee's waist. They lunged across the grass and mud toward the cabin. Like a three-legged race, hoisting Brenda Lee by her belt, Ethan trying to match her stride, pull her along. He heard the report of the rifle again but didn't take his eyes from the cabin. The arm of his slicker flopped loose and tangled beneath their feet. They left it. Another step. Then they were there. His elbow knocked against the screen door.

"Don't fire," he called to Cassie.

She opened the back door, crouching, the shotgun cradled across her body. Cassie grimaced at the blood blooming from Brenda Lee's side.

"It's him," Cassie said. "The guy I saw go into Bob's with Jody. I saw him."

"You're sure it's him?"

Cassie nodded. "He's still got the hat on."

Wearing white in a landscape dominated by greens and earth tones was a stupid move—an overconfident move. Their own uniforms weren't exactly camouflage, but a sight better. Ethan set Brenda Lee down on the floor and examined the wound. Rich dark blood had soaked her shirt and the waist of her trousers. He hoped the bullet hadn't grazed any organs.

Ethan ran water and field dressed the wound with a reasonably clean tea towel. Cassie took position near the window, keeping watch with the shotgun balanced on the ledge. The exit wound on Brenda Lee's hip wasn't much larger than the entrance wound, which suggested Nazareno Fulci was firing a medium-caliber round at high speed, and hadn't hit anything vital. Deer rifle, .38 or .30-30 maybe.

"Are there other guns in here?" he asked.

Cassie didn't turn her head from the window. He was starting to like her. "Rifle in the closet. Jody brought it out once for us to plink cans."

He loosed Brenda Lee's belt and used it to hold the towel in place, freeing his hands. His officer was seething in pain, but conscious, watching him work.

"I want to help," Brenda Lee said.

"Sure. Rest up a bit first. There's plenty to do."

He remembered feeling helpless after the IED. Lying among the bodies of Ben Henriquez and Brad Dobbs. Unable to check on his friends or move himself to safety. Waking up in the medevac, numbed but conscious. Being transferred from the base in Bagram to somewhere in Germany, stabilized for the flight home. The next time he woke up he was in a bed in Bethesda, Maryland, after the first surgery and before the second. He remembered learning what had been taken, familiarizing himself with what was left.

"There a radio here?" he asked Cassie.

"At the neighbor's. Charlie with the chainsaw. He lives a mile or so down the trail."

Ethan found a green nylon rifle bag in the closet, smelling of mildew. Inside was a rifle the same vintage as the shotgun, small and with a plastic stock. Chambered for .22 long rifle, it wouldn't be a match for their adversary's firepower. Still, it was something. He found half a box of cartridges on the closet shelf.

Pulling out the feeder tube and loading the rifle, Ethan thought over their options. Nazareno might not be alone—in fact it was almost a guarantee someone was out there with him, someone familiar with the terrain. The shooter knew Brenda Lee was injured, could guess they didn't have cell reception, no means to call for assistance. Nazareno could charge the cabin, which would be risky. Alternatively he could wait them out, see if they tried to run. With the creek behind them and a mountain to the north, their options for escape were limited to the road and the trail. From his vantage near the hill, Nazareno would have no problem picking them off.

Outgunned and out-positioned, with an injured officer and a scared witness. Brenda Lee wasn't at death's door, but she'd need medical attention in the very near future. A future they wouldn't have if Nazareno kept them bottled up in the cabin.

The sight on the rifle was crude, just a bead on the front end of the barrel. No binoculars in the cabin, no telescope. Ethan could approximate where the shots had come from, but by now Nazareno had probably moved—inching closer, he'd guess.

No good alternatives, and yet he felt calm settle over him. Danger simplified things. No worries other than those immediately at hand. Eldon Mooney's campaign to cost him his job, the woman he loved renewing her wedding vows to someone else. Even the death threats seemed detached from him now.

He overturned the card table and propped it in front of the window, giving Cassie an extra barrier of protection. He drew the curtains. As he reloaded Brenda Lee's pistol, he explained what he was planning.

"I need to know exactly where this guy is firing from," he said. "So in half an hour—thirty minutes exactly—I want you to open up. Both barrels. When he returns fire, I'll see him, and his attention will be on you."

He draped Brenda Lee's slicker over the rocking chair, making a steeple of the hood so it looked like a head could be under it.

"Before you fire, slide the chair where it can be seen from the window. Not too obvious, so it looks like someone hunkered down. I want him to take a shot at it."

"What if he hits me instead?" Cassie asked.

"Probably best if you don't let that happen."

He handed the pistol to Brenda Lee and positioned her where she could cover both doors. "In case they breach," he said. "How you feeling?"

"Pissed off, to be honest. I don't much like being shot."

Ethan took up the rifle, took a steadying breath, and eased open the porch door, scanning for any surprises. Nothing but grass and the creek a short distance away.

"Half an hour," he said.

He ran stooped over, zig-zagging as well as his ankle would let him, heading to the water. The bank turned from spongy grass to rock, and then he was over it, plunging into the creek up to his waist.

A sharp stinging cold, the creek bed rocky and uneven. The water's source was somewhere northwest, up the hillside. The current crept by slowly, but he fought it, circling upstream, staying low.

A trained soldier would prepare against an enemy circling behind. He was betting on Nazareno's overconfidence. What could the three of them do, trapped in a cabin, at least one of them injured, with only one road out? No threat to a professional.

If Nazareno worried about anything, it would be reinforcements arriving from the west along the trail. He'd keep them bottled up in the cabin, work his way closer. Maybe parlay through the door. Promise them no harm if they surrendered. Then shoot them all.

It was slow going, trudging along the creek, keeping his head below the edge of the bank, the rifle raised out of the water. He had no idea if the damn gun would even fire. The ammunition was old enough to fail. *He* could fail.

As the incline increased and his waterlogged ankle started to scream with pain, it was harder to keep steady. After wending upstream for about twenty minutes, he ventured a look over the edge of the bank. He was close to the bushes where Nazareno had fired from, but his adversary had moved nearer to the cabin by a hundred yards or so. There he was, Nazareno's back to the creek. Ethan was looking over the shooter's shoulder.

He heard footsteps nearby, directly to his left, and crouched, making himself small, part of the creek bed. The steps got louder, the figure not even trying for stealth. Maybe twenty feet downstream from his hiding place. A shadow loomed over the bank and he heard the sound of piss. Jody McCandless hummed the chorus to "Disco Inferno" while he relieved himself in the grass.

From here he could shoot and kill Jody, even the odds. That would alert Nazareno to his plan and cost him the surprise he'd crawled here to gain. Nazareno was the more dangerous one, he reckoned. Ethan waited till he heard Jody zip up and tramp back before peering out again.

"How much longer?" he heard Jody ask.

Nazareno shushed him.

Jody might be the one paying Nazareno's fee, but in the bush, the man in white was running things. Jody deferred, though not quietly. He fidgeted, digging a furrow in the grass with his heel. Eager for this to be over.

Crawling on his stomach, gun in hand, Ethan slunk his way closer. Nazareno was occupied with the scoped rifle; Jody had a pistol shoved in the waist of his camo-patterned cargo pants. A red jerry can sat in the bushes nearby. That was the ultimate plan: use gasoline to burn away the evidence.

How close was it to half an hour? Ethan didn't dare look at his phone. Patience in battle was a tough quality to cultivate. Snipers could be in one position for days at a time, not moving at all, waiting for a window on their target as short as a fraction of a second.

He'd asked one for advice once, a woman from Texas. "You can't take your mind off what you're doing, not even partways. But your mind is gonna pull away on its own." The sniper had held up her fingers, as if counting off. "What you do is keep it surface level. Lists are good for that. I'm partial to geography, so waterways, state capitals, that sort of thing. Thinking without thinking, that's the key."

Lining up the rifle beads on Nazareno, Ethan kept his mind away from the topics he tended to feel too deeply about—women, his family, regrets, and things left undone. Instead he rattled off lists, itemized, sequenced. Books he'd enjoyed, favorite actors, places he'd visited with remarkable countryside. Stehekin belonged on that list. Music was an easy one. Take his favorite artist, list his albums in order. *Strait Country* was first, then *Strait from the Heart. Right or Wrong* came third, fourth was *Does Fort Worth Ever Cross Your Mind?* What was fifth? Seventh was easy, it was called *#7*. So which ones was he missing?

By the time he'd got to George's mid-nineties era, he saw movement in the cabin window. The peaked hood of the jacket was only an outline through the curtain, not convincing as a human head. But Nazareno focused on it, aiming from one knee.

He heard the shotgun blast and saw a gust of powder vent from the cabin window. Too far away to be a danger to the attackers. Nazareno fired, smashing the glass and knocking the chair aside. Seeing the shotgun barrel still protruding from the window, Nazareno adjusted his aim. Ethan shot him.

Bullets were wild things. Ethan had seen a .22 target pistol leave a significant hole in a man's skull at close range, and had heard from Frank Keogh how a thick leather jacket once deflected a .38 slug. His first shot caught Nazareno high in the shoulder, his second in the left breast as Nazareno spun, looking for where the shot had come from. Next to his target, Jody McCandless stood slack-jawed, head swiveling as Nazareno inched toward cover.

Ethan missed his third shot, aiming at Jody. He saw Nazareno sight along the horizon without the scope, moving the barrel toward his position. Ethan aimed and squeezed the trigger, catching his target somewhere above the collar.

Nazareno surprised him by popping up, running pell-mell for cover. His destination was the bushes where he and Jody had been hiding before. Maybe Nazareno had an ATV stashed there. Or additional weaponry.

It didn't matter in the instant, retreat was retreat. He sighted on Jody, who was watching his subordinate run, dumbstruck at the turn of events.

"Drop your gun," Ethan called. "You're surrounded, Jody."

"Surrounded my ass," Jody said.

Ethan aimed at the grass by Jody's feet, fired. Only the trigger wouldn't pull. The feed had jammed. Meanwhile, Jody McCandless was gripping the deer rifle Nazareno had dropped.

"Don't try it, son." Ethan changed his voice, doing his best impersonation of Charles Bronson. "Next one's aimed at your head."

"Bullshit. We saw you."

"Saw some of us."

Nazareno's footsteps faded. Ethan scanned the bush but couldn't see anything. He waited to hear the sound of an engine. Nothing. Maybe the killer had fainted out there. Three wounds could do that.

"I got the shot," he said as if speaking to someone else. Jody's head whipped around. Doing his best impersonation of Frank Keogh, Ethan said, "Take it on three, son" and then answered as himself, "Roger that, Frank."

"You're all alone out here," Jody said.

"Three."

"Your deputy or whatever she is is either dead or on her way, and Cassie's alone in there. Has to be. I seen you. That's how I know it's only you."

"Two," Ethan said.

"You think I'm that dumb? You really think I don't know your cop tricks? What, you sneak an entire platoon up here?"

Ethan racked the bolt on the .22 loud as he could, chambering a round he wasn't sure he could fire. "One."

Jody's hands went up, the deer rifle falling to the grass.

"All right, I give," he called.

Moments later, as Ethan cuffed him, Jody swore.

"God*damn*it, I *knew* you were alone."

39

Ethan waited in the cabin with his prisoner and the injured officer while Cassie Maxwell ran to the neighbor's and radioed for help. A matter of trust; he found he trusted Cassie. Jody scowled at him and didn't speak.

Soon a search and rescue helicopter set down in the field near the cabin. Paramedics strapped Brenda Lee to a trauma board and hoisted her into the chopper. They asked if anyone else needed immediate first aid.

Ethan, soaked and muddied from his crawl along the bank, said he was fine and dandy.

"What about that one?" the paramedic asked, pointing at Jody.

"He and I are gonna have a little talk."

A second chopper was beginning to comb the hillside for Nazareno. Ethan had searched the brush where he'd last seen the killer, finding blood on the trampled stems, footprints leading up the mountain, but no visual. Maybe his third shot had hit something vital. If not, Nazareno wasn't likely to forget him.

Collecting his pistol and rain slicker, Ethan led Cassie and Jody down the trail. The rain had abated, and the going down was easier—at least for two of them. The second time Jody stumbled, Ethan uncuffed him, snapping the bracelets on in front.

"I could move even better with free hands," Jody said.

"But then you might take it in your head to run."

Cassie, loping along faster than them, turned back to spit and say, "Let the bastard fall."

Ethan's own footing was easier at Jody's slower pace. He took the frequent slopes and ledges of the trail with feet pointed sideways, hands free to grab a branch or pull his pistol should Jody bolt into the brush. Above them, jays squawked.

He'd already read Jody his Miranda warning, so questioning the prisoner wasn't likely to result in an answer. Instead, he spoke with Cassie, glancing at Jody to gauge his reaction.

"I only said yes because I needed the money," Cassie told him. She was wearing a poncho and hiking boots a size too big. Even so, she walked circles around the two men, pausing at times for them to catch up. "He said all's I had to do was show the man at the bank Laura's ID. Easy-peasy. He said Laura couldn't travel no more, so I'd be doing both of 'em a favor. Then, night before I'm s'posed to go, Jody tells me I'll be crossing the border *as* Laura. Got me the tickets in her name and everything. Brings me a backpack looks just like hers. Had me dye my hair."

"Shut your face," Jody said.

Cassie laughed. "Last order you ever give me, Jody. After what you did to Bob, I hope you rot."

"I did nothing," Jody said.

"Sure, 'cept ask me do I know someone who can meet me on the train with a change of clothes, take the money off my hands. You set him up."

"Shut up."

Cassie hung back, scooped a handful of dirt and rocks and pelted Jody's back with them. Ethan's prisoner swore and spun around, a murderous look on his face.

"You gonna let her do that?" Jody asked.

"Ain't nobody telling me what to do," Cassie said.

"How did you and Bob work the hand-off?" Ethan asked, figuring there'd be less friction if Cassie was answering.

"Jody had his sister sell us seats that were one car apart. That way we knew which washroom to head to. As the train pulled in to Bellingham, I holed up in there, switched the sign to vacant soon's the passengers got onboard. Bob did his part beautifully. He knew the kind of hassle I could get in if it turned out wrong. He wouldn't'a said nothing, either. Why'd you have to kill him, Jody?"

She aimed a kick at Jody's ass, leaving a muddy imprint. Ethan stepped in before she could deliver another.

"That's assault," Jody said. "And it was witnessed by an officer."

"Give me five minutes alone with him and I'll show you assault," Cassie said.

They were nearing Stehekin. Through the swath of Douglas fir Ethan glimpsed the gray-blue water of Lake Chelan. The *Sea Pig* was still roped to the end of the jetty.

"Maybe you can clear this up for me," Ethan said. "You spent the train ride north in the bistro car, right?"

"Sure did," Cassie said. "Had a burger, got my drink on. I figured since Jody was paying expenses, why not live it up?"

"And no one was with you?"

"Nope. I had my instructions. Don't talk too much to other passengers, don't draw no attention. 'Mousy gal with a yellow backpack' is the impression I was s'posed to make. So that's the impression I made."

"You paid for your drinks in cash?"

"With Jody's money."

"And you asked for a receipt?"

"You don't got to ask, they give you one each time you pay."

"What do you mean, 'each time'?" Ethan asked.

"Ain't you ever bought a beer on a train before?" Cassie shook her head as if she'd encountered someone totally naïve. "They don't let you run a tab in the bistro car. It's a cash and carry type situation. Each item you buy, you got to pay for it first. You pay, you get a receipt."

Ethan grabbed Jody's shoulder to halt their progress down the last leg of the trail. On his phone he had a picture of the receipt found beneath Laura Dill's body. He held this up so Cassie Maxwell could see it.

"That's what I ordered," she said. "But that's four hours' worth of drinking right there. Each of those rum and cokes I bought separate. Then I switched to beer so's I wouldn't be too hammered to get to the B and B Jody booked for me."

"The burger was yours too?"

"Came out of a microwave, but I've had plenty worse."

"So this receipt isn't yours."

As proof Cassie dug a hand-knit wallet out of the pocket of her slacks. She rummaged through the billfold, pulling out paper slips and dollar bills. She unfolded one and handed it to Ethan. The receipt bore the rail line's logo, the date, a bill of $13.25, and the words PAID IN CASH.

"Told you to get rid—" Jody said, catching his mistake, eyes flicking to Ethan's to see if it landed. He bolted, dashing off the trail into a patch of ferns, high-stepping like a cadet running over tires on an obstacle course.

Ethan followed, moving at a slower pace and watching for the inevitable. Sure enough, Jody stumbled, but instead of crashing to the forest floor, he seemed to disappear into it.

When he approached the spot, Ethan saw why. The ground fell away here, sloping down to meet the next turn of the trail. Jody had fallen six feet and was sprawled in the muck.

Cassie caught up to them, laughing. "The great criminal mastermind," she said.

* * *

At the jetty, Maxine Duke sat on a pier smoking a cigarette. She threw it into the water as they approached. "Been waiting since forever," she said. "Saw the choppers and assumed the worst."

Noticing the mud spackled on his uniform, and the wet fatigues clinging to Jody's legs, Maxine headed into the visitors center to find some newspaper. "No sense mussing the *Pig's* upholstery."

"No," Ethan said, "we wouldn't want that."

40

Very few sights seemed as right as Jody McCandless in a cell. Ethan took a moment to appreciate that. Jody had been charged with attempted murder, plus a host of lesser offenses. Only a couple of years ago, his brother had sat on the same bench. Seth's trial had taken months; Ethan wondered if Jody's would drag on as long.

But it still wasn't enough. Ethan didn't have proof that Jody killed Laura Dill. Cassie Maxwell could connect Jody to Bob Galvin's murder, but she hadn't actually witnessed it. And without Nazareno Fulci in custody, Jody would no doubt blame his subordinate.

With Jody locked up in the county jail, Assistant DA Hayley Hokuto was busy preparing a search warrant for the McCandless property. There wasn't much left for Ethan to do. Cassie was giving an official statement to Moira Sutcliffe. Ethan listened for a while from outside the room, then drove home to Blaine.

In his absence, the most exciting event was the discovery of Jody's ATV. A patrol officer had spotted it upside down in a culvert near the I-5 onramp. Mal Keogh had gone over the vehicle, taken prints, but as evidence it was practically useless. In court, Jody could claim that whatever they found had been left after the ATV was stolen.

All told he was away from Blaine less than a day. Yet Ethan felt he was returning to an alien place, one of those *Twilight Zone* worlds were everyone in town has disappeared. Brenda Lee Page's cluttered, unoccupied desk at the station underscored this. His senior officer had been airlifted to a trauma center in Wenatchee. Brenda Lee was stable, and according to her husband Terry, would be home in a few days.

"The search team wouldn't say much about what happened to her," Terry said over the phone. Ethan had spoken to Brenda Lee's spouse maybe five times in his life, mostly at the annual Christmas parties. A nice pleasant man with a disheveled beard who ran an accounting business out of a spare bedroom. They'd never talked about anything more serious than the Seahawks' chances, or whether Naomi or Wynonna was the better Judd.

Ethan explained as concisely as he could what happened, stressing Brenda Lee's bravery. He offered what assistance he could. It was an awkward conversation. Terry Page was in shock, for the first time realizing that what his wife did for a living put her in danger.

"It's like something you read about," he said. "Has this kind of thing ever happened before? I mean to her?"

Ethan could think of a half dozen occasions where violence had threatened to flare up, and Brenda Lee Page had stood calm alongside him and the others. But he didn't answer.

"If you need anything, call me directly," he told the shaken husband.

The town wasn't empty, but the faces he saw—the temporary desk clerk, the reserve officers on the overnight shift, the new waiter at Lucky Luk's—all seemed to stare at him as if Ethan had been the one to change. Like they knew something about him he didn't.

Since last time he'd gotten strange looks it had been on account of Jay Swan's news stories, he pulled up the homepage of the *Skyline*. The top story bore the headline *Mayor 'Deeply Unhappy' With New Chief, Sources Say*. Instead of Jay's name, the story had appeared under the generic 'Skyline News Staff' byline.

Blaine Mayor Eldon Mooney has repeatedly expressed "serious concerns" over newly appointed Chief of Police Ethan Brand's fitness for the job, sources inside City Hall confirmed Saturday afternoon.

The "sources" were anonymous, very likely Mooney himself. The "serious concerns" were vague. The article hinted this likely connected to the chief's medical records. The way his ankle and foot felt after a day spent hiking and crawling through water, Ethan could almost wish to be relieved.

He didn't have to wonder when he'd be asked to defend himself. The mayor had left him a voice mail, summoning him to a special meeting of the City Council Monday at ten AM. "Hate to do this to you, Ethan, but some of us have concerns that are, well, pretty darn concerning. We'll wade through all this Monday morning, and don't worry for even a second that you won't be given ample opportunity to explain your side of things. Till then."

Ethan had known that as chief, he'd face his share of opposition from City Hall. He'd expected more when he fired Cliff Mooney. What he was beginning to realize, though, was that the mayor cared less about his nephew's future than about Ethan defying him. This hearing was payback for a personal insult. The mayor was a small and petty man, unconcerned that his scheme might hurt the investigation into Laura Dill's murder.

If these were his last days as chief, Ethan decided, he'd spend them making sure the case was solved properly. That meant finding evidence to charge Jody McCandless and Nazareno Fulci.

Speaking of. Search and rescue had combed most of Cascades National Park, and the shores of Lake Chelan, finding no sign of Nazareno. The Ocean Beach Hotel confirmed that he'd checked out Friday morning. Ethan wondered if Nazareno was dead. Three shots, he ought to be. But then people had survived far worse.

When he arrived home, Ethan examined both doors and swept the yard before entering his house. No sign of disturbance. No notes or elk hearts or other gifts.

Once he was certain he was alone, a different emotion gripped him. The emptiness of the house, the memories each room held, swamped him with a deep sense of gloom. The bedroom where he and Jazz had made love, where later on, after his separation, he'd brought Steph Sinclair. The kitchen where he'd scrambled eggs and scraped margarine on toast for the kids on Christmas morning, Ben and Brad protesting that they could open presents on an empty stomach. Ethan turned on lights throughout the house, as if illumination could chase away those feelings. All the light accomplished was to create deeper shadows.

And still no sign of his coyote.

Amused at his own sense of concern, he punched in the number for the Whatcom Humane Society, was put through to Animal Control. A cheerful-sounding operator asked what seemed to be the matter this evening.

"I was just wondering if there's been a call out to Blaine in the last few days regarding a coyote," he said.

"Have you spotted one, sir, and are you certain it's not a dog?"

"Actually I'm calling to see if *you've* spotted one recently. One with blue eyes."

"We've had several interactions with coyotes near Blaine, but we don't record the eye color."

"No, of course," Ethan said.

"We encourage citizens not to interact with wild animals."

"Thank you."

"Generally speaking, if you leave them alone, they'll do the same to you."

Ethan hung up.

Strange that he attached feelings to the disappearance of a wild animal. Talking to the coyote had felt silly, but had helped to curb that sense of being alone. Seeing her prowl the yard had made him feel connected to the world rather than cut off from it. He'd associated her with this new stage of his life, with being single and being chief. Absurd, but he'd felt at peace with the coyote nearby. Since its disappearance, nothing had seemed to go right.

He needed a pet, maybe one of Jon's kittens. Loneliness made people loopy.

Tomorrow would be better, he thought, stepping off the porch into the quiet hallway. Tomorrow always meant hope. Then he remembered tomorrow was Sunday, and what that day was going to bring.

Hope. What a silly and far-fetched idea.

41

"Couldn't ask for better weather for matrimonials," Moira Sutcliffe said. "The Sinclairs must have paid off the weatherman."

It was true. The morning had arrived rosy and clear skied, with distant clouds the color of whipped honey. The sun was peeking over Mt. Baker. The day seemed to promise warmth and calm. To someone, anyway.

Ethan trailed Moira through the tall grass along the side of the McCandless property. The house was being searched by Heck Ruiz and a half dozen officers from the WSP. Hayley Hokuto had succeeded in getting a search warrant signed off by a judge, comprehensive enough to cover Jody's house and property. Among the items listed in the warrant were one backpack, mustard yellow in color; a sum of money amounting to eighty thousand dollars or thereabouts, bundled as Cassie Maxwell had described; and a long, thin blade matching the dimensions of the puncture wounds in Laura Dill's side.

Ethan tried to feel optimistic about the search. That was proving difficult, because of the ceremony that lay ahead that afternoon, and because of what he knew of Jody McCandless. Finding a tire tread was very different than finding a bloody knife and a sack of money. Jody wasn't stupid. If those items were on the property, they would be well hidden.

Jody's mother had once grown corn and beans in the backyard. All that remained were a few weathered stakes and some empty furrowed rows, overgrown with dandelions and rhubarb. A fire barrel, a compost heap—these would have to be gone through too. But their current destination was the large shed along the back of the property. Despite a decade of neglect, the roof was mossy but intact, and the siding hadn't warped. The lock on the door still held.

"I didn't happen to bring a key with me," the lieutenant said. "Did you?"

"'Fraid not."

"What a shame. We came all this way."

Moira had brought a pry bar with her, and now easily splintered the frame. The door eased inward. Neither of them carried a flashlight, and pulling the chain on the ceiling lamp did nothing. Each wall held dozens, maybe hundreds of tools. Picks, shovels, augers, hoes, long-handled pruning shears, every kind of rake and broom. Two wheelbarrows were tipped up. Saws and hammers hung on nails. Close to the door was a large mound with a nylon dust cover.

"Another ATV?" Sutcliffe guessed.

But removing the sheet revealed a sit-down tractor. Above it, the ceiling beams boasted several nests and webs.

"Everything you'd need to pretty this place up is in here," Sutcliffe said. "Three kids, none of them handy. Must've been a disappointment to Joe McCandless."

Ethan crouched, stepping to the side of the door so the sunlight fell on the concrete. Dirt and shreds of ancient leaves, paper scraps, stains from motor oil.

"I don't think Joe was much of a handyman," Ethan said. "I spent some time at his cabin."

"Yeah, we heard about that." Moira was too much of a professional to ask for details, but she was interested.

"This morning I looked up the property history. The previous owner put in the well and septic, then sold the place to Joe for a dollar. Probably to settle a debt. The McCandless family didn't improve it much."

"Not sure what you're getting at," Moira said.

He gestured at the walls. "Awful lot of tools for a guy who can't use 'em."

"Maybe he's a hoarder," Moira said. "I watched a show one time about a guy like that. Couldn't even get rid of used Kleenex. You imagine?"

There were no footprints on the cement floor, at least none visible from the door. Behind the ATV, though, Ethan saw a cigarette butt, an empty can of Diet Dr. Pepper.

"You know what just struck me?" Moira held her arms out to measure the width of the door. She turned to the tractor and bent at the waist, hands still out at the same measurement.

"Looks a little like you're doing the robot," Ethan said.

"I'm surprised you know the name of any dance that's not done in a line."

The lieutenant's measurement made her point. Head-on or sideways, the tractor was too wide to fit through the door.

"Does he tip it on its side every time he does the lawn?" Moira asked. "Not that the lawn is in any great shakes. Get on the other end of this, will you?"

The brakes were off, and they wheeled the tractor to the side, but not before Ethan inspected the wheels. Searching the shed brought back memories of searching homes in Garmsir. The family waiting outside while they searched for assault rifles hidden under cribs, explosives being brewed beneath the floor. Fear and irritation on both sides.

Beneath the tractor was a sheet of cork smelling of machine oil, as if put there to stop a leak. Moving this revealed a three-by-three square indentation in the floor, a hinged metal door attached to it.

"Now I could be wrong," Moira said, "but is this what they call a secret compartment?"

"Sure looks it."

Ethan examined the contours of the door. No wires or other traps visible. He lifted the handle. Nestled inside, wrapped in translucent bags, were a half-dozen inch-thick bundles of dollar bills.

"The proverbial fat stacks." Moira opened one, fanned through the bills. Fives and tens and twenties. "What do you think, that look like the eighty grand listed in the warrant?"

"More."

Below the money was a trash bag full of orange pill vials—OxyContin, oxycodone, hydrocodone, T-3s. Most with prescription labels from Canadian pharmacies. Almost all of them expired.

Ethan examined the labels, finding one that read *Dill, Laura. Take 1 to 2 tablets every 4 to 6 hours as needed for pain.* Someone on the other side of the border was writing scrips for Jody's people.

The dead woman's name was on several other vials, Cassie Maxwell's on a few as well. One of the other names surprised him: Lorraine Rusk, Collin's mother. Ethan wondered if Lorraine's family knew she worked for Jody McCandless.

Not that he was anyone to judge. Fifteen years ago, when his own prescriptions had run out, he'd bought black market pills like these. Money handed to a woman in the parking lot of the Blue Duck. A man tossing a similar-looking vial through his truck window. His money, his need, had fed the McCandless organization or one just like it. His shame kept him from celebrating now.

"Jackpot," Moira said.

But it wasn't. Yes, the money was consistent with what had been listed in the warrant. And the scrips connected Laura Dill to Jody's criminal enterprise. But no weapon, no backpack, nothing to state conclusively that Jody murdered her.

The evidence had to be somewhere else.

42

On the back porch of the McCandless house, Heck Ruiz swigged from his water bottle and wiped his forehead. Ethan and Moira Sutcliffe studied the framed picture he'd found. An aerial photo of the property, taken sometime in the 1990s. Giles Road was a dusty gray ribbon. The McCandless property still included the acreage on the other side of the logging road, as fallow then as it was now.

"Please tell me you found the knife cached behind the picture frame," Moira said.

"No knife, but looky." Heck held the photo flat. His finger tapped a small gray rectangle set back from the road on the west side. "That look like poured cement, Chief?"

Ethan squinted. The structure could have been concrete, it was hard to tell. What was curious was its position.

"Say it is cement," Moira said. "Why's that anything?"

"Well, what were the sons of guns building there?" Heck asked. "And where's it at now?"

The three of them walked through the house to the front, pausing as Sergeant Rao summarized her findings. Several personal possessions likely belonging to Laura Dill, clothing and toiletries and the like. No backpack. A wide variety of kitchen cutting implements. None matching the blade.

"The victim clearly lived here, ma'am," Rao said. "We can't say to a certainty much more than that."

"Keep looking," Moira said.

The front yard was overrun with police cars from both agencies, plus an evidence van. Ethan had parked his truck on the shoulder. Heck Ruiz consulted the photo and pointed across Miller Road to a section of field not so different from the rest. Maybe a bit flatter.

"That's where it was," he said. "If the family had a secret hiding place built into the shed, maybe they have another one there."

"Good eye," Ethan said. "Only problem, that field's not included in the warrant."

"So we'll call the DA and get a new one written up," Moira said. "Not sure if a judge will sign off based on a decades-old photo. Any idea who owns the property?"

Ethan nodded. "Bit of a thorny issue."

The lieutenant opened her prowler and extracted a thermos and several paper cups. "Thorny issues make me thirsty," she said. "Coffee, gents?"

As she poured, Ethan explained that Frank Keogh and his business partners had recently taken possession. Finding a murder weapon, or anything else linked to criminal activity, could hurt Frank's reputation, to say nothing of putting him in legal jeopardy. Better to ask him for permission to search. Moira agreed.

The coffee only served to whet their appetite, and Moira sent an officer for McDonald's. By the time Frank Keogh's new Mercedes pulled onto the shoulder behind the Dodge, Ethan was finishing off a McMuffin, feeling less famished but still exhausted. And the day had only begun.

Frank shook hands, dressed in a red checked shirt and high-waisted Wranglers. "Still finding my retirement fashion sense," he said. "How's this all going?"

"It's going," Ethan said. In the presence of his mentor he felt deferential, uneasy posing the questions he had to ask.

His hesitation proved well-founded. After listening to Ethan explain what they suspected might lie under his property, Frank stared at the spot, thumbs hitched over his belt. He shook his head.

"I been over that area a few times prior to the sale. There's nothing there."

"A quick look would confirm that."

"Not gonna happen," Frank said.

Ethan had foreseen the discomfort of having to ask, weighed that against the damage of a search warrant. He hadn't even considered Frank might say no. Used to taking the man's counsel, trusting his moral compass, Ethan had to fight down an instinct to simply nod and do what he was told.

"Two people have been murdered, Frank. It doesn't bother you the killer might have used your property to dump the evidence? Might have done it just to put one over on a cop?"

"Ex-cop," Frank said. "If it was my own personal property, the answer might be different. But the land is a corporate asset, and I have fiduciary responsibilities."

"Fiduciary hell," Ethan said.

"If that's all, I got a short stack of whole wheat pancakes and a bottle of sugar-free syrup waiting on me."

He walked beside Frank to the door of the Jeep. "You won't even take a look yourself?"

"I'm not police anymore," Frank said, his voice soft but threaded with steel. "My priorities are different. You can push me, you want to, but this ain't an argument you can win."

* * *

Moira Sutcliffe promised to try for a warrant for the adjacent field, but didn't seem optimistic. For the rest of the afternoon, the lieutenant's good humor was gone. Whatever evidence might have been found on Frank Keogh's property didn't matter now. The concrete square was another dead end. The damn things were piling up fast.

The rest of the search turned up little in the way of evidence. To Ethan, the most significant discovery was what they found in Jody's closet—and what they didn't find. On the floor of the large walk-in space were three molded plastic cases for firearms, plus three unlocked trigger guards. The guns themselves were missing. The rifle and handgun Jody and Nazareno had wielded at the cabin accounted for two sets of cases and locks. That left an automatic pistol still at large.

Tension settled on Ethan's shoulders. If Nazareno Fulci managed to get off the mountain alive, he'd be armed.

Part of him, hell, most of him, wanted to pack it in for the day. The search, the investigation, the council meeting looming on Monday—it was all too much. Overwhelming. Let someone else deal with it.

But there was no one else. After a moment of feeling sorry for himself, Ethan climbed into the truck and pointed it toward town.

He could interview Jody, knowing there was insufficient evidence, and hope the smuggler let something slip. Jody's lawyers would probably advise their client to keep quiet. Or Jody might claim Nazareno had forced him to participate, might point out that he hadn't actually fired at anyone himself. He could end up released on bail, and the murders, which he either committed or ordered someone else to, would still be unproven. Guesswork, when it came down to it. And once he was free, what would stop Jody from destroying whatever evidence might be left?

Alternatively, Ethan could make another run at those closest to Jody, his sister and the two known associates. Sissy McCandless would have the best knowledge of the homestead, any hiding places her brother might have. But just how far had Sissy broken from her family? Would she be willing to go that much further?

A faint hope, but Ethan couldn't summon to mind a better one.

43

A short lineup crowded the counter of Breakwater Travel. Sissy McCandless was explaining what was meant by "All Included" to Jolene Whitley, who lived at the senior center on C Street. Ethan waited behind Arnie Rasmussen, another energetic retiree, who asked for the same Greek island cruise package as Mrs. Whitley. Sissy asked if Arnie would mind being on the same evening flight as her previous customer, perhaps even sitting next to Mrs. Whitley.

"No," Arnie said. "I suppose that would suit me just fine."

After the door shut, Sissy grinned and leaned over the counter. "That's the third cruise those two have taken together. Always buying separate tickets, as luck would have it ending up on the same flights, with adjacent berths. Romantic, isn't it?"

"I'm not much for cruises," Ethan said, swinging the OPEN sign to CLOSED. "Can we talk?"

"That tone of voice, it can only be about Jody." Sissy removed her glasses and cleaned the lenses on the corner of her vest. "I know my brother's in custody."

"You know what he did?"

Sissy nodded. "I wish I could say I was a hundred percent surprised."

From behind the printer stand came a rustling sound, paper bring crumpled. A person hiding behind it would have to be small or in a crouch.

"You have company?" Ethan asked.

"Nuh-uh. So what about my brother?"

"We're searching the homestead right now."

The information didn't seem to faze her. Nor did the rustling sound. Sissy reaffixed her glasses, set her hands on her hips. "Like I said last time, I only go out there for the odd holiday."

"I know about the shed."

She didn't pretend not to know what he meant. A good sign, Ethan thought.

"So you know," Sissy said. "That has nothing to do with me."

"I need to know where else Jody would hide something."

"You're asking me to—"

"To help me locate evidence in the murder of two people. I'm asking you to do the right thing."

"The right thing," Sissy repeated. "Well, that's a matter of perspective, isn't it?"

"Not to me, no."

"I haven't even taken my lunch break yet," she said. "It's a little early for an appeal to my sense of civic duty."

"To your sense of what's right."

"You're aware my last name is McCandless? Asking me to do what's right, you must be what my mom would call 'plum desperate.'"

"Won't deny it," Ethan said. "But you're different from your brothers. I'm sure the town hasn't always treated you that way. Here's your chance, then, to prove it, to make that difference clear to everyone."

"And incriminate my little brother. I'm not sure I care what anyone thinks that much."

Ethan leaned his hands on the counter, imploring her. Sissy looked around the travel agency office, a humble workspace that had taken a thousand sacrifices to carve out as her own. Sissy licked her thumb and wiped away a smudge from the countertop.

"Laura Dill was living at the house," Ethan said, keeping his voice emotionless, letting Sissy supply the drama for herself. "We found Laura's stuff, her clothing and toothbrush, her shampoo and her comb. Know whose old room those things were in?"

Sissy didn't answer.

"Sitting on the same porch you did. Staring out the same bedroom window. Out at Giles Road, wondering if *this* was the best that life had to offer. Asking herself if she could ever get free of here, of your brother. What that better life might look like."

"I know what you're trying to do," Sissy said.

"Laura stood up to Jody, the way you stood up to your folks. No more, she told him. I expect Jody tried everything to change her mind. Bribery. Threats. Lies so obvious they both knew he was full of it."

Sissy was staring at the floor now.

"I don't have evidence to prove this," Ethan said, "but put yourself in Jody's shoes. Parents gone, Seth in jail, you on the straight and narrow. The runt of the litter is suddenly all by his lonesome, and here's this young lady standing up to him, saying she's done being used. Do you think your brother would let her go? Or do you think he'd smile at her, one of those wide Jody McCandless smiles, and say 'Sure, babe, whatever you want, it's all good.' All the while he's planning—"

"Stop," Sissy said.

"'Sure, darling, I'll even help you earn some walking around money. I just need to borrow your ID for a while. I'll pay you for it, and you don't even have to make the trip. And by the way, Laura, how 'bout one last ride on the ATV?'"

"Please stop." Sissy's index finger wiped at the corner of her eye.

"Ever ride double on an all-terrain vehicle?" Ethan asked. "You put your hands round the waist of the driver, same as a horse or a bike. I bet Jody drove that first part out from the house. Up and down the brush, along Portal Way, heading out to the train tracks. I imagine it'd be fun. And when Laura asked could *she* drive, Jody brought that vehicle to a stop. He let her climb on and get comfortable. He sat behind her, put one hand around her waist. And the other drove the knife in between her ribs."

He didn't have to describe the rest. Laura Dill falling to the brush, unsure what had happened, realizing too late. Jody riding away from the scene, turning back to make sure he hadn't left anything behind. The train passing by, carrying Cassie Maxwell and his money, providing an alibi of Laura still alive. Ethan gave Sissy time to dwell on this.

After a long pause, the rustling sound all that broke the silence, Sissy said, "I can't tell you where something is if I've never seen it. I don't know my brother's business, where he hides things. Wish I did."

Ethan nodded. He'd tried.

From behind the printer stand, a small fuzzy head peeked out. A tabby kitten, trailing from its mouth a balled-up scrap of paper.

"I got this little guy yesterday," Sissy said, cradling the kitten. "Someone from the police station came in to put up a poster and asked if I wanted one. I still haven't settled on a name. What do you think of Westfalia?"

"Like the Volkswagen van?"

Sissy nodded, kneading the cat's shoulder blades. "My daddy used to drive one. Me and Seth learned on it. Then Seth wrecked the transmission, and my daddy gutted it, so it was just this big beige box in our yard. Sold the tires to a neighbor. That old Westfalia sat for years till it was all rusted out. Weeds growing up through the floor. Seth always said he'd hire a flatbed some day and take it to Mo's, but he never got around to it. I think he decided it was just easier to dig a hole and bury it."

"In the yard?"

"Yuh-huh."

Sissy brought the tabby to the counter, where Ethan could pet him. The kitten looked apprehensive as his hand smoothed the fur over the small head, purring and closing its eyes.

"He likes you," Sissy said. "Maybe Westfalia's not the right name for a gregarious personality. Don't know why I thought of that van. Sorry I couldn't help you."

Nodding, grateful, Ethan gave the kitten an extra scratch under the chin. "You never know where help might come from."

* * *

Most of the team had gone from the McCandless house, and what remained was focused on the interior. Ethan found he could now park right next to the porch. Moira Sutcliffe greeted him with a lackluster wave.

"Glutton for punishment, huh?"

Her look of defeat turned to incredulity when he dropped the gate on the Dodge, slinging out a pair of shovels and a brand-new metal detector.

"You know how to work one of these?" he asked, passing her the headphones the manager at Outdoor Outfitters had rented to him. "The damage deposit was three hundred bucks. I think I broke two hundred worth bouncing it around."

"They have one at the station in Bellingham," Moira said. "What am I hunting for?"

"A big box of West German steel."

In half an hour they found it, following the route around the side of the house a large vehicle would be most likely to take. Far back, behind the compost, was a mound of bark mulch. The Westfalia had been tipped on its side, half-buried and then covered over with cedar chips. Scraping those away with a shovel unearthed the sliding door of the van. Soon Moira Sutcliffe had it open, flashing a light down into the gutted interior. She called out to Ethan what she saw.

"More shrink-wrapped bundles of cash," she said. "Couple bricks of our old friend the 'suspicious white powder.' And would you look at that."

She beckoned him over, held the light so it shone down on a fringed leather sheath. Nestled inside, the black plastic handle of a long knife.

44

Jody McCandless had rolled up the sleeves of the prison jump-suit, pulled the front zipper only halfway up his chest. He shuffled diffidently into the hard interview room, his well-dressed lawyer Woodrow Gaines holding out the metal seat for him. Gaines perched himself on Jody's right.

Ethan had water on the table for them, offered coffee and tea. No takers.

"Before we get started," Gaines said, "Mr. McCandless would like to share something with you."

"A confession?" Ethan asked.

Jody met his eyes. "I was as shocked as you were by what Nazareno done. I wish I could have stopped him, but I was afraid for my life."

"So that's how you're playing it."

"I have too much respect for the law to shoot at an officer. Especially you, given your service to this great country." Jody kept his lips pursed, stifling his smirk.

"You ran from me," Ethan said.

"I was"—Jody looked over at his attorney, who mouthed an "M"—"momentarily disoriented. Y'know, from stress, being held hostage and all. The cuffs brought all that back."

"Mr. McCandless is willing to provide information to help capture Mr. Fulci," Gaines said.

"If I buy into his interpretation of events, you mean."

The lawyer nodded. "We'd naturally expect consideration for our solicitude."

"Solicitude. Good word."

Attorney and client shared a look, and Woodrow Gaines continued. "We have a phone number Mr. Fulci gave to Mr. McCandless, as well as a possible rendezvous point."

"A rendezvous implies your client was planning to meet up with him," Ethan said.

"That was Naz's idea, not mine," Jody said.

"Does your client think he can locate Nazareno for us?"

"All we can promise is our good faith cooperation."

"So in other words, I get a number this guy *might* answer, a place he *might* go."

The lawyer folded his hands. "I gather that's a good deal more than you have at present."

Ethan leaned back in the chair, surveying both of them. No doubt Gaines had a draft of an agreement in his briefcase. Jody seemed to feel confident it would be accepted.

"If you can make that deal with the district attorney, you have my blessing," Ethan said. "Finding fugitives is the job of somebody else. My job, what I'm interested in, is the murder of Laura Dill."

Evidently Woodrow Gaines hadn't been informed of this possible charge. He asked for time to consult with his client alone. Ethan left them in the interview room. In the office, he instructed Mal Keogh to turn off the room's surveillance camera and microphone.

"What do you think?" he asked Mal, who'd been watching on the monitor.

"I wouldn't make a deal with Jody McCandless for anything."

"Your father did."

"And I'm not him," Mal said, an edge to the words. "Giving Jody a pass in order to find a guy he obviously hired? That makes zero sense, Chief. That's working our way down, not up. Just my opinion."

Ethan was inclined to agree, but there were other factors. His own safety among them.

"Nazareno is a stone killer," he said. "The kind that would hurt a civilian without blinking. If we can scoop him up before anyone else gets hurt, that's worth the trade."

"You said yourself he's not our priority," Mal insisted.

"If I've learned anything being chief, it's that priorities are complex. You have to do what you can with what you've got."

He watched the younger man consider what he'd said, not thinking his words would convince Mal. Ethan wasn't totally convinced himself.

"If it gets the person who shot Brenda Lee, I guess a deal's worth it," Mal said. Seeing Ethan's surprise, he added, "Oh come on, Ethan. She and I quarrel, but Brenda Lee's part of the team."

Woodrow Gaines knocked on the interior side of the door. Interview ready to resume. Mal flicked the mic and camera back on.

"When you see me rap my knuckles on the table," Ethan said, "three times, like I'm losing patience? That's when you bring in the knife. Got it?"

"Will do, Chief."

Ethan entered the room.

Before he'd taken his seat, Gaines had peppered him with questions. Whether he planned on charging Jody immediately with the homicide of Laura Dill, and if not, then when, and if so, what effect that might have on the offer they'd all but agreed to?

"Like I mentioned before, I'm not the DA. For now let's focus on what your client can tell me about the murder."

"Before Mr. McCandless speaks to anything, we need to know what evidence you're prepared to produce."

"Enough that we don't need his confession," Ethan said. "This morning we executed a search warrant on his property. Jody can tell you what we found."

Ethan watched the smuggler's expression. Jody knew about the warrant, and knew they'd find Laura's things in the house. Maybe he even anticipated them finding the hiding place in the shed. But Jody's face showed confidence, even boredom.

"What are you proposing?" Gaines asked.

"That if your client admits to the murder and helps us with Nazareno, I'll do what I can with the DA," he said. "Otherwise I'm not so inclined. And busy."

"Surely you don't expect Mr. McCandless to confess to a homicide he isn't charged with and didn't commit?"

"That his position?"

Gaines wrote something on the legal pad in front of him, cupping his other hand so Ethan couldn't read it. The lawyer held up the pad in front of Jody's eyes. Jody shook his head.

"We're happy to discuss that at a later date, but right now we're concerned with the charges at hand."

"Tell me about the rendezvous point," Ethan said.

Jody made sure his lawyer had no objections before speaking. "There's a dude in Wenatchee who's got a speedboat, ex-forest ranger or something. He took us up the lake to the cabin. Was gonna wait at a campground partways down the lake till we signaled him. So I got his number, plus the campsite where we, I mean Nazareno, agreed to meet him."

"After you killed me, my officer, and Cassie Maxwell."

"We had no clue you were even there." Jody scratched his nose. "Naz was after Cassie because she might've seen him do something to Bob. I dunno what, I wasn't there."

"Cassie says different. She saw you enter Galvin's house with Nazareno."

"Maybe it was someone looks like me." Jody brightened at his own suggestion. "People are always getting mixed up, like Laura and Cassie, right?"

"Putting aside whether or not you were there, why kill Bob Galvin?"

"The hell do I know? One minute Naz is picking up the money, cool as can be. Then he's asking is there anyone else knows about the switch. Next thing I know, he's strangling the guy—I mean that's what I heard."

"So why did you hire him?"

"No one hired anyone," Jody said. "Naz just showed up. I tried to get away, but you know, the guy was vicious."

Jody was different from his brother, Ethan decided. Seth McCandless would never admit to being a hostage, not even for a reduction in sentence. Jody had a less fierce sense of pride, and was smarter. A different kind of dangerous.

"So you don't know him."

"Nope."

"He was never staying at your home? Never on your property?"

"Nuh-uh."

Ethan rapped on the table three times. "That's what I wanted to hear," he said. "I don't want any confusion over whose this is."

As prompted, Mal brought in an evidence bag, making sure the knife inside was visible. Spots of blood clung to the steel.

The change in Jody's expression couldn't have been more drastic if the victim herself had walked in and pointed an accusing finger. Ethan watched as Jody tried to get hold of his emotions, rein in his shock.

Woodrow Gaines only knew the reaction the knife produced in his client. He demanded another private consultation. As they spoke, Assistant District Attorney Hokuto had arrived at the station. Ethan briefed her on what they'd learned. When Gaines knocked on the door again, Ethan and the prosecutor entered, ready to deal.

Woodrow Gaines stood and cleared his throat. "My client would like to make a voluntary statement concerning the unfortunate death of Ms. Dill."

45

"The motive was what we couldn't ever get straight," Ethan said, hands fidgeting with the ends of his tie. Hospitals still made him uneasy, the colorless, officious atmosphere reminding him of his time at Walter Reed. "Laura handed over her passport thinking it would only be used at the bank. One teller would see it, during a busy time of day, then give Cassie access to Laura's safe deposit box. Simple. No reason Cassie had to cross the border posing as Laura. But that was Jody's instruction to Cassie. She didn't know she was being used as an alibi for murder."

"Didn't Laura suspect anything?" Brenda Lee Page's voice was weak and slurred from painkillers. She listened attentively, propped up in her bed. Her husband Terry had gone to the cafeteria to give them a moment to themselves.

Sitting in the visitor's chair in his best suit, Ethan felt a fear for his senior officer, a relief she was going to be okay, emotions he hadn't let himself acknowledge before. The bullet had only damaged flesh, and Brenda Lee was expected to recover, good as new. But it had been closer than he'd wanted to admit.

"According to Jody, the switch was actually Laura's idea," Ethan said. "She told him, 'You got other girls who look like me. Let one of them go. She gets caught, I'll just say she stole my passport.'"

"Brazen," Brenda Lee said. "Laura was smarter than we gave her credit for."

"And more self-aware," Ethan said. "Blending into the background was something she counted on and used. People overlooked her, allowed her to work her way inside."

"She was plotting against Jody?"

He nodded. "Laura started out collecting scrips for him, pills for quick cash. She saw the real money was in being a courier. Not just what Jody would pay for moving his cash across the border, but what she could steal while doing it. A few hundred here and there. It added up. Want some water?"

"Please."

Ethan poured from a beige plastic pitcher into a beige plastic cup with a straw.

"How did Jody find out?" Brenda Lee asked.

"You'll like this," he said. "Laura told him. She said he was leaving himself open, and that she could help him do better."

"And maybe work her way closer to the top," Brenda Lee said. "In place to one day take over. With Jody none the wiser."

Ethan knew he had to tell her eventually. "Jody is claiming he was Nazareno's dupe, held hostage while we were being shot at. He didn't think the gun he had was loaded. His lawyer insists this be included in the agreed-upon facts of his case. In return, he's helping to bring in Nazareno."

Brenda Lee's reaction was a tired spreading of her hands. "I see."

"I wanted you to hear that from me, and have a chance to voice any objection."

Ethan noticed her hand creep up to the dial for the morphine, surreptitiously, as if not wanting him to know. Brenda Lee eased her bed down a notch, pushed away the table holding her water.

"I understand why you have to agree to it," Brenda Lee said. Her eyes had closed, and her voice was fading into a morphine haze. "Still sucks."

"Sure does." Smiling at her, Ethan stood up. "I'll leave you to heal."

"Hey," Brenda Lee murmured. "Do me a favor?"

"Name it," Ethan said.

"Give my best to Wynn and Steph."

In the hall, he checked his messages. A text from the search and rescue team leader, Billie Suzuki. *Campsite located.* Ethan phoned her from the truck.

"I'm standing next to your missing man's tent," Suzuki said. "He camouflaged it pretty good. We found a freshly dug hole with some bloody bandages and clothing inside. Some burnt papers, too."

"But no Nazareno." Ethan's mood darkened.

"He's cleared out, probably in the last day or so," the search leader said. "We got a report from the marina of a missing twelve-footer. With that, Mr. Fulci could get down the lake, and from there, who knows?"

"All right." Ethan thanked her.

"We'll keep looking," Suzuki said. "For what it's worth, Ethan, I don't think this guy is in much shape to cause anyone grief. Least not for a long while. He lost a helluva lot of blood, and if he's not holed up somewhere licking his wounds, it's likely he just dropped dead out in the bush somewhere."

Ethan doubted it.

He drove out of the hospital parking lot, fighting back feelings of regret and foreboding. If he'd taken one more shot at Nazareno, if he'd aimed that half second more . . . One day he might have to answer for that error.

But today had its own miseries. He looked at the clock in the Dodge's instrument panel. It was ten past five. He was late for the ceremony.

* * *

How many hours and how much money had gone into transforming the beach in front of the hotel? The pink steepled roof of a tent was visible blocks away. The beach itself had been scrubbed of broken shells and trash, even raked in places like a Japanese garden. No parking anywhere close. Ethan drove the Dodge up onto the curb at a diagonal. Parking was one of the perks of the job—a job he might not have much longer.

Mercy Haze was stationed by the front flap, wearing a white tuxedo and mirrored shades, the uniform of party staff. She nodded at Ethan. "The show's about to start," Mercy said.

He could hear canned music from inside, the gabble of a crowd. "You working security?"

"Mr. Sinclair offered triple time, and my kid needs glasses."

First Cliff Mooney, now Mercy Hayes. Blaine PD officers past and future, working for Wynn Sinclair. That didn't sit well with him, though given the town's economy it was probably unavoidable.

"Carrying?" he asked, not seeing a weapon in sight.

"No, but in thirty seconds I can have a half dozen people here who are." Mercy tapped her earpiece.

"You see a blonde man, maybe in white clothes, driving a Mazda pickup, you call them ASAP."

As he was speaking the music swelled and stopped. Feeling like a sinner entering a revival meeting, Ethan stepped into the tent.

The back flap had been drawn open, so that the couple would take their vows with the Pacific providing a backdrop. There were no empty aisle seats, nothing near the back. Ethan made his way down toward the middle, feeling disruptive, out of place.

Mei Sum waved from halfway down. There was a free chair next to her and Walter. He tried not to impose himself too much as he climbed over people, pressing between rows.

"Pretty boring so far," Mei said, prompting a head shake from her father.

Wynn Sinclair waited at the front, his tux a silver-gray, immaculate. Wynn Junior stood next to him, the teen swinging his arms anxiously. The reverend bent his head so the sound technician could affix a wireless mic. The speakers began to play strains of Mendelssohn's wedding march. Heads turned and the crowd made a noise of awe and appreciation.

"Whoa, Jess looks pretty," Mei said.

Ethan felt like the last to turn his head. Jess Sinclair preceded her mother, carrying a heaping spray of pink carnations which matched her dress to the shade. Her face was impassive, eyes focused on the water. Steph Sinclair's dress was strapless white lace with scalloped shoulders, white ribbons in her braided hair. She smiled, sweeping her head to each side of the aisle in turn.

Ethan wondered if the ceremony would include the part about whether anyone knew a reason why the couple shouldn't be wed. Or re-wed in this case. *Speak now or forever hold your peace.* Forever seemed a long time.

46

The Ocean Beach Hotel and Supper Club was given over completely to the celebration. After the ceremony on the beach, guests were treated to a seafood buffet and an open bar (with a strictly enforced two drink limit). Ethan took both his drinks together, a double greyhound, the same pink color as the wedding decorations.

The chairs had been cleared from the restaurant to create a dance floor, one that extended outside through the double doors. Picnic tables had gone up nearby. On a small bandstand, a guitar player tuned up, and a drummer gave a few tentative whacks to the kick drum.

A hand slapped Ethan's shoulder with force. "The man I wanted to see." Eldon Mooney's tie was fish scale patterned and silver, his cufflinks silver anchors. Mooney had taken more than two drinks, it seemed.

"You prepared for tomorrow?" the mayor asked. "I do hope you realize this isn't a personal matter. It's strictly what's best for the community. We need an able hand at the helm."

"I have nothing to hide," Ethan said.

The mayor's smile only grew broader. "Your service as an officer will be fully credited. And I hear you're close to finding that young woman's killer."

Ethan didn't tell the mayor Jody McCandless was already in custody. Partly out of disdain for Mooney, partly because he didn't yet consider Laura Dill's homicide closed. Not until Nazareno was in custody as well.

Ethan caught Mooney glancing at his ankles, as if looking for evidence of the heel plate and amputation. The mayor smiled and trailed off to join another cluster of citizens. Ethan headed to the bar, and all but strong-armed a refill.

More musicians were approaching the bandstand. A feeling of not belonging flared up as the noise swelled. He'd put in an appearance, as promised. Staying any longer was inviting more heartbreak. He wanted to be by himself.

Pushing his way toward the exit, he was swept up in the counter-flow of well-wishers. The bride and groom were passing him, heading to the dance floor. Applause. What could he do but stand there and clap with the others?

As the couple passed him he forced a good-natured smile. Wynn was beaming, having himself a wonderful day. And why shouldn't he have a wonderful day? Wynn Sinclair had everything else.

Steph's smile was equally radiant, but she avoided looking his way. A minor tilt of the head and Ethan was out of her sight. Maybe that was a kindness.

He watched the couple join hands and square up, hips in line. He recognized the first song: "Carried Away" by George Strait.

"Now you're just rubbing it in," he muttered to his drink.

Arlene Six Crows was holding court at one end of the picnic table. Dr. Sandra Jacinto, Timothy and Yvette Lemieux, and a few others he didn't know were gathered around the councillor. Ethan joined them, nodding that yes, it was a lovely evening, and wasn't Steph's dress something, and what a terrific couple. He shrugged off any worry about the meeting tomorrow. When he left, he refilled his glass with table wine.

His wedding to Jazz had been a backyard affair. Her parents attended, along with a few friends, Frank Keogh among them. A nice quiet ceremony. It hadn't been enough to bind them forever. Maybe if they'd gone all out like this, rented an entire hotel. He doubted it.

The night was getting colder. Inside, he could see Wynn still dancing with an elderly relative. Steph was nowhere in sight. He dumped the wine in a planter and left the glass balanced on the edge. Before he left he needed to congratulate her. That would complete the day's humiliations. It would end things right.

Steph wasn't in the dining room or on the beach. The kitchen was bustling, but the bride wasn't there, either. Her daughter was. Jess sat with Mei and a few other teens watching video clips, giggling. One made a half-assed effort to hide a bottle of beer at Ethan's approach.

"Your mother around?" he asked Jess.

"Taking photos in the mezz. Why?" The teen girl was curious about his intentions, though not willing to voice this with her friends.

"Just want to say my goodbyes."

"It was a nice ceremony, wasn't it?"

Was she rubbing it in? If anyone was entitled to do that, it was Steph's children.

"Real nice," he said.

The mezzanine was up a short flight of stairs, strewn with flower petals. After three hours of being trampled by guests with sandy shoes, the flowers looked like scraps of pink confetti. In the hotel's conference room, a trellis had been set up for wedding photos—wedding *renewal* photos, he reminded himself. The photographer was drinking beer alone. No sign of Steph.

At the top of the stairs he heard her voice—hushed, insistent. "Not now," she was saying. "We'll discuss it at home."

Knowing he was intruding, but ready to get it over with, he climbed to the third floor hallway. Steph held the shoulders of her son. Wynn Junior's cheeks were puffed, rubbery looking. The kid turned his face away as Ethan approached.

Seeing him, Steph Sinclair's reaction was to drop her grip on her son, hold her hands together as if to keep from reaching for him. A red thumbnail pressed into the opposite palm.

If they'd been truly alone—

"Just wanted to say," Ethan said, and paused, tongue on his teeth, thinking of what words he could manage in front of her son. "Everything was lovely tonight." *You were lovely tonight.* "Thanks for the invite." *This has been hell.*

"You being here meant a lot," Steph said. He imagined her words were as carefully chosen. *It's hell for me, too. Just ask and I'll go with you.* Maybe that was wishful thinking.

"Say good night to Chief Brand," Steph instructed her son. Junior turned further away, arms crossed, hands buried in the folds of his jacket. Like his older sister, it was clear he knew, or at least suspected.

"It's all right," Ethan said. "Tough night for everyone." He nodded a goodbye.

Two steps down he heard the boy speak. "Liar."

He recognized the voice. Turning, he saw the pistol in Junior's hand. A target pistol, small caliber, both hands wrapped around the handle.

Steph was the first to react, putting a hand on the barrel over top of Wynn Junior's. The boy struggled, elbow flailing. Ethan took the top steps, moving toward the barrel as Junior backed up down the narrow hall.

"You're gonna ruin everything," Wynn Junior said. "You're gonna take her away."

Junior's eyes were shut, his voice quavering with sobs. Ethan doubted the kid could even see him. Steph again reached for the gun and the boy turned, slashing out with the weapon, the barrel leaving grease on her dress.

"You left the elk heart on my porch," Ethan said. "The phone call, that was you. The bullet through my tailgate."

"You were gonna take everything."

"Junior, I'd never," Steph began to say.

"*Don't lie to me.*" Wynn Junior sniffed, moving the gun back to Ethan, taking one hand off it to wipe his face.

He could die here now, gunned down by the child of the woman he loved. Almost a poetic way to go. Ethan had come to think of death as something that followed you, like your shadow, looming over a shoulder, snapping at your heels, but always behind or below. Now death hovered in front of him, waiting, and had in fact always been there. His own demise decided by a sobbing fourteen-year-old. Ethan was afraid.

"All right, kid," he said. "No lies."

"You were gonna take her away."

"If I could have, yes."

"That makes you a liar. You all are. Pretending nothing's wrong and you're all friendly but really you're just . . . liars."

Junior's hands chopped up and down, the pistol moving from Ethan's hairline to his groin. Steph didn't move.

"Your mother made a very tough decision. She loves you an awful lot. More than anything. You know that deep down."

Wynn Junior's hands circled, the barrel pointed at the center of him.

"Adult choices are tough, Junior. They involve giving things up, trying to do what's best for more than just yourself. Trying to think what's good long-term."

"She was gonna leave with you," Wynn Junior said.

"Not in this life." His eyes moved to Steph's, hers reflecting back the pain in what he said, the truth of it. He turned back to the boy with the gun. "You have an adult decision to make. Think about yourself and your mom, your sister, and your dad. And me."

"I hate you."

"That's your right. Ask yourself if hating me from juvie is any improvement over hating me from right here?"

Junior's arms fell. He rested his head on his mother's wedding dress. Steph gently turned the barrel to the floor and worked the grip from Junior's fingers. She held it out to Ethan, and when he took it, she wrapped her arms more completely around her son. Her voice was a whisper, a plea, a command.

"You won't say anything."

He shook his head, pocketing the gun. Mother and son were weeping together. He gave them the hallway to themselves.

* * *

The band had packed it in, replaced by a DJ. Only a few couples remained on the floor. The hotel staff were dropping silver domes over the leftover shrimp and lobster. Wynn Sinclair stood among Arlene, Mooney, and a few others, all smoking cigars.

"Care for a stogie, Chief?" Wynn offered. Maybe there was a gloating edge to his words, or maybe he was just drunk and happy. No crime in that.

Ethan handed him the target pistol, offered no explanation, and left.

47

Monday morning, his last day as chief, Ethan Brand made the final adjustments to his dress uniform in the hallway mirror. He filled a Yeti travel mug with coffee and took it out to his porch.

There, crouched on the bottom step, was the coyote. It licked its chops and bounded to a safer distance near the shed. The pale blue eyes regarded him with curiosity and no fear.

"Hold a good thought for me today," he asked the animal.

An hour later he stood in the council chamber, waiting for the councillors to file in. The hearing had drawn a crowd of two dozen, filling most of the room. Frank Keogh had come to lend support, sitting with Mercy Haze in the front row. Terry Page had left his wife's bedside. "On her strictest instructions, if they open the floor, I'm to tell them Brenda Lee doesn't want the job. She'll resign if they take it from you."

He took a reading of his own mental temperature. Surprisingly, he didn't feel all that bad. If his career ended today, so be it, he'd find some other occupation. Laura Dill's killer was in jail, and the threats had been stopped. Not bad for a few days on the job.

Part of him wanted to fight, to sue for discrimination and wrongful dismissal. To explain why he'd hidden the injury, what it was like to have people treat you as diminished. At the same time, he felt he shouldn't have to explain anything; his record spoke for him. Frank had wanted someone familiar enough with violence not to resort to it, and Ethan had done that. For the most part, anyway.

Sissy McCandless was in a seat between Sally Bishop and Jon Gutierrez. Sissy had a needlework project on her lap. Madame Defarge, he thought, knitting at an execution. Behind her sat Mei Sum. Cliff Mooney sat at the very back, his cast stretching out into the aisle.

The door behind the dais opened and the councillors entered, faces solemn, taking their seats without preamble. Wynn Sinclair had left last night, taking his bride on a second honeymoon. Both children had accompanied them. Ethan's eyes moved from Wynn's empty chair down the row of faces. Even Arlene Six Crows seemed grave. Eldon Mooney, who was probably jubilant inside, kept his expression formal as he called the session to order.

"This was to be a hearing as to the fitness of our chief of police," Mooney began. "However, the council has met privately, as some of this information is medical in nature and therefore confidential. Chief Brand?"

Ethan nodded up at the dais.

"The council was furnished with indisputable proof that four-teen years ago, during a patrol assignment in the Helmand province of Afghanistan, you were critically injured. That you have, that you wear, a prosthetic. Do you deny this?"

"Nope."

To his surprise, the small crowd didn't murmur or exclaim. Silence.

"The council has considered this at great length, from every conceivable angle. Unless you have something new to offer, a statement you'd like to make. Would you like anything added to the record?"

"No statement."

Mooney nodded, flipped the page in front of him. "You were confirmed by council after being recommended by your predecessor, Chief Keogh, is that correct?"

"It is."

"And did Chief Keogh know of your infirmity? Sorry, your injury?"

"I did, Mister Mayor," Frank called from his seat. News to Ethan. "He got zero special treatment because of it. Went through the same training, did the same job as everyone else. I take responsibility for bending the rules. My call."

"This is total BS," Mei called.

Laughter, shushing. The mayor called for order. If he'd had a gavel, Ethan was sure the mayor would have rapped it.

"The council's decision was difficult," Mooney said. "Whatever deception was involved in concealing this injury has to be weighed against the commendable job you've done. We recognize that your work led to charges being laid against one of the persons responsible for the murder of Laura Dill. While the other is still at large, we congratulate you for this."

Ethan settled into an at ease posture.

"Council must be governed by the wording of our Police Act, with regard to the fitness of officers. While your personal circumstances might be exceptional, as a general rule, an amputation impedes the performance of one's duties."

Mooney was drawing this out, making sure every word landed. Yet instead of glee, Ethan saw only resentment.

"As clear as it is that you cannot serve as a police officer," Mooney said, "there is no language to the effect that you can't serve as police *chief*. Therefore it's the council's recommendation—a unanimous recommendation, by the way—that you continue to serve as chief of police. We wish you good health in the performance of your duties. God bless."

A rally of applause, a few groans, voices uttering congratulations. Ethan barely heard them. Stunned and trying to process what had happened, he watched the mayor speed-walk back through the door of the chamber. The rest of the council gathered themselves. Arlene bumped her fist on the dais in victory and beamed at him.

Frank was on his feet, arm around him, shaking his hand. "As it should be," Frank said, adding in a softer voice, "How the hell did you pull that off?"

He could only shake his head.

Walking up to the exit, hands patted his back. He felt confused, almost dizzy, not a little overjoyed. Jay Swan asked him for a comment, but Ethan couldn't think of a cogent reply. He promised them an interview soon.

Outside it was spitting rain. In the parking lot he looked at his phone, saw an incoming call from a number he didn't recognize. An 808 area code. Was that Hawaii?

"Good morning," he said. "Is it morning there?"

"Early morning." Steph's voice was bright, less strained than it had been the night before. "I'm in the lobby of a hospital in Honolulu. We're staying for a few weeks, to see that Junior gets the time he needs to rest."

"Not the most romantic honeymoon," Ethan said.

"My family is all here. That's the best I could hope for. Thanks to you."

Ethan had found himself walking to his truck, but now turned toward the beach. The tide had returned debris and seaweed to the sand.

"Something tells me I should be thanking you and your husband," he said.

289

"Eldon is a politician. He owes Wynn more favors than you can imagine. What better time to call one in?"

"Thank you, Steph," he said. "And thank your husband for me."

"It was only right."

"I love you."

The words came out almost on their own. He didn't qualify them. Steph didn't answer immediately.

"What are you going to do now?" she asked after a moment.

Ethan looked toward the water, which that morning seemed truly endless.

"I think I'll walk for a while," he said.

* * *

An hour later, circling back to his truck, he noticed the lights on in Breakwater Travel. Sissy McCandless was alone inside. Ethan knocked, wiped his feet, and entered.

"Congratulations are in order," Sissy said. "Maybe I can sell you on a celebratory cruise? Mazatlán is going on sale next week. If you haven't been, the beaches are lovely."

"I just got my job back, not sure I want to take time off just yet."

"Suit yourself," Sissy said. "Something else I can help you with?"

"Just wondering what'll happen to your brother's house."

"Well, it's the family house," Sissy said. "Seth and Jody didn't exactly do upkeep. It needs some work."

"Will you move out there?"

"Eventually, I imagine so. Why?'

"Things worked out pretty well for you," Ethan said.

"Not following, Chief."

"The middle kid. The only girl. I can't imagine what that was like in your family."

"No, you can't," Sissy said. "What's your point?"

"Your older brother inherits the family business and wrecks it. The younger brother is too ineffectual to do much better. He's even got one of his couriers living in the house. No separation between work and play for Jody. Soon this woman, Laura Dill, is trying to call the tune. And Jody's too weak to stop it."

"It's just who my brother is," Sissy said.

"Now you're running things, you won't make the same mistake."

"Running things?"

Ethan put a hand on the counter in a disarming, just-us gesture.

"You helped me find the knife, enough evidence to put Jody away. I don't doubt he killed Laura."

"Then what are we talking about?"

"We're talking about a brilliant woman who watched her family make all the wrong moves, who finally saw her opportunity to take control. A woman who knew what to say to Jody to make him mad enough to kill. Who helped him plan it out, offering the train tickets. This woman even convinced her brother to hire a professional killer, just in case Jody couldn't go through with the murder."

"I don't even know how to respond to such lunacy," Sissy said. "I run a small business."

"And you studied graphic design. That receipt was a fake, but it pointed to the dead woman being on the train, just as you wanted it to. Same as the burnt remains of the backpack."

"You're reaching, Ethan," Sissy said.

"Jody could be manipulated into killing Laura. But eliminating Bob Galvin, trying to do the same to Cassie Maxwell—those were cover-up crimes. Someone wanted to make sure they'd never talk."

"My brother."

"Jody had cash and evidence buried on his own property. He knew Cassie. No, killing Bob was about concealing who hired him, something Jody would only care about if you drilled that into him. You know what's funny?"

"I have no idea what you find funny," Sissy said.

"When Jody confessed, he claimed he only went along with the trip to the cabin because Nazareno threatened him. I thought he was minimizing his involvement. But it's true, isn't it? You had Nazareno force him to help."

"What other crimes do you think I committed?" Sissy asked. "Did I kidnap the Lindbergh baby?"

"Forgery," Ethan said. "If I looked on that computer back there, I bet I'd find one of those photo design programs."

"I still dabble, sure."

"And maybe, saved somewhere in its memory, is a mock-up of the receipt we found beneath Laura Dill's body. You made that receipt, and made sure it would be found on her body. You led us on a hell of a chase, Sissy."

"If you want to take a look at my computer, please go ahead," Sissy said. "But, Chief?"

"Yes?"

She wasn't looking at him. Instead her gaze rested on the floor, where her kitten sat, sleeping on a quilted cushion.

"If I was as low down and devious as you claim," Sissy said, "would I really have used my business equipment? I mean, wouldn't someone smart use a second computer for a thing like that, maybe even a second printer, and a roll of receipt paper different from the kind I use in the store? That's how someone smart would do things, wouldn't they?"

A smile of understanding passed over the counter between them. If Ethan had worn a hat, he would have doffed it to Sissy McCandless.

"Not so different from your brothers after all," he said.

"Don't be dense, Chief," Sissy said. "There's a huge difference. They're both in prison, and I'm about to open for business."

Acknowledgments

Thanks to Marcia Markham, Thaisheemarie Fantauzzi Perez, and the entire team at Crooked Lane Books.

Thanks to agent extraordinaire Chris Casuccio at Westwood Creative Artists.

Thanks to Nathan Ripley for the encouragement, and to Brian Thornton and Jim Thomsen for I-5 details.

And finally, thanks to Larry, Patsy, Clint, and John D.